Southe

Teresa Matthes

iUniverse, Inc.
New York   Bloomington

Southern Rain

iUniverse books may be ordered through booksellers or by contacting:

iUniverse
1663 Liberty Drive
Bloomington, IN 47403
www.iuniverse.com
1-800-Authors (1-800-288-4677)

ISBN: 978-1-4401-7125-3 (sc)
ISBN: 978-1-4401-7126-0 (ebk)

Printed in the United States of America

iUniverse rev. date: 8/27/2009

SOUTHERN RAIN

Waudean looked at herself in the mirror, with hope in her blue eyes, thinking I am really doing it, I am going up north. With her high cheek bones, ocean blue eyes, brownish brown hair, petite frame, brushing her hair, Her Mama, with sweat on her face, walks in, you know child were goanna miss you here, I here it is cooler up north. There is a blessing right there.

Waudene, put down the hair brush, walked over and hugged her Mama, I am only going up north to finish my schooling, mama, Mississippi, does not have a college that I have picked my specialty in , mama, looking with a little smile, but Waudene, could see Mama holding back the tears, you know Waudean, they don't have whimper willow tree's I heard , up in the north, you are going to miss this small little town, I know Mama, but it's only for a little while.

Waudene, you know, your sister is going to miss the heck of you, Your Papa, child I think he already misses you and you have not even left yet. Mama wiped her tears away from her eyes. PapA, walked in and said,

In morning we all take you to the bus station. Papa, walked out like I was Dean was leaving for good. Papa, said as he turned around I love you, Waudene, Papa, I love you too. Mama said child, a mother's love does not stop or slow down, just because her child is old enough to leave home for any

1

reason, when you get married, and children of your own, then waudean you will know what I am talking about then.

That is sure some engagement ring Hank put on your finger, yaw know Waudene, this man just plum loves you, and can not wait to make you his wife, Mama said, I know we do not have a lot, but we love you and your sister so much, The lord has made sure we have lacked for nothing,

Mama, giving Waudene her bible, Mama, I have my bible it's in the suite case, Well Waudene, you do not want to get out in this world with out your bible, and keep the the lord in your soul. , Mama, Waudene, looked at her, I know where I come from, mama, you and papa, did a fine job raising me and Pauline, Dean smiled at her Mama and gave her a hug.

We do not get up in the morning with out "Thanking the Lord, and praying before each meal, we know, we do not know how some days how we even got food, with this recession, and all. The lord always provides, have faith my child and do not ever forget that. Oh, mama, I love Jesus, Well, child I am gonna get on back in the kitchen and get supper ready.

Mama walked out, sweating and hot, not a breeze any where. But waudene saw the tears Mama was fighting so hard to hold back.

Lord this is one hot day, Waudene, is hoping for some kind of breeze, any kind of breeze lord, if the wind would just blow a little, Waudene, walked in the kitchen, Mama, I think I heard papa's car pull up. Child goes and makes sure you ant's leaving anything behind, that you will need at that northern Nursing school. Yes mama.

Waudene, walked back in her bedroom, and heard her sister Pauline and papa walk in, supper ready, oh, most, putting plates on the supper table now, yaw all wash up, and supper will be ready.

Papa, knocking on waudene's bedroom door, you alright child, Yes sir, papa. Just making sure I am not forgetting anything, papa was a small frame man, small little town, in Mississippi, knew papa as a loving the lord, and his name had value,

Waudene, knew this day was hard in the 1940's,

Well, be ready in the morning child, your mama, and sister, and me will take you up to the bus stop. Papa, had the same old car ford falcon, blue , if cars had air conditioning papa's did not,.

Papa, had built this house, as Waudene looked around, , beautiful house, southern porch, sure felt good, on a hot southern night, and tonight, was the last night , even though the tree's are sweating , it's that hot Waudean thought. Shortly, she would be gone. Lord, knows I'll be back though she thought to herself. Waudean, this heat is just too much at times, I will not miss this heat.

Dinner is ready yaw all, Pauline and Waudene, and Papa came in and sat down , papa took off his old gray hat, we all sat down and that's one thing looking forward too, time with family. Mama fried chickens, made biscuits, and gravy, cooking over that hot oven, lord made this kitchen seem like 110 degree's inside. We all sat down, Papa, said, Lord, thank you for this food; we thank you for today's hard work and earnings. Guide us with wisdom. Please, keep our youngon safe while she is going up north for her schooling. Amen. Thank You papa, for that wonderful prayer, Pauline and wauden, and Mama said.

After supper time, it was time for waudene and Pauline to do the dishes, mama, you going out side with papa, to sit out on the front porch? Your papa works hard; I am just being right out side, if yaw all need anything.

Mama and papa were out side, Pauline and Waudene doing dishes, I sure wish I could afford to buy mama and daddy a fan, by my lord those things are expensive, think you gonna miss this place asked Pauline?

Waudene, looked at her sister, and said oh yes, it's all I have ever known, since mama and papa, moved from phildelphia, ms, by horse and wagon, You know Hank, is just plum acting funny, acting snappy with people, That is my fault, waudene said, With me and Hank engaged I think me leaving for schooling, is bothering him, more than he is trying to let be known. Waudene, these dishes is about done, sit down, I want to speak with you about something,

How can you leave Hank, for schooling? Oh, Pauline, I do not want to leave Hank are you all, but I had to pick a specialty in nursing and that will take me to Missouri. I just did not have a say in this.

I want to help babies. Pauline, a small framed woman, a little heaver set than her sister, I know, it's just hard on all of us with you leaving. Besides I guess I will be the one feeding them old chickens, and that mean old rooster, out back. Pauline said sometimes I just want to throw the food at them, but I know they are our meals. Waudene, looked at her and said, well if you get angry or upset about anything, just ring one those chickens' necks, and your feel better. Both girls just laughing.

Pauline, looking at her sister, and grabbing her hand, I just could never leave Dade, he means the world to me and all, Mama and Papa like him , that is a Blessing, can't do nothing in this town, if some one does not approve,

I know waudene said. Dade , would not even consider letting me go off to some school, I know for a fact , up north, with those Yankee's, Hank, makes me wonder, Waudene, said, wait, Hank and I discussed me finishing my nursing school, and he knows I am still a virgin, and he is going to be the one. Hank , always wearing his Sheriff uniform, if not in that his old gray shirt, with his old gray pants, Lord, sometimes, I just wish Hank , would wear something different,

Well, Pauline said, you know, Hank is a sturdy man, and dresses up for church. What more do you want form him? Waudene, looked at her sister, it's would be nice if Hank, now and then would get dressed up, even if it is to the old café in the small town. The only one in this town, old faded out wood floors, smells like burnt grease half the time when you go in there,

Dean, said, it would be nice if there was a fan, you know Waudean, Pauline said, with a smile, I heard in town the other day, they might put a fan or two in there. But next year or so. Pauline said, a man's clothing is not everything, I know that, said waudean, but just now and then it is nice to see a man dressed up.

That's all I am saying. I love Hank, Well Waudean said looking at her sister

When I get Graduate, I will be back, Hank and I will be getting married, and living next to you, and Mama and Papa, if I do say so myself, those are wonderful plans

Oh, Pauline, yes, I love Hank, my gosh, yaw know Dean, a lot of girls would love to be in your shoes' , Hank is the sheriff, and he is a God loving man, he is so kind , even to the colored. Folks and that are just rare.

I just don't think you are going to get a better man than that, Waudene, said, please just be happy for me, I will be back before you and Dade get married.

Well, I have all my stuff packed for school, but I feel like I am forgetting something, Pauline, with a little smile. Looked at her sister, that's a sign, do not go.

Waudene, said, I will write, I have saved up so I have a few stamps, and Mama gave me a couple of enevolpes to write to you all. Hank will be at the bus stop to see me off tomorrow too.

Pauline, looking at her sister, well waudene, do you really think that man is going to let you go up north, with out seeing you off. Waudene, knew how much Hank loved her, it is a blessing he is willing to let her go.

Well, I am going to going outside, and tell mama and papa good night, big day tomorrow,

As waudene, went in bedroom , looked around Lord, I am gonna miss this room, pulling the cover back , waudene fell on the white cotton sheets, I done took a cool bath, and still hot as ever in this room,

Waudene could feel the sheets sticking to her back, waudene got up and went and got some baking powder, at least that kept the sweat off her back,,

Waudene heard her sister, Pauline, said hey thought you might be asleep with you leaving and all tomorrow, it's so hot, Pauline said, last night hear I will get a piece of paper and fan you with that , that's your breeze for the night, Waudene laughed, Pauline fanned her sister for a couple of minutes and waudene was sleeping. Pauline went on her room and went to bed.

Waudean, heard the roster crow, opening her eyes, Lord it was going to be another hot day here, I can feel the sweat already,

Waudean, went in took a cool bath, got ready, Mama, Papa, and Pauline were waiting for her in the kitchen, Waudene, walked in the kitchen, Mama had cooked smoked fried ham, eggs, and biscuits, Mama, your meals are always so good, I wonder if they cook like up north? Mama shook her head, child I just do not know what they do up north.

Not long after everyone was done with breakfast, Papa, said with sadness in his eyes, well lets' get on going up to that bus stop, Papa, grabbed his old hat, and Waudean , grabbed her suite case, looked around one last time, What am I thinking, I will be back, before I know it. Out the door they all went, all got in the car, papa opening the door for all of them,

Pulling out of this drive way, felt so strange, Waudean , when you get up north, I just wanna know if it is true or not, that white folks and the black's folks eat in the same place, will you let me know? Waudean said "Yes" Pauline if I pass by a place and see that, I will write you and let you know. Child papa said, you sure walking in a different world, be careful, Satan is every where child, Keep your faith, yaw hear me? Yes, papa.

Pulling up to the bus stop, the old greyhound bus was waiting for people still to arrive, that's one big machine there, papa said. Well, I best be getting on that bus if I am going. Papa, helped waudean, with her suite case, and Hank, about scared the heck out of us all, hey, there, yaw all. Waudean, these here are flowers for you, and this letter, please do not read the letter until you are on that bus,

Oh my , these flowers are beautiful Hank, but they will die on the bus , I have nothing to keep them in, as beautiful as they are, may I just give them to my Mama, while sure you can, Hear you go Mama, as she handed her the flowers, Mama said Good by, with tears just a rolling down her face. Waudean hugged everyone,

Hank, the last one standing, if I did not love you so much woman, you know I would not be agreeing to this, Thank You Hank, for your kind understanding. I will be back before you know. I love you and I miss you all.

Waudean, is on the bus, waving good by still, That greyhound bus is pulling on out, Lord, would you just look at the smoke come out of that engine, all that's how they make those big machine today, sturdy I tell you, Hank said. Papa, said I am gonna get the family back home and get on to work, I am heading to work myself said Hank, tipped his hat, as he got in the sheriff car.

Waudean,, trying to get comfortable on this loud bus, and strange people, Waudean so quite and shy, next thing , some woman with gray hair, and, smelled like a rose petal, very proper lady, said I am going to visit my sister in northern Mississippi , with a firm grip on her purse.

You know it is her birthday, and I am gonna surprise her with my visit. That will be a nice birthday gift, Waudean said, , well, child you are awful young to be going to place by your self, I noticed you do not have no wedding ring on, Waudean, said , I am going to finish my nursing school.

The lady, said I am Wilma, and I know you girls today, want to work outside your home, and do things, who is going to take care of your man, as pretty as you are , this is a man in your life right? Yes Mam, I plan to marry him, when I am done with nursing school, they do not allow a woman to be married and go to college, and it is one or the other. That's under stable if I do say so I. Yes, mam. Dean said.

Wilma, grabbed a book, and offered waudean an apple, no thank you Wilma; I just had a big breakfast and full still, so kind of you to offer.

Waudean, reached in her purse for the letter Hank had given her, Has she open the letter, a little piece of paper fell out, reaching for the floor on the bus, she picked it up, and there was a picture of Hank and Waudean, ,

Wilma, leaning over to look as hard as she could at the picture, well lady, that is one fine looking fellow, going by his uniform, he must be a police officer, is that so, Waudean, said yes Mam, as she looked at the picture and smiled.

He is a wonderful man, he treats me so well, and when I go up north and finish my nursing school, you see, I be on my way back to Mississippi to be is wife.

Well, you sure are lucky, in my day and time a man who was engaged to a woman , he just did not allow her to go someplace and get some education, times sure have changed, Yes mam, they have said Waudean.

Waudean, put the picture in her wallet, and read the letter, Wilma, trying to lean over , oh child that must be your love letter, pardon me, I have forgot my manners, That's quite alright Wilma,

Waudean, went on reading the letter, My Dearest Waudean, , I am missing you as I write this letter , and you have not even left yet, my heart earns for you , knowing you will be back , is like waiting for my next breath. I have never loved a woman like I do you, which are why I have agreed to allow you to go on up north and do that schooling. I know you have stamps and stuff to write, but I will be writing you at least two or three times a week. I will put stamps for you to write me back, they are so expensive, I will pay for that.

Waudean, when you get lonely just look at the picture of us, that I have put in this letter, I have the same picture of us myself, and I will do the same. This town is really talking about how you are going up north with the Yankees, but don't you pay no attention to all that gossip, people just talking is all, do well in school. I love you, and I can not wait for you to be my wife. To enjoy the rest of my life with you. Love, Hank.

Waudean, wiped a tears starting to roll down her face, Lord I sure hope I am doing the right thing, leaving and all. She thought.

Child, here is a tissue, said Wilma, must have been one heck of a love letter to put you in tears child. Thank You, for the tissue, I will be fine,

It's gonna be a long trip I think I will try and take a nape waudean said to Wilma,

This bus is hot, they said it had some type of cooling system, Waudean, said, I am so sorry but I am gonna try and rest my eyes, I have been up early. Oh, I will not bother you, Waudean, Wilma said, you go ahead and get your self some rest.

Waudean, fell asleep, with Wilma with a loud voice sitting right next to waudean, child, is a rest stop, wake up, if you got to use the rest room, or want to get a drink of water , they have it here, Besides, I need to get up , tired of sitting,

Waudean, yes, mam, I am getting up and waudean, and Wilma walked off the bus together,

Waudean, powder her nose, fixed her hair, used the rest room, got some water, , looking around, excuse me sir, as a man walked passed her, is this still the state of Mississippi,? No mam, you are in Arkansas, my lord Waudean said it sure is pretty here, and not as hot, the wind blows, ⸻

Yes mam, the man walked away.

Waudean, heard her name being called, loud voice , turning around to see where the voice is coming from, there is Wilma, child get on the bus, what are you day dreaming about, my gosh, child I have been looking for you.

With everybody back on the bus, and here this big old greyhound bus is taking off , it is sound loud, said Wilma to too Waudean, Yes, mam.

Waudean, said I thought you were getting off in Mississippi, I did say that, but I paid extra fair, see here this bus is going to Missouri, and coming back to Mississippi, I have never been out of the state of Mississippi, and at my age, with no husband, I would at least like to see what a northern state looks like, and the people well you know rumors, they say blacks and whites eat in the same place, image that, Yes mam.

That will be different. I don't have any one to go home to except meddling neighbors, and my flower garden. They both can wait.

Waudean, said no disrespect but I am going to go back to sleep, it makes the time go faster. Child you go right on ahead, don't mind me. I am just looking away at the scenery.

Well, time flew by alright, Wilma loud voice , woke Waudean up again, child , you must not have got any sleep last night, you sleep a lot, and the bus is here in Saint Louis , Missouri.

Waudean opened her eyes, grabbing her purse, and looking watch, well it was nice meeting you Wilma, I hope you enjoy your visit with your sister back in Mississippi, same here child, you take care.

The bus is suppose to be here for three hours before it heads back to Mississippi, so I have time to look around, Good luck on your nursing thing child.

Waudean, said "thank you" and walked off the bus, to get her luggage she waited her turn and the called her last name Barrett, Waudean, walked over the sweaty man, with a old gray hat, looks kind of like papa's hat, Waudean thought.

As Waudean, took his luggage, thank you sir. Waudean, looked around, nothing like where she had come from, tall buildings, people walking fast, northern people must be in a hurry all the time.

And, the college is supposed to be right around the corner from here. Waudean looked at the address, ugh, this luggage is heavy, I miss Hank already, "Thank God" it not a long walk" she said to herself.

With, her pressed dress, and black heals, black belt, walking to the college, she seen her College of Nursing School. L.

Waudean, walked in, to admission, next, with a loud voice, Waudean, walked up handed her papers to the lady, Yes, here is the key to your dorm, you will be sharing your dorm. The papers read them they have the rules to school. Just you know, no smoking, no cursing, and if you're late, well just read the papers I gave you, and I wish you well. Next, the woman called out.

Waudean went walking around and found her room, walking in, this room has air condition, it sure felt good no to be sweating.

So cool in this place, what a difference.

There sat a med size woman, with coal black hair, is the first thing Waudean noticed about this woman in her room,

Well Hello there, My name is Betty, as she stood up, and said here let me help you with your suite case. "Thank You" My name is Waudean, but I liked to be called Dean, if you do not mind. Of course not, Well Dean, I will give you the tour after you get your stuff unpacked and settled in, that way tomorrow you will not get lost. That sounds good, Thank You dean said.

Dean had just sat down on the most comfortable bed, Betty came in, you about ready, and you know there is not a whole lot to get to know.

But better knowing, than being lost on the first day. Oh, can I see the classes you are taking, we might have some together, sure, Dean, handed her paperwork, oh, my Gosh, it this great, we have all our classes together, that is good news I agree Dean said. Dean looked at Betty, the weather is so much cooler than Mississppi, I, would pray for rain, that always brought a breeze.

After the tour of the school , Dean said look at the time, I used to being in bed by now, Betty said oh, I am going to take a bath, and get ready for bed, well you go on right ahead, I am going to bed Dean said. Betty in the bathroom heard Dean praying.

The next morning getting too classes was not hard at all, Dean had the hang of where everything was right away, Betty was right , now a whole lot to learn as far as where the classes were. Rules, were on giant poster boards every where.

Everybody seemed really friendly here so far, it was not long before Betty and Dean, became very good friends,

Dean, put the picture of Hank on her mirror, Well, Betty said he a nice looking guy, and does he work for the police or something? Yes, he is the town sheriff, Betty, giggled, the town sheriff,

Dean, looking surprised, yes I live in a little town in Mississippi, and Hank is the Sherriff there, and He is a kind man., and Hank would do anything for me,

He would never let me down, and I would never let him down. And Dean, said I think is an attractive man.

Betty, brushing her hair, well kind and nice looking, you have best of both worlds Dean. Yes, I do feel very Blessed that he picked me.

Betty, looking at Dean, well didn't you pick him too, well dean said of course, but where I come from, people in the whole town that makes a silent remark on rather a couple should be together, and nothing can be done in canton, Mississippi, Blacks live on one side of town and the whites on the other, no one has to tell any one, we do not cross over the tracks, it's a silent rule.

And if you did a person could not do with out anyone knowing it. And then it's all over town,

. That sounds horrible, you will like Saint Louis, there so many people they do not have time to gather around and decide if they like the way your life is going. Dean raised her eye brows, wow, that kind of sounds nice.

Months had rolled by letters went back and forth to Hank and Deans family.

Dean, was reading the last letter and Hank sounded so lonely, Dean knew she was lonely, home sick all of it.

Betty and Dean were both have a great time in college and there grades were something to be proud of. Hey Betty, said, this Saturday night, I agreed to set us both up on a blind date, they are about are age, and suppose to be attractive men.

Wait a minute Betty, Dean, said, as she turned around with a Hank's picture in her hand. I am engaged to a man back home. I know that Betty said, but my gosh, girl, Betty said a little even louder.

It is a blind date, not a shot gun wedding. See here Dean up here in the North it's just called meeting people, and doing sin.

So you will be alright. And

Dean you got to get out a little while you're here, all the time, Dean you need to get out and see things, and mingle with people.

That does not make you trash, because you meet people, my gosh, let's live a little we are young.

Before you go back to Mississippi, don't you want to say, hey Saint Louis, is big and lot's of things to do and see? Dean put Hank's picture back on the mirror, and looked at Betty and said

Well, I sure wish you would have discussed the blind date with me, No Betty, said , because you would have said no Betty, I need to study. Or write my family or Hank a letter. This way, it's just getting out and meeting people. Betty said, smiling have some fun.

Dean,, not excited at all and it showed asked Betty where are we suppose to meet these men, and what time, It's that fancy restaurant down the street, not far from here, How did you set us both up,

Betty, said I will be honest with you, my one friend I have made here is and lives here, her name is Helen, she works at the restaurant, and Theses nice men come in all the time and Helen, as some what got too know them, Any way, it is this Saturday night at Seven o'clock. Be ready, ok. I reckon I will.

Dean, glanced at Hank's picture, and thought of her family back home, they would be so disgraced , going to a place that servers alcohol, and loud music,

One meeting, Dean, thought.

Saturday night came quicker than Dean wanted, she knew she only had one nice dress, she had worked so hard for, Betty and Dean, after putting on the make up, and teasing there hair, with Dean's blue dress, with a v neck collar, and small white pearls, Betty, said, I have white pearl ear rings that will go perfect with your necklace,

Dean tried them on and what a difference ear rings made, Well Thank You Betty. Let's get going since we are walking, it's not that far, Dean, said as they walked Betty, I am glad to get out, I know I am not going to do anything I regret ,

Dean realize getting out and meeting nice people, no harm in that, Betty, by the way, I wanted to tell you earlier, your dress is beautiful. Well, Thank You, Dean, Look there, the merry way restaurant,

Dean, walked behind Betty as they walked in, looking around, well I do not see anyone looking for us , maybe we should leave Dean said, Betty said, look two well dressed men, are standing up, and walking towards us,

Dean, noticed the tall man walking toward her and a smaller man next too him, dean, hugged Betty, my gosh, his suite he is wearing must have cost a year's worth of wages, be quite Dean, here they come.

A tall handsome man, with blue eyes, and Black hair, and smelled nice, reached his hand warmly out too Dean, and said I am Ed, you must be Dean, I was told you are pretty.

But I believe Helen, should have said you are the most Beautiful woman in the world. Dean, caught herself blushing, the smaller man reached out too Betty, and said I am Russell, you dashing woman, let's get back to our table, I have ordered you ladies a drink said Ed.

With all four of them sitting around this huge table with a white linen table cloth, and candle light in the middle, beautiful music playing , Dean, found herself impressed , people really get out and eat like this.

The waiter came quickly with the four drinks, vodka and tonic, Dean, about choked on the first sip, Ed, said you alright, I just do not drink alcohol , oh, Ed, smiled you want something else, maybe ice tea, But, since you paid for the drink, I will try it again,

Dean, looked over at Betty, and she was drinking just fine, and giggling away, everybody y making small talk,

The waiter came back, Sir, with his black and white uniform on, here are the menus', and I will be back in just a moment to take the order from you all,

Ed, gently put his hand on Dean's and said, well sugar, what would you like to have? Dean did not see anything that looked liked what she was used too, oh Ed, please order for me, which impressed Ed.

The waiter was back , and Ed had placed his order for himself as well as Dean, Betty, and Russell, looking confused at the waiter, ugh steak for me said Betty, Russell, make that two steaks medium rare. And more drinks said Russell.

Time went by quickly and small talk was comfortable, Ed, said they are playing a beautiful song, May I have this dance?

Dean, too her surprise said yes, it was some kind of orchestra music, not Elvis, which she heard all the time.

Dean, said this is very nice, as Ed, slipped her into his arms, Dean, felt something, she knew the minute Ed held her in her arms.

Dean, was feeling something she had never felt before, My God Dean, thought this man, is so kind and gentle, Ed, pulled Dean even closer while slow dancing, Ed looked into Dean's eyes, and said you are wonderful and a beautiful woman. I am a lucky man to be dancing with you. Dean's heart started beating faster. Dean was getting goose bumps as Ed held her. Dean knew she did need to be dancing with Ed, but my God it felt so different and so soft and kind.

The song ended, Ed kissed Dean on the cheek "Thank You" for the best dance of my life. Dean smiled back, you are welcome.

With every one back at the table, Dean across the table, Betty, excuse me but let's go to the ladies room, oh sure Deanne, oh, my, Excuse me, Ed , we will be right back, Ed stood up to let Dean, out of the booth table, once in the ladies room my .

Gosh Betty, Dean, grabbed Betty's hand, look in the mirror, you are acting a little tipsy, stop drinking, drinking that alcohol, and drink water or something , we can not afford to get kicked out of school, your right, I will eat something too.

Dean, powder her nose, she noticed she was having a good time, even though Betty needed something to eat.

Back at the table, Ed stood up and let Dean in the booth, and Russell was barley eating the salads the waiter had brought while Ed and Dean were dancing.

, Betty, The waiter had just came to the table, the waiter laid lobster and steak for Ed and Dean, Russell and Betty with the steaks and sides orders. They way they served food here and layer everything out, it look like a table of food that came from a magazine thought Dean.

Dean looked at this food, far cry from ham and hand picked beans out of the garden. Ed, notices Dean, was looking tense, anything wrong, because if there is, I will have to fix it for you, No, this looks really nice,

Dean, was trying to get her lobster out of the shell, and having trouble. Ed , said please, let me help you, Ed, got the lobster out of the shell, sprinkled a little lemon, and butter on the lobster for Dean, there you go , "Thank You" you are a such a gentleman, Ed, was impressed with Dean, Dean and

Ed finished there meal, and Betty was almost done, Russell did not eat much. But drank a lot, Dean noticed.

As time went by that night, everyone was getting along just fine, small talk turned into all four of them giving out there phone numbers.

Betty, said now when you gentlemen call us you have to make sure you say you are our brothers, we are not allowed to date in the college were attending. I see, Ed, said no problem. With, the night get close to the end, Dean, looked at her watch, oh Betty, we have to go, my gosh we can not be late getting back,

Ed, stood up to let Dean out, and walked her out side, can I drive you to your school, Oh, "Thank You" for the offer, but it is just around the corner,

Betty and Russell were right behind them, Betty and Dean, Thanked Ed and Russell again for a wonderful evening. And taking off the high heals, they ran back to college.

Almost out of breath, and back in there room, we made it by three minutes,

Betty, catching her breath, you have to say , you had a good time, I seen it, on your face Dean, Dean, started walking into there bathroom, keeping the door cracked, yes Betty, it was more than I have ever had the pleasure of dining like that. But Dean, I did not expect you to give Ed your phone number to the school, or much less take Ed's telephone number, Well, I fooled myself too.

Months rolled by, and every Saturday night, and spare moment they all spent together,

Ed had learned he had a virgin on his hands, and Dean, had learned Ed, had been married before, with two children in the state of California, that he failed to mention at the first dinner.

Ed, seen Dean, had little money, and did not come from money, a loyal woman, as he told his brother Russell, a woman you can trust. He was falling in love with her, Ed told his brother Russell.

Letters, were still being sent back and forth to Hank, not as much though, Dean, wrote her family as much as possible, and Betty, noticed Hank's picture was gone from the mirror,

Hey Dean, Betty said, where is the picture of Hank at? I have put it in my wallet. It makes feel strange and guilty, I am not too proud of myself right now.

, Betty, said, come here Dean, sit on my bed, we need to talk

Dean, sat down , with a guilty look on her face, hey, Dean, it's ok, you met someone who happens to be in love with you, oh sure , Betty, but Dean, knew she had fallen in love with Ed, and she could not make it go away. Her heart said one thing, and her mind told her Hank. It was tug of war of the heart and mind.

How do you know Ed feels that way?, Dean said with a surprise look on her face, Betty said Ed's brother Russell whom I am seeing just as much as you are seeing Ed, told me that's how, for a second Dean, could not believe how her life was changing, I can not , just not go back home,

My God, Betty I gave my word I would be back after school,

My parents oh, if they knew I was out on doing what I have been doing, I just can not tell them, it would break there hearts, Dean, you have not done anything, there as been only a couple of times, when, you and Ed, went some place , different and spent time alone, like Russell and I did.

Well, Saturday night came again, and all four were together, at dinner the four of them sat. laughing and having a grand time, Ed, took a fork tap on his drink, and that got everyone's attention at the table, Ed, took out a red box with a white ribbon, and opened the box, and there was the hugest diamond ring Dean, had every seen,

I would like to ask to be my wife, Dean, found herself saying yes. And kissing him,

Betty, about dropped her drink, my gosh woman that is a huge ring. Ed's ego only grew with that remark. Yes, I agree said Dean. Ed, put the ring on Dean's finger.

Once back at school, Betty was getting sick every morning, she found out she was pregnant, oh Betty, Dean, said maybe you can hide this until we graduate.

I hope so.

Does Russell know, yes, we got married by the justice of the piece? I will not let the school know. You did not even let me know until now, very good with secrets I see said Dean. Betty said I trusted you, I thought my life would be married then children. Dean said I know, I thought Hank, and now my heart says Ed.

Time went by, school found out and Betty was kicked out for being with child. Russell has a house ,

I guess I messed up pretty bad , oh no, God wants this child or you would not be still with this child, God has another road for you that's all Betty.

, Dean, you sure have a way, of making a empty glass look full. Dean, hugged Betty, let me know if I can help I am here for you. Thank You, said Betty.

Dean knew she had to call her parents, because she and Ed got married them at the justice of the piece only Dean did not tell Betty, or anyone else.

Ed gave her money all the time, for clothes, or about anything she wanted. Dean, learned Ed, had a distributing company. Quite a few, some in Memphis, some in Chicago, and Saint Louis, But Dean was so in love, it took her heart and mind by surprise.

Dean, found out if she could not be with Ed, she did not want anyone else. Not even Hank.

Which broke her heart, because the left Hank out either way she went? I should have never slept with him, with rushing thoughts, Mama, told me about this, once you sleep with a man, you will love him for ever, nothing in the world can change that, because the Good Lord, only made you to give your virginity to one man.

The weather was changing, cooler up here, Ed, bought her the finest clothes, Dean, said I can not go home dressed like this, mama and Papa, will not agree, they will think the northern people are just in to clothes, and I have lost my way with the Lord, thinking to herself, it sure has been a while since I have been to church, Dean, grabbed her purse and went to the nearest church, and prayed. Dean, cried when she prayed, with all her being. Chills went out to her body; she got up after praying and left the church feeling much better.

Dean, and Ed, went out for dinner, which is so funny, looking at Ed, they call supper down in the south, and up here in the north they call in dinner. Odd. Don't you think? Yes, baby.

Ed, said as before you finish school, we need to look at new houses, the recession is pretty much over, and the economy is picking back up.

Dean, leaned into him, and told him that she could not tell her family about him being divorced they just could not accept something like this right away, or two children he left behind, she could image her papa's expression and are how Dean let them down.

This day and time, you don't marry a divorced man whom made a choice to leave his family.

Dean convinced herself the day will come when she would be honest with them.

Ed and Dean, found time to look at houses, they purchased a brand new four bedroom house, with two living rooms, a dish washer, brand new side by side refrigerator, the whole house had new furniture.

Ed, put a fenced in back yard. Landscaping with trees and bushes. And bought Dean, a new Cadillac. Dean, could not believe her eyes.

Ed, had a red convertible Cadillac, and he had bought her a white one. Over whelming,

Dean knew it was that time to make the call, to her family and to Hank. Dean, was getting a headache just knowing what the would be said on the other line.

Time went by, with her palms beginning to sweat, Dean made the phone call and Mama answered the phone,

Dean told her almost everything, that she is married, mama had tears, Dean heard it in her voice, oh my Lord Child what have you run off and done? Mama, you will like him, mama said she understood but dean would have to be the one to break the news too Hank and everyone else, on why she was not coming back to Mississippi.

As Mama, heard all about Ed, she wished Dean, well, and put Papa on the phone, the conversation went the same,

only Papa said, Dean what kind of church did yaw all get married in, Papa, I will talk more, I am not being disrespectful, I just don't want to run up the phone bill. God bless you my child and call any time and we would like to meet your husband Ed, as soon as we can.

Yes sir, I understand Papa, They said there Good by's. And Dean, felt some what relieved then it was Hank she had to call next. But, Dean feeling guilty that she was not honest with her mama and Papa.

It would break there heart. Dean, found her self sneaking and smoking cigarettes, it calmed her nerves, and she told herself. Not on school grounds did dean ever try to smoke.

Betty called from time to time and was getting bigger with the baby growing in her. Dean try her best too cheer her up, but with Russell drinking more and more was not helping.

It was Sunday, and she had mail she had not open ,
Dean seen a letter from Hank, Dean opened it , and read it and cried, Dean, knew Hank did not know she had married someone else, it was time to make this horrible call.

Dean, called Hank, her hands shaking, and her mind being focused on what to say, and how to say, what was going to destroy Hanks heart.

Dean made the call , Hello its Dean, Hank said Baby wow, I have not stopped thinking about you , and let me tell you Dean, that land you and I look at , a while back , I have made up mind , I will buy this for you.

You love that area with the flowers. Dean, I am sorry I have been rambling on, how are you Dean? Hank, heard the tears in Dean's voice, and the trembling. Hank, I do not know how too say this,

Hank said oh my lord, are you ok? Dean, yes, Hank I have some bad news. Really bad news, Hank got silent, what kind of bad news, just tell me.

Dean, said Hank I met a man up here and I , Hank , this is really hard , tell me about the man you met Hank said firmly. I am trying, Hank I am so sorry to tell you like this, but I got married. Hank, yelled how you could do that, Dean, tried to explain that she had not planned any of this, and was so very sorry she had hurt him and let him down.

, Hank was mad and hurt at the same time, Dean, knew he had every right to be that way. Silence on both ends for about a two minutes, Dean, you will Reap what you sow.

You can quote me on this. I know you are a wise woman, but you are making a mistake, Do you hear me? Before Dean could not answer while crying,

How could you make a fool out of me? And how could you leave me here thinking we had a life to share together?

Dean, kept saying over and over how sorry she was as she cried, Tell me Dean, if you're so in love and happily married, you do not sound like it. You're not happy you just are confused. I am, I am just so sorry that I hurt you; silence was on the phone,

I can not talk any more to you Dean, Dean, tried to say Good By, by Hank had hung up on her.

Dean took his engagement ring and mailed it back to Hank, with a note that said, I am truly sorry for the pain I have caused you.

God as my witness I did not mean to hurt anyone or let anyone down. Hank I hope one day you can forgive me. Love, Dean. And the letter was sent off.

It was not long before Dean, had graduated from school, she knew mama and papa could not afford to come up and see her graduate, and they would not take a hand out from Ed. Or any one else for that matter.

Ed and Dean moved into there new home, Dean was feeling so happy.

Ed knew with Dean's looks, she could open accounts for him very easily, it's hard to say no to a good product, and a pretty face,

Ed talked Dean, into working with him instead of using her nursing degree.

Dean said but I had worked so hard for that nursing degree, you are limited too how much money you can make, Ed, said, this here, we set the limit.

Dean and Ed, went places .
, Dean could not image taking trips too the ocean, Ed and Dean also took trips with Betty and Russell, Betty was do any day,
But it did not stop them from going on long trips. And Russell drinking all the time, it was embarrassing Deans said to Betty, I know. Betty said.

A Year had rolled buy, and Dean, just loved the smell of fall, not hot at all, the tree's had so much color, always a nice breeze, and the site of snow, came shortly, the whiteness and it was soft,.
Ed, made her a snowman, first one she had ever seen in real life, Dean, Ed called her, yes honey, come on out here I want to show you something,
There in the front yard, was a snow man, with roses, Dean, laughed and said the snow cold will kill those flowers, well go get your flowers, the snowman is holding. Dean, loved Ed sense of humor, but he also was always on the go.

With a year gone by, Mama and Papa came up, Pauline and her family could not make it, Pauline had just had a baby boy named Charles.
Mama, and papa just loved the house, they did not care for the high price cars, and the air conditioning, papa, said Dean, why do yaw all two living rooms?
Oh Papa, that's just how Ed wanted that's all. Mama and Papa did stay a week and went on back home.

Dean, hoped see could see them soon, Dean cried when they left. That feeling of when is I going to see my family again was on her heart.

Dean, found out she is going to have a baby, oh my gosh, Ed and I always go here and there, and seems no time left over for anything but sleep.

More accounts were opened, which to Dean's surprise it was more money than she had ever seen in her life.

Dean, found her so out of place going from a slow place in Mississippi, to opening accounts all day long, and no time for anything else.

Dean and Ed travel a lot, too much to take on some days, months had rolled by, and Ed was out of town again,

Dean, found her self going into labor, she walked as hard as she could to the next door neighbor, and Marla, open the door,

Oh, My gosh Dean, Marla, open the door and helped Dean, inside, with painful sounds and moaning, please get me to the hospital Marla, oh Dean, I can drive, let me get my husband Howard, Dean was moaning, and sweat was all over her face, this hard labor Dean said.

With Marla, running to get her husband, leaving Dean, what sounded like Dean, was in hard labor, and oh where is your husband?

With moaning sounds he is out of town Dean said. Howard got Dean, in the car and drove her Hospital. , Dean, Howard asked do you have a telephone number for Ed so I can let him know you're in the hospital. , No, Ed, usually calls when he is out of town, but I have no idea what hotel he is at.

My husband Ed is supposed to back today. Well, when I see him I will get him the news about you.

With more hard labor pains, Dean, could not even say "Thank You"

Dean, found herself in tears, because she knew she all by herself, God help she said out loud, , oh you will be fine the nurse said, you are about ready, so I will get a wet towel and put in our head that helps some,

The Doctor walked in and took a look at Dean, and said we do not have much time, you have a baby that is wanting to come on out.

Dean pushed, sweating and screaming the pain was so bad, the Doctor raised his voice, you must do better than that, if you want this baby to come, out.

Dean gave long hard pushes, finally the doctor said, one more push and that's it, we're almost there, and the doctor said come on you can do this.

Dean, with sweat all over her body, oh, one more push, yes the Doctor said, here is your new baby boy

, Congratulations you have a baby boy, but, the nurses had odd looks on there faces, Dean, could feel something is wrong, the doctor said we will be back; we are cleaning up your baby boy.

Dean said Dr. Oh with a big sigh. I want to see my baby. And hold him.

The doctor said Dean, I will be back the nurses are cleaning up the baby, just rest and I will be back in. Dean laid back, taking a big breath, thinking I am just anxious, there is nothing wrong with my baby.

. Dean, thinking I am a mother. What a wonderful feeling. Dean, smiled. I know he is beautiful.

The doctor walked back in this small white room, and walked up too Dean, and said I need to prepare your baby did not form all his parts of his and hands and toes.

Dean, turning pale, and feeling sick.

the Doctor grabbed Dean's hand I am so sorry to tell but your baby has no fingers and no toes, the bones were formed, but no growth after that.

Dean screamed no, this can not be happening, Dean, was crying and shaking, so hard the Dr. called for a nurse , the nurse came in quickly give Dean, a valium to calm her down.

The nurse gave dean the medicine and Dean was calmer, but Dean had so many questions. The Doctor grabbed Dean's hands please, calm down, some times things like this happen. Dean, said please fix my baby's hands and feet.

The dr still in the room, Dean, I will give you the name of a plastic surgeon and these plastic surgeons can do a lot.

The Doctor said right now I need to give you something to calm down; your blood pressure is going to go up even more. The valium is not working like it shoud.

The Doctor gave Dean a shot for her blood pressure; the doctor knew she could not have another valium so soon.

The Dr. left and gave Dean Time to calm down, the Dr. walked back in Dean Room checked her blood pressure and it was fine.

Dean, I am going to go get your baby now and bring him in, Dean, sitting up in bed now, waiting for the Doctor to return with her first new born son.

It was not long and the Doctor walked back in holding a wrapped up new born, the doctor leaned down, and Dean sat up with her arms reaching for her son.

Dean, now holding her baby, and looking at his face, he is beautiful, my son is fine. The Doctor said, Dean, take the baby out of the blanket, Dean, did and Dean's face, had horror on her face.

My baby , oh my God, looking at her son, Dean, looked at the doctor , do something please, I am begging you to fix his fingers that are not there and his toes, Tears and pain rolling down Dean's face.

Dean, was over whelm with racing thoughts, Dean said, Doctor how did something like this happen?

Dean's heart was beating so fast, why me, Dean asked out loud, Some times, things happen like this, I am sorry Dean.

As the Doctor touched her hand. Your baby, other wise is healthy.

The nurses will come in and get him and they will do the first feeding,

Dean, since you are not breast feeding, I think that would be best if the nurses feed him first, you need to try and calm your self down the doctor said.

, Dean, found her self crying so hard, the Doctor calling for the nurses.

The nurses came, the doctor explained to take the baby and feed him, Dean, is not breast feeding and my patient needs to calm down more The Doctor looked at Dean sad eyes' Dean, I am going to give you a little something extra to calm down, the valium was not strong enough. Ok Dean said.

The doctor gave Dean a shot. Dean, just starting to feel relaxed.

Ed, walked in the room, and Dean, started crying, she could even tell him about the baby, the doctor, took Ed out side the hospital room and explained everything.

My lord how did this happen, and what can be done?

I will give you and your wife the name of a plastic surgeon, they can do a lot, and it is the 1950's. , the Doctor, looked at Ed, I just gave your wife a shot too help calm her down, but tonight we can give her something to help her sleep.

But we need your permission to give your wife that medication.

The Doctor said I will give her something they call valium to help at home, it a pill she will take as needed. . Of course give my wife wants she needs, Thank You; we will give that shot to her later on tonight.

Ed, walked back in the room, with a dozen of Red roses in his hand, and a smile that made Dean feel so glad her husband was by her side.

And he grabbed Dean's hands and put them together in his Ed, said "Thank You" for giving me a son. Dean, tears rolling down her face, she said nothing,

Baby with calm and loving words do not worry we will get the best plastic surgeons money can buy, and things will work out.

He is healthy the doctor said, he is not going to be a cripple, unless we treat him that way.

The nurses walked back in, with a wrapped up little baby, Dean, reached her arms out for her son, here you go, we will be back in little bit, to get him, since you are not breast feeding, we' will keep your baby boy in the nursery.

Dean, UN wrapped her son, and she almost lost her breath; he has no fingers and no toes, oh Ed, my God. Calm down Dean.

Dean, you know this you have seen the baby, Dean, looked at Ed, I can not believe our son has no fingers or toes, he will be handicapped.

Ed grabbed Deans hands and said

Things will work out. Dean, felt horrible. I do not know what I did to cause our baby to be born with no fingers or toes, tears rolling down her face, as she took the baby's arms into her hands.

Dean, things are going to work out, you are getting up set about something that can very well these days be fixed.

Dean knew the medical field had not advanced like the way Ed thought it had. Ed, said let me hold the baby.

Dean gave him to her husband and said, Ed, said I am going to name him after my brother , the one who died in a Tran wreck ,

We will name him Julius , that's a beautiful name Dean said, Ed said my brother was a good person. Ed kept holding the baby, and the doctor walked in the hospital room, I am sorry to interrupt but I need to take the baby and Dean you need to rest.

Ed, said I am going to go home, I am going to ask the Doctor to give you something to help you sleep, ok Ed, Ed, leaned over the hospital bed, and said I really do love you .

Ed said Dean, I am leaving I will have everything ready for you and the baby when you get home.

Dean, was out of the hospital, and a year had went by nine operations, passed by, on Julius, the Doctor's used the skin off his legs to make fingers, which were all different shapes and sizes.

The Doctors told Ed and Dean, there is nothing we can do about the toes; the bones did not form all the way.

But we can make still more progress with his fingers, Dean, asked can his fingers be the same size and shape on each finger,

The Doctor, said I am sorry each finger, the bone did form on some but not each one, but we are doing the best we can.

Ed, said well for fifty thousand dollars, this all you can do? Ed shook his head,

Dean, found she working and taking care of what Dean, called a handicap child, Ed, said no more words like that.

Dean said I am tired of people looking at my child like he is not human. Ed, looked at Dean, and said, there are kind people and mean people in the world, your not going to change that. Our son will be fine.

Dean, was getting tired, working, taking care of the house, and by now two years have gone by, the doctors did all they could for Julius,

Dean, found out she is going to have another baby and scared with her second pregnancy, she prayed all the time, God please let this child be health all fingers and toes.

Time went by quickly, and Dean had a baby girl,

Ed showed up, went into the hospital room where Dean is, and with the dazzling smile, and diamond ear rings for Dean.

Ed, said I seen that beautiful baby girl, we will name her Jennifer. Dean said that is also a nice name. Did you know someone by that name asked Dean?

Ed, looked at Dean, and said no, I thought it was a pretty name for our baby girl?

Dean, looked down, with an open box, Oh, my I did not see these diamond ear rings, why? Because I love you. " Thank You" Ed. I feel so loved, I know how lucky I am, you are faithful, and kind, and a loving man. Ed, kissed her on the lips, Baby, you are the one, the makes my day. He winked at Dean,

Phone calls went back and forth to Mama and Papa, and Pauline. Pauline had her second child as well a little girl they called Rhonda.

Dean told Ed, she is really missing her family, and she reminded Ed, that her and her Mama's birthdays were on the same day. July 10th.

Ed, was not too agreeing to let Dean go down to see her family, there is money to be made, grabbing his vodka and tonic, and looking at Dean, with amazement,

Dean, saw and felt he did not want her too leave, but it was about making money,

Times were changing, things were getting invented, lot's of work going around, people dressing in all kinds of styles.

Dean said it would only be for a week I will take both the children with me. I guess go own down there and see your family, but I am staying here to make us money.

Ed, was not happy, but agreed.

Dean, was getting ready for her trip, she had called her mama, and told her she was on her way, and would be leaving in the morning.

Mama prayed she would make back home safe, a woman traveling with two small children, you're a brave woman Waudean, mama, and I miss you and will see you when I get there. I love you, and again I will be leaving in the morning.

Dean, I have question for you, yes Mama? How does Ed, let you travel alone with those children, does he not worry about you? Mama, Ed loves us, he has business to take care of, Dean, heard the disbelief in her Mama's voice, ok.

We will all be waiting on you child. Dean avoided the question. Dean, starting feeling like that's all Ed, wanted was money, and her pretty face too open the accounts. But, she could never love a man more than Dean, loved Ed.

Dean packed the care and the children and was gone by five am. With a note on the table for Ed, Dearest Ed, I will call when I get there to let you know I made it safe. Thank You, for being a wonderful husband, love, Dean.

Dean was long gone on the highway, with two small children asleep, which made the trip so far easier. And her hand map in her lap, just in case she needed directions.

But Dean knew her way.

Dean prayed she would not see Hank. She prayed a lot.

Ed, got up and seen the empty house, not a sound, of anything that sound like a family lived there. Dean, thought about how Ed's ego was changing the more money he was making the more his ego was.

Dean liked the money, but not the mountain high ego Ed had.

Dean had made it to Mama and Papa's house, getting her children out of the car, papa came out of houses, and that old screen door was a sight for sore eyes, and Mama's rose bushes never looked better, and those roses Mama grew, everyone loved them

Huge roses in bold colors, it looked like a rose garden of love.

Hugging Papa, with happiness in his voice, said my child we prayed you would make it with no problems, we knew the Lord heard our prayers, let me get your luggage for you, "Thank You "Papa. Papa, said I notice you have leather suite cases, fancy things .

Papa, Ed, uses them as well for his business trips, I see child.

Walking into the house, with Julius and Jennifer, mama, kissed Waudean, let me see my grandchildren, oh they are just a blessing, mama and the rest of Dean's family did not even react to Julius fingers, but Dean, noticed how could they not.

Dean knew she had a loving family.

Jennifer, with her naturally curly brownish hair, was a picture perfect baby, your young eons are a just lovely,

Julius, has your Papa's eyes I think, Dean, smiled yes Mama, I think so too. Jennifer is about the prettiest little girl I think I ever seen. With her southern accent.

Sitting down at the table, mama walked over here I made you a plate of supper; I thought you might be hungry and all. There is enough for children as well.

Dean, ate, butter beans, fresh picked corn, with butter cornbread, never tasted to good, I miss this food Mama,

I do not think I realized how much you can miss something, until, and you are around it again. , child eat up, you look so thin, everything all right with you,

Yes, mama. Just tired. I need to call Ed; I will call him collect so it will not be on your bill,

Dean, gave the children the bath in the claw foot bath tub, which brought back so many memories, Lord, the kids were tired from the long trip, and Dean, thought she as soon as she called Ed, she was so tired so would take a quick bath, and get to bed.

With the kids in the beds sleeping like babies,

Dean, made the collect call it was about eight o'clock or so. The operator, came back on the phone, and said I am sorry there is no answer at that number, to Dean's surprise, Ed should be home, odd, maybe he went and visited his brother Russell and Betty, and they were not doing so well, the last Dean had heard.

Papa said I have to get up with the sun in the morning, so I'm off to bed, Papa, had said the family prayers' to end the night.

Dean, found herself sleeping so comfortable, until about midnight, she slowly got out of bed, and used the phone, collect call from Dean, to this number, one moment please, the operator came back on the phone I am sorry, there is no answer at the number, Dean, could not believe it, Ed, must have worked so hard he didn't even hear the phone ring Dean said to herself.

Once back in bed, she finally dosed off, and got some sleep.

The children, woke her up, Dean, could smell Mama's breakfast, helping Julius, go to the rest room, he could not button his pants, the Doctor had told Dean, after the next operation he should be able to do that. Jennifer, pretty much went to the bathroom, washed her hands, and could not wait to see smiling grandma, her reached out for her, when Jennifer walked in the kitchen, ahead of Dean.

Well child did you sleep well, yes, grandma, it's hot down here. And in here. Oh you will get used to,

Pauline and her two kids walked in about that time, Dean, walking Julius into the kitchen, with smiles, and hugs, Pauline, said look our children are not too far in age difference,, Dean, smiled, Dean, knew she had been so busy with Ed and the business,

Dean, had not realized until that moment, she was missing on a lot of family time. Pauline, said oh, what beautiful children you have, and Dean, said the same about hers, that's a shame about Julius, but I am sure he will be just fine,

Yes, Dean said looking at her sister, Mama said nothing. I am going to take Mama out for he Birthday , at the catfish house, she always wanted to see what there food is like, Pauline Dean, said, you and your family are invited to come, oh my we really do not have the money to be going out to eat , we have food at home.

Oh, no , this is my treat, I would be so pleased if you all would come to dinner with me and Mama and Papa,

Pauline, lit a cigarette, you know that is one of the finer places to eat here, it will not be cheap, Dean, said this is my treat, I miss you all . Please, come.

Papa, and Mama, drove with Dean, and the children.

You still driving these fancy cars, its cold up in here, oh Papa, that air conditioning, Dean, turned down the air condition. Pauline rode with Dade, she did not drive, and Dade's ego could not handle a woman driving, that's a man job.

Once in the restaurant, they all seemed to be getting along fine.

The waitress came and took there orders, the only thing you could get is catfish, and side green's as side orders, everyone is drinking ice tea, or lemonade.

, Dean, found she was feeling very blessed, to have her lifestyle.

Everyone was eating, and laughing about old times,

Pauline, said, oh my Gosh, grabbing Dean's hand, my lord, your wedding ring, is the size of walnut, beautiful, if I do say so myself, Dade, was not real comfortable, seeing his wife, admire how big his sister n laws wedding ring is, Papa, said, just material things,

pretty, but there is more to life, than big diamond rings.

Pauline and everyone else were about done with supper, the bill came and Dean paid for everyone in full.

Well, I guess you doing pretty well for yourself to be able to take us all out like that; we sure do appreciate the nice meal, Dean. Papa said.

Dean replied I am glad you enjoyed in Papa. Well, Dean went and paid the bill, Pauline helped Dean, with the children as the left the restaurant.

Dean, road back in style in her red convertible Cadillac. Dade and Pauline in there old pick up truck, and Mama and Papa, on the same old faded ford Falcon,

Once back home,

Dean, tried calling Ed again, same answer the operator had told her no answer at the number. Papa, said did you ever get a hold of Ed, Dean, found her self telling Papa, a little white lie, the phone lines are having problems connection or something, well it is a far place away, as papa removed his hat.

Dean was struggling with the fact she did not come out and tell the truth, she can not get a hold of her husband. Part of her wanted to stay for ever, and part of Dean, wanted to be home in the next breath, what kind of man, thinks more of making money than paying respect at your father n law passing away.

Dean and all were sitting outside, Dean, went in one more time to try and make the call to her husband again, sounded like the same operator and Dean, and were getting embarrassed.

As Dean, hung up the phone, she had noticed what Papa, had made, was still hanging on the same wall, the Ten Commandments, she rubbed her finger across the wood plaque, and Jesus hanging on the cross.

Wow, this pretty, Dean, thought it would be nice if Ed would want something like this in our house.

Dean, reminded herself, Ed., loved her, she knew that, when we go some place, people we don't even know, said we look like the perfect couple.

Dean, was getting worried, had something happened to Ed, with racing thoughts, she heard papa's voice, coming Papa, said now listen up Dean, I know you are smoking them cigarettes, you might as well go ahead and smoke in front us all, don't be hiding things like that. I am not proud of the habit you done picked up.

Dean, grabbed a cigarette, which in dean's mind, and released so weird pressure about her husband never answering the phone.

Dean, said as she watched her two children run around having fun, I am so sorry to cut this trip short, but I best be getting home, Pauline, says, with a smile, that Yankee man of yours can not stand the site of you be gone,

Dean, smiled, just need to get on back home.

Well, you are a grown woman with a family you know what is best.

Before you leave Dean, can I talk with you? Smiling at her sister Pauline, of course. Mama said I will watch your children while you girls go talk. Thank You mama Dean said.

Pauline and Dean, went into Dean's old bedroom, it seemed cooler in there, Dean, sat down on her old bed, Pauline next too her grabbing her hand, look I am your sister, tell me what is going on, you have this worried look on your face since you got been here,

Dean, said I can not get a hold of Ed, starting to sweat, Pauline's eyes wide open, her mouth dropped, you mean too tell me Ed, does not know if you and the children even made it here safe?

Dean, put her head down, with a low voice Yes, I am worried about him, and it's not like him. Dean, was so anxious to get a hold of Ed, Dean was not having a good time with her family.

You sure the operator dialed the right telephone number, that long distance calling is strange, I know, when I call you Dean, its gets confusing at times.

I do know maybe, Dean, knew she had give the right telephone number,

Dean, got up , Well Pauline, that's why I want to get back home, things just don't feel right, why didn't Ed come with you and the children, ?

Dean turned around its business it's all the time about making money. All the time, Dean found her repeating herself.

Grabbing her leather suite cases for her and the children Dean, started packing her and the children's clothes.

Well, I thought you were worried about Hank and all, you know how it ended between yaw all. To be honest with you, I really have not thought too much about Hank, after all we are not together, but since you brought name up, I guess he is doing fine?

Pauline crossed her legs, well, after you broke his heart and all, Hank, really was not fine, his kind of got bitter towards the town, and I guess life. But, folks around here finally quite talking about it, except bertha, she will talk about to her dead ancestors if she could. She is teaching that old stupid bird she has in the house to talk, some kind talking bird. I heard for myself, that bird does talk, she brought in town,

Dean smiled. Same old bertha, does she still curses up a storm.

Dean asked. Pauline said, her and the bird said bad words, she done taught that parrot how to say things we would not even say on are worse day.

Bertha, as got a bad mouth on her. Dean agreed. But sometimes, she can be funny too.

I am helping Mama, as much as I can, Papa is getting to old to mow the grass, and Dade mows Papa's grass.

Pauline, I am sorry I am not here too helping more. Pauline, looked up and her sister, my gosh you have a wonderful life up north, I'll be alright.

Pauline, could not help but be a little jealous of Dean, diamonds, fancy cars, coming back home affording to take everyone out for supper. Sounded better than picking beans out of the garden all day.

Dean, got the luggage in the car, went and gave everyone hugs and kisses, and left everyone in tears, not knowing when they would see Dean, again, and watch the children grow up.

With Dean and the children in the car and pulling out of the old dirt drive way, she felt odd, like she belong here and up north, like Papa said, you can't pick corn and pea's at the same time.

The trip went by quick, Dean drove a little faster than she should have, but she wanted to be in house , the children are sleeping,

Dean, lit up a cigarette, amazing she thought I know these things are bad, they help me with the anxiety.

Time went by quick and dean, was pulling up in her drive way, Ed's car was there, what a relief, the children, were excited they knew home.

Opening the door, there Ed was on the phone in the kitchen, Dean, thought what is going on, Ed, ended is phone call quickly, went over to Dean, and said, you are home earlier than I thought,

Dean, put her arms around Ed, that is because I have missed so much , that I had to come home, I tried calling many times, Ed, with his eye brow's up, Really now, I have been in and out, trying to make us money, but grabbing her hand , it was lonely here with out you. Dean did not bring up how many calls she made to Ed again.

Ed, went picked his children up, Ed, smiling at the children Hey did yaw all have fun down there, Julius says yes. Jennifer said the car ride was long. Teresa, nodding her head, Ed took that as yes.

The kids went in there rooms as played, as Dean, said. Well,

What did you do while I and the children was gone, just business baby?

By the way how is your family doing? Fine replied Dean. I wish you would have been there. Ed said I told you why I was not going. Dean did not bring up that conversation any more.

Let's go out with out the kids, tonight for dinner.

Infact I think we should go out to the first restaurant where we met, and then go by Russell and Betty's house, ask the next door lady if she will baby sit the children, Dean, organized it all , Marla, was so eager to always help Dean, liked that Marla seemed like family . Dean paid her well.

Ed and Dean, went out dancing and drinking, had the time of there lives, drove by Russell and Betty's house, things were awful,

Russell, is leaving Betty, with two children, and he is not going to help out at all.

Ed said we can not stay long, I am sorry to hear about yaw all not working out.

Dean, hugged Betty, call me, I will help you in every way I can. Betty said, I just can not believe I gave up my nursing degree for this man, who left me with two kids. Tears rolled down Betty's eyes.

Dean, sent child support payments to Ed's ex wife in California. On a regular basis. The little boy is Edward, and the little girl's name is Jacqueline. Ed's ex wife, was also named Betty, she had sent pictures of the children.

, When Dean could she sent money to Betty, who had no job, and Russell did not care if they ate or not. Horrible husband Dean Thought and horrible dad. Poor Betty, if she could have only stayed on school Dean thought.

If he did care no one could tell. Dean, seen she could afford to send her parents money almost every two weeks, she knew Pauline was doing what she should have been doing for her parents if she would have stayed in Mississippi.

Dean sent a little money to Pauline, knowing she is doing so much for Mama and Papa.

The years rolled by, more money in the bank than Dean every thought she would see in her life time.

Now it was 1962, and Dean, is about to get birth to another child, she knew she had pretty much stopped going to church, but in her heart she prayed, Lord, let this child be healthy.

Dean's third child came in the world April 7th 1962, Dean, was happy the cold weather was gone, and trees were starting to get green.

Dean, had a healthy baby girl, all fingers and toes, the only problem was the cord got wrapped around the baby throat, but the Doctor, took care of that and, the Doctor told Dean, your baby girl is healthy,

Ed came to the hospital, with his charming self flirting with the nurses and the nurses flirting back

Dean, was upset, I seen and heard you with those nurses,.

How could you, Ed, grabbed her hand, because I tell a woman she looks nice, that is not flirting, that is being polite.

Ed said by the way I have named this baby Teresa. Dean liked the name too. Dean did not bring up to Ed about him flirting with the nurses anymore.

Dean knew she was so tired, from opening accounts and traveling, trying to take care of what Ed, called a home,

Ed and I are never there she thought to herself. , Ed, said, looked when you get out of the hospital; I have a surprise just for you.

Ed, kissed her on the cheek, again I went and seen our pretty baby girl, you are just the most wonderful woman in the world to me, you do not need to get upset, over a compliment , Dean, thought , Ed is right, what is wrong , he did not touch her or anything.

This marriage will never end,

Once back home Dean, tried to keep up with the business, kids, and traveling it had taken its toll.

With Dean and three kids to take care of , Ed knew a house keeper was in deep need, He told Dean, hire a full time house keeper, to run this house and take care of these kids, he needed her with the business.

Dean, waking up at 3:am, not being able to sleep, she went into the kitchen, looked around her pretty house, and looked at the diamonds on her hands,

Dean, lit a cigarette, and got a glass of wine, and started crying, this is my place to take care of my children, as she finished her glass of wine, the phone rang, she looked at the time, it was almost 3:30 am, she answered, and the woman on the other end of the phone, asked if Eddie was there, Dean, could tell this woman was some what drunk.

Why I am his wife, how may I help you? Well Eddie, told me he is single, and the drunken woman wanted too argue with Dean, that Eddie, said he would help me out with my rent,

Dean, and said really, where do you live, the drunken woman hung up.

Dean, found herself drinking one more glass of wine before she went to bed,

Dean, also took a valium, she had left over the doctor had given her.

Dean, woke up,

Ed, was taking care of the children, and told Dean, good morning, with instructions to hire a housekeeper today if she could today or soon as possible.

And that he also reminded her of the surprise he had for her, that as soon as she hired the house keeper, he would show her, what he had for her,

Dean thought this must be some surprise; we can not take the kids, a housekeeper now. Ed was getting demanding as his money grew.

Dean, said has she drank her coffee and smoked a cigarette, a woman called last night about 3:30 am or so, she said Eddie, was suppose to pay her rent,

Ed tuned around, that must be the one lady, she is a drunk and down on her luck, since her husband had died, I felt sorry for her, and told we could help her.

This woman who is she?

Ed, turned around a friend of Russell's, Your brother does not even support his own children, and this woman is his friend, that we are going to help out and pay rent for her, Dean, you always said, it's a blessing to help out someone, what is wrong with you? Dean, said, you never mentioned her to me, where she lives or anything, Baby , as he touched Dean's shoulders, that's because I was going to give the money to Russell to give to her,

Dean did not want to talk about this drunk woman anymore. But Dean wrote a check out to Russell's ex-wife to help with bills and the kids, with a note, keep this between you and me. Call me anytime you need something or just a friend to talk too. Loved.

Dean, went to the unemployment office, the unemployment office, had someone in mind right away ,

Dean, felt so lucky, they allowed Dean, to interview her over the phone, they were eager to find Donna a job.

Dean thought she sounded wonderful, and a sweet and trusting voice

Dean, got the directions, and interview Donna in person.

Dean could tell she is wonderful with children, Donna agreed to work and Dean went and picked her up. This is really a short notice Dean said. No Donna said I have been looking for the right house keeping job.

Dean, knew Ed, wanted somebody now, she knew she did not want to disappoint Ed. And Ed did not like to be disappointed.

And Dean came home with a woman in her early twenty's with an hour glass figure, and a face that belonged in Hollywood, dashing woman.

Dean, pulled up in the drive way, with Donna, once inside the house Donna, said she would love to work for the both of them. And Donna "Thanked both of them" Pay, with free room and board.

Dean had no problems with Donna, she was a great housekeeper, and the children loved her, Teresa was about three years old give or take when Donna came,

Donna did very well with Julius and Jennifer as well. Donna took extra care with Julius fingers and helped get him a lot, Jennifer, did fine.

Dean, found herself gone more than at home, traveling here and there, wore out most of the time,

Dean, also noticed Donna, and Ed got a long real good, Dean, thought to herself, Ed, may not go to church, but he would never cheat on me, just never happen Dean, said to herself. Dean knew where she came from, woman did not break up other woman's homes. Its was just plum unheard of.

Ed, told dean, after you get a good nights rest we are going some place in the morning after you wake up.

The next morning Dean, and Ed had woke up to a wonderful breakfast, the children, were all dressed and playing.

Everything is working out fine, you are doing a wonderful job, great job for your first day Ed said. Too Donna, Ed said with a smile, as he touched her shoulder.

Dean, did not react, Ed, is just being polite, what would the world be like if we did not give a compliment,

Dean, soul searched and realized, Donna, is a woman, but Ed, is a faithful husband.

After breakfast, Ed said, Dean told Donna, Dean and I will be gone most of the day, you will not be able to reach us, but we will be back before dinner.

Ok Donna, said with those pretty white teeth, a body any man would look at twice. I will have dinner waiting for you all.

How does six o'clock sound for dinner time, we might be back by then or sooner. Ed and Dean left, in the care and were gone.

Ed said it's a beautiful day, as Dean lit a cigarette, yes, it does appear that way. Ed, turned on the radio, JFK is on the radio giving his speech.

That is a good man, changing things for the better,

Ed said, Dean, said I agree but do you think things will really change for the colored people, not in the south Ed quickly replied it will take years for the south to change. The people are not eager for any type of change.

The drive went by some what quick, Dean, realized they were way out of city limits, seeing cliffs, and huge tree's and not much in between, no stores.

Turning to Ed, honey where are we going?

It's a surprise, it not too much farther, they enjoyed the ride being alone together, with Dean's head on Ed's shoulder. It's been a long time since we have done this, just us together like old times, Ed said. Dean, said this man loves me so much, I can feel it.

With the car slowing down,

Ed said Dean, close your eyes until I tell you too open them, Dean, did that, with anxiety, the car stopped, and the engine turned off,

Ok, Sugar, open those baby blue eyes, oh my gosh, look at that two story house, with wrap around porches on each level, and the farm animals, cows, and pretty white horses, with a white fence, and flowers every where.

What a long drive way, Ed, said look across the highway, Dean, and saw a white fence, around a lot of land, what is that over there Dean asked, that is the other side I bought as well. It's beautiful over there as well, spring feed wide creek, and parts of that creek across the highway is quite deep.

But that grass needs to be worked on, before I take you over there, weeds are up to my knees. Ed said.

Ed said and it's not a dirt drive way either, Dean, looked at him, like he was referring to her parents,

Ed, my Papa, has a dirt drive way, a quite frankly I really do not see any harm in that in a dirt drive way.

You will soon or later, you don't live there anymore, and you do not belong on dirt drive ways, sugar, I think of you is why I say these things. I look out for you when you are not looking out for yourself, you're a sweet woman, but you can be naïve at times

Dean.

Dean, did not like that remark, Ed, I am smart woman, I earned my education to work in any state I choose. Ed, laughed, out loud , looking at Dean in the eye's baby you will be using that nursing degree, now really , look around do you think a nursing degree could have purchase all this. Ed, laughed you are kidding yourself woman.

Dean lit a cigarette and said no. I reckon my nursing degree would not have bought all this. But I am grateful that you think of me, and our children. I should have not snapped at you like that Ed, I am sorry. Ed smiled its fine baby. Ed, said you know I fell in love with you because you are smart and beautiful, but I need to help you not be so naïve about the world.

Both of them walked up to the house, Dean said it seems bigger now that I am right next to it, well sugar go on in, it's yours after all.

Dean, pinched herself , yes, I am not dreaming, feeling guilty, if this man did all this for me, and here I am getting upset over some drunk woman calling the house, Dean, reminded herself, how lucky she is.

She walked around the entire house, Honey, Ed, I am upstairs, and the master bed room is just so large, this whole house is. I don't think I have ever seen a pretty house, a fire place in most of the rooms.

Ed, smiled as he caught Dean on the swirling stair case, and held her in her arms, so are you happy?

You make me happy, but yes the house and land is just plum over whelming. How much land came with this home, Ed, kissed her four hundred acres, and its highway frontage?

Dean, said let's go out side and look around its breath taking, Dean, thinking back this house looks like the governors house back in Mississippi.

Dean, felt really good and guilty, thinking about her sister taking care of Mama and Papa, and Dean was over five hundred miles away.

Dean, heard Ed calling her, take a look at that, a small water fall in the back, Ed, said when I purchased this property I did not noticed how small that water fall is. It's so pretty.

Dean said. It's small and needs to be removed. Or we can make it large enough to see it.

Dean noticed how full of himself Ed was becoming. Not attractive at all to Dean, but Dean kept her thoughts to herself.

Dean, reached for Ed's hand as they walked around , well I am glad you like it, on the weekends we will come here, I love would love to have a big garden down here Dean said, Baby , as he kissed

Dean, there is enough room for all types of gardens. Enjoy yourself. Don't forget how much I love you Dean. Dean said I love you too. Honey Hush, with a smile, Ed's favorite saying.

So many beautiful trees, the wind slightly blowing it sure felt nice here, Dean said.

I noticed the house has furniture in it, Ed said, yes, the people left it there, the beds I did replace,

Everything else they left behind. Dean, looked at Ed, do you find that odd, to leave such nice things behind.

People can be strange. Ed took Dean, by the hand into to the house and to the master bed room and they made love.

Dean, is so happy and excited, she wanted to call her sister Pauline, but she knew it would sound like boasting, and Dean, seen the change in Ed, and Dean, said I will invite them all up and make it no big deal, I have always been a quite and reserved woman and plan to stay that way.

Once back out side, Dean, noticed how beautiful the tree's are, tall and so green. The air smelled so good here. Ed, said you must really like the farm, you have mentioned the trees here a couple of times, Dean, said I just never thought I would be a part of something so beautiful.

Dean, clean up, and noticed the time, Ed, do you think we should head back home? Yes, baby doll, let's go. When Ed said let's go, he did not mean in a minute or two, he meant now.

Back in the car heading home, Dean said I just want to tell you here and now, "Thank You" for being the best husband a woman can have for a soul mate. You really are my best friend,

Ed, smiled, you too sugar, Ed, turned on the radio and bobby Vinton was playing Roses are Red, Dean, fell softly asleep on Ed's shoulders

Dean woke up when they she looked around and could see they were close to home, looking at time, my gosh Ed, I can not believe I fell asleep like I did. Baby, making money is not easy, it takes a lot of us sometimes, and you will be getting your rest with Donna, there now.

You, are my main concern you and the children.

Dean, smiled, and light up another cigarette, you sure are smoking more these days, I know I have noticed that myself Dean said too Ed.

Time went by quickly as Ed, pulled in the drive way, Donna was outside playing with all three kids, Dean, looked and knew that was her place, trying to be in two places.

Dean tried and it took all her energy. Getting, out of the car,

Dean, and Ed, said Hello, and Donna and the kids followed them inside the house, Dinner, was in the oven be kept warm. Donna had cooked ham, and all the things that went with it.

Ed did not hesitate to compliment Donna, on her wonderful cooking.

Dean, said it was very good, "Thank You", Dean, noticed the house is spotless, laundry in all done,

Dean, felt relieved, and guilty she should be doing this instead of Donna, Trying to tell that to Ed, would be a waste of time.

The conversation of Dean, seeing and being around the children more, did not come up.

Time went by quickly and easier, Dean, got up and went to work opening accounts, and checking on the ones to make sure everyone was happy with there service. On the go all the time.

A little over a year and went by and Dean, came home early, Ed, is was suppose to be home to take her out to dinner, was gone, Donna, and the kids were gone.

Odd, but peace and quite. Dean walked around the house no sign of anyone.

Dean, waited , and waited, about dark time, here came Ed, with Donna, in the front seat, and the children in the back of the car,

Donna, had a smile on her face, Dean, thought, I had that same smile too. They all had smiles on there faces. Donna seemed very happy.

Dean, waited for them too come into the house, Ed, said hello Dean, how was your day, I worked hard, How was your day Ed, with Dean looking him straight in the eye, it's was a great, took the kids to the farm, let them play,

Dean, lit a cigarette up, what you took Donna, and the kids down to the farm, why? Ed said the kids wanted to go and play at the farm, the little sheep, and so on.

Why are you asking, because I thought that was our place to for our kids and as husband and wife to do that? Not Donna's.

Ed, walked over too Dean, look here, I was trying to show the kids a good time, you read to much into things you need to stop it. Ed said it's not you. Dean said it's odd.

Donna, walked out with out saying a word, and went and got the kids there baths, Ed, we were suppose to go out to dinner you said tonight, that is why I came home early, to a empty house.

Oh Baby, I am so sorry, I forgot all about that, I was just trying to show our kids a good time on a nice day,

Why Did Donna have to be there? Because I am having a private lake built down there, and there is a man I wanted to talk to about getting that done, Dean, smoking her cigarette, you never said anything about a private lake. I Am now, and do not start the Donna, thing up.

You have nothing to be jealous of , it's all for you and are not seeing this, You Dean are a smart and pretty woman, Do you really think Donna , is over you in anyway?

You must be out of your mind, woman. If you think that.

Dean said well are we going out for dinner. Baby, the kids were hungry I stopped and got us all something,

Dean, said nothing. Dean, put her head down, you did not think of me, or you would have brought me something back. Ed, said I knew you would get your self something too eat, I forgot. Blame it all on me Dean, is that what you want too hear? Dean, knowing Ed, is trying to hard to confuse her.

Fine, Ed. I am tired and I am going to take a bath. Dean went too bed, Dean did not feel like eating now.

Dean. Laid there thinking on her silk sheets, looking at her wedding ring,

This can not keep up, I am finding myself jealous of a woman, I hired. But thinking to her self, woman did not back stab woman where she came from.

Just did not even cross the line of degrading them selves. Dean, thought how could I have missed it Ed, doing this?

Mama and a great marriage.

But something is not right, I know my heart, as she convinced herself, Ed. Would never cheat, maybe flirty at times, but he would not cross the line. Fading over to sleep she saw Mama's roses, and how good it would feel to just go home, just for one day.

Dean, rolled over and woke up late around midnight, and noticed Ed was not in bed. Dean, checked on her children, they all looked so comfortable and so peaceful.

Dean smiled as she shut the kid's doors. Looking around for Ed, him and Donna, were just a laughing away in the back living room,,, with a reserved look on Dean's face, she walked in, Oh baby Ed said, I thought you were fast asleep, I was, but when I woke up, normally you are in bed by now, oh me and Donna were talking about this and that, I really could not sleep,

Dean said I think it's all about time we go to bed, Donna agreed and Ed followed Dean, to the bedroom.

The next morning, Dean, got up and Ed was still sleeping, Dean's breakfast was made for her and her coffee waiting for her, Donna was out side playing with the kids, she really liked Teresa, playing ball, and teaching her how to tie her shows, smiling make faces, and acting like a child herself. Donna was great with all the children.

Dean, said hello to the kids, ate her breakfast, and left for work, and it seemed like a long day.

Dean, came back home tired, and the kids were asleep, they should be awake it's not that late.

Why are they sleeping, as Dean, walked to her bedroom?

Donna coming out of the bedroom as Dean walked in, Dean noticed her top was missing one button undone, her hair appeared messed up.

Donna, I want to talk to you later.

Yes Dean. Let me know when. You want too talk too me. Donna was nervous and Dean could see it.

Ed came out, Dean did not say one word, Baby, the kids are sleeping, and I think you and I should go out to dinner tonight,

Dean, felt so tired, but she wanted to spend time with Ed, Ed got dressed up in his suite and tie, looking dashing and charming,

Dean fixed her self up. Out they went, Dean, had a great time. Ed, said now in the morning I have to go to Memphis, I will be gone for a while, I will call you. There is money to be made there. Dean, smiled said I understand.

The next morning Dean, told Donna, Ed is going to be gone for a while, you have been doing such a great job with the children and all,

I will get to your room after I get done with what I am doing Donna, said, No need for that I made my bed my whole life, I know it's part of your job, but I will take care of Ed and I bedroom this morning, Donna, seemed anxious.

And Dean, acted like she never seen this in Donna,

Dean went to her and Ed's bedroom shut the door and smelled the sheets, and it was Donna's perfume. And one of Donna's socks left in her bedroom, Dean, came back out and said

, when I get back I will take care of the me and Ed's bedroom., No need to go in there Donna. Dean said. , Donna, gave Dean a serious look and said ok.

Donna had her hands full with three children. She played out side a lot with the kids, who grew attached to Donna. While out side, a lot of neighborhood men, had no problem waving and saying Hello to Donna.

. Dean came out, she passed Donna, who was playing with the children, and I will be back in a while. Ok waving by, the kids ran to the car, by Dean, and Dean said no, stay with Donna, mommy will be right back.

Dean got in car and drove to the unemployment office and got the same lady, oh hello there Dean, is your name am I right asked that lady, I remember from before.

That's right, well come up here no one is here, the economy is picking up, leaves us really not doing a whole lot, what brings you here?

Dean, said Donna, is not working out, too the lady sitting behind the desk, oh, really is there anything we need to know about, is

Donna stealing or anything else we need to know about as an agency? Dean, crossing her legs, with a tight grip on her purse,

No Donna just is not what I am looking for in a housekeeper that's all. I do not mean to bother you, but do you have any one older, say in there forty's or later?

Yes, your in luck Dean, we do, I have this one lady in mind, now I have to warn you ahead of time a lot of people do not want to even hire her because of her limp with her leg.

Dean, with a surprise look on her face, why, would no one want too hire her because of a limp, well it was because of polio the unemployment lady said. Sad. I, agree said Dean. The unemployment lady looked at Dean and said, so sad,

Dean looking down and then back up at the unemployment lady, Dean, thinking of her son Julius, is this how people are.

And you know that's just how some folks are, she is a lovely woman, loves children, let me get her file, the lady came back, and said, yes, her husband is dead, she has raised his children, and what we have on file is she is seeking employment as a housekeeper, Her name is Okle, and she can do a lot of things, the polio she had, makes some people just stare, you know. Dean said I know very well how that must feel.

Dean, thinking of her son Julius.

We'll I have no qualms about a limp, May I please call her from here, and see if she is what I may be looking for,

Of course, the lady gave Dean,

Okle's telephone number, and the call was made, Dean, introduced herself, and explained the three children and what needed to be done, and sometimes her and Ed would be gone.

Dean discussed the pay and the free room and board. Dean explained also Ed.

. Okle said I can start this Friday if you like, that will be fine. But Dean said I would like to come to your place and interview on a personal level, Dean said, do

You are it possible to do that now? I know it is short notice and all. Okle said no problem. Here is my address,

Dean said I will leave now. Dean smiled at the unemployment lady and said Thank You so much for your help. Dean, left and drove to Okle's address

Dean, showed up, and Okle was just fine, your limp does not bother me. I can do about what anyone else can do, Dean, said no need to explain.

Dean, said why would that be a problem , thinking of her son Julius, as she listened to the Okle, well every place I tried to get a job, they mentioned my small limp., Okle, said I think it makes people uncomfortable.

Dean told her I was hoping you could start Friday, like you said to Okle, that's fine with me.

Like I told you Dean over the phone Friday is just fine. I will have my stuff packed and Dean, said I will come pick you around nine in the morning. Well thank you Dean. And thank You as well as Dean walked to her car.

Once back home Donna, was doing laundry and the going to fix a wonderful dinner, any thing special you would like to have for dinner Donna asked Dean,, what ever you choose Donna, but after dinner I would like to speak with after the children are bathed and asleep. Again, Dean seen how Donna began to act nervous.

The pork chops and all were great, you did a nice job. Donna, let me do the dishes and you can take care of the children, Dean, was not happy out about what she was going too do.

Papa voice is a blessing so you can be a blessing, Dean, sighed out loud, Dean, cleaned off the table and loaded the dishwasher put in on the cycle.

Dean started cleaning the dinner table, thoughts of Hank crossed her mind, what he was doing, Dean, talking to her; Hank would have never done the things Ed has done to me. When Dean was down cleaning the table, Dean sat down and smoked a cigarette.

Donna, walked in with her tight fitting clothes, beautiful teeth, and Dean, still saw how young and innocent she looked.

Donna came in the kitchen well the kids are all bathed and in the beds, Julius and Jennifer are sleeping, but Teresa is almost asleep,

Teresa tends to fight her sleep, Oh, Dean, did Teresa tell you I taught her how to tie her shoes? Dean, smiled at Donna no, but I noticed she was doing that all by herself. Thank You for teaching Teresa that Dean said.

Donna, I have some news, Donna, feeling uncomfortable, I, am going to have to let you go, things are not working out here for you here.

Donna, started crying you know it was not all my fault, your husband, as Donna looked up too Dean's eyes, and Dean, said what is not your fault, your husband has tried things on me,

Dean said how many times, as Dean lit up a cigarette, Donna said too many too count, Dean, said then why did you not come to me as woman to woman and talk too me.? Donna wiped the tears from her eyes.

Donna, put her head down, Because Ed said to tell you nothing, Dean, grabbed Donna and said you listened to him. Dean, was angry, but refused to show it. Dean, calmed down and realized Donna, was between and rock and a hard place.

Dean started feeling the same way. Dean, said Donna, you are a very pretty young woman,

Donna, you're smart, do something with your life. Dean said.

Dean said as she lit a cigarette I am going to tell you something, Dean, looked at Donna please sit down Donna. Dean said it's uncomfortable with you here, I thought things would work out, but for a lot of reasons it is not, and Donna, I am not aware that it is not all you. But,

Donna, it does not matter right now, the main thing is I need you to be gone. Dean, felt tears coming, Dean, thinking I can not believe I am getting rid of Donna, really because of Ed.

Donna, with shame on her face, and crying said fine I will call my sister and she will come get me and my stuff.

Dean, said wait, I do owe you money for this week,

Donna, had a deer in the head light look on her face, Donna, looked at Dean and said, I did not work a full week of work. , Donna, I would feel more comfortable with you having money in your pocket when you leave this house.

Dean said, as she lit a cigarette.

Donna agreed and walked away, Donna packed her stuff and her sister came and got her. Thank God she is gone, Dean said out loud, Dean, realized and thanked God, for her children not hearing what she had said.

Once Donna, was gone , the children really did get attached to her, Teresa cried for her, it did take a while to calm Teresa down, Dean, told the children, something had come up and Donna had to leave.

Friday, came, Marla the next door neighbor is coming over to watch you kids, and I want to behave and listen to her. Marla, knocked on the door and Dean, told her to come on in. The kids sat on the couch, Dean, said I am leaving now I will not be gone long.

Dean drove down to get Okle,

Okle, what kind of name is that, said Julius, and she is old. Not like Donna, which made the other two children upset.

Marla, said stop that kind of talk your mother would be ashamed of you three kids. You will be nice to this lady.

Time, went by and Dean, pulled up in the drive way, the three children ran to the front window, to look at her. I told you she was old and she looks mean, Stop it said Marla, Dean and Okle walked in the house, Okle one by one. Met the children, and took a quick tour of the house she would be taking care of.

Sitting down with Dean, in the living room. I see no problem, Marla, was introduced to Okle, Okle, and wore a plaid dress, flat shoes, black framed glasses, and grayish curly hair, nothing like Donna. , Dean, heard the kids talking.

Marla said it was nice meeting you, and if you ever need anything Okle, I am right next door. Okle, smiled. And said Thank You, and Marla, before Marla, could shut the door, Dean, said Marla "Thank You" for watching the kids for me. Marla smiled anytime, and shut the door as she left.

It was quite that night, Ed would be home tomorrow.

Okle and Dean talked. For a long time. They seemed to really like each other; it was not long before Dean knew she had a true friend in Okle.

The children were going to have to get used to you Okle, and that's all there is to that Dean said. As she lit another cigarette up.

Now, Dean, do you all like anything special, or will you let me know what you want cooked for dinner?

Dean, told Okle, what Ed liked, and what the kids eat. And there snack time. Okle loved her big room.

It was getting late, and they said Good night to each other like the best of friends.

Dean, woke up the next morning, and went and took a shower fixed her self up, came out of the bathroom,

And it smelled like Mama's cooking, Dean, came into the kitchen,

Good Morning Dean, I noticed you have them can biscuits in the refrigerator, I am used to making home made biscuits' and gravy is that ok with you. Wonderful, Okle,

Dean, said this looks like and smells like my Mama's cooking. A wonderful sight for sore eyes. I really miss this type of cooking. Okle, with a half smile "Thank You" Dean.

The children have ate already,, they listen well, Teresa's hair is snowball white, like Julius I see, where does Jennifer get her dark curly hair from.

Well, just between you and me, Dean said, Ed wears a taupe, but he was a natural blond, I have the dark hair. ,

Okle turned and smiling that makes sense then. But your children good are well mannered. , they are in the front living room watching TV all three them, not a peep out of them.

Okle said I tried to keep the comfortable and quite while you slept. Thank You for that Okle.

I am not going to work today, I have a feeling Ed will be home early this morning, and I want to be here when he meets you.

Okle, said well that some feeling you have, some man just pulled up in the drive way, in long red car.

Dean, looked out the window, yes Okle, that's Ed., Dean gently put her and on Okle hand remember what I said our little secret. The kids, yelling Daddy's home, yeah.

Ed, walked inside the house, and smiled, Dean, I am home Baby.

Dean, came into the front living room and kissed Ed, and hugged him, you were so missed. I was, that's glad to hear Ed said. .

Ed gave each child a hug. But Teresa, would not let go of her Daddy's leg, as Ed tried to walk, I was missed, Teresa, let go of Daddy's leg, and you kids go out side and play.

Ed, said now Teresa you come back in, I want too show you something, Teresa came running back yes Daddy, with those big blue eyes waiting, go in your room I got you something,

Teresa ran in her bedroom, a little puppy. Teresa, so happy, grabbed the puppy and came out to show everybody what Daddy had got her,

Dean, said a puppy in the house, with a shocked look on her face, Ed, said this puppy will stay out side, I seen it and I knew Teresa would just love it.

What about the other kids. Ed said, as he looked around the house, Julius and Jennifer has no interest in a puppy.

I did not know what to bring them back, but you can take them shopping and get them something. Dean lit up a cigarette,

Ed, Julius and Jennifer are going to feel left out, you brought Teresa something, and not them.

There older and they will understand Ed said. I got Teresa the German shepheard puppy , and look at her out side playing with it already, Dean, said look , that is not fair to the other kids,

Dean, I got Teresa something and this discussion is over.

Ed is walking into the kitchen, he stopped and Okle, turned around and said Hello, I am your new housekeeper, is there anything I can get you. Ed, with no expression on his face, said no, but nice too meet you. I am Ed.

When did you start working for us, just the other day, I must say to you Ed, you and Dean have a nice home?

Dean, came in later, Well Dean Ed said, you did not tell me about Okle, well if you would have called like you said you were when you were out of town,

Then I would have had a chance to tell you about Donna leaving and Okle being hired. Ed smiled at Dean, Where's Donna gone too.

Dean said why you want to know, just curious no body belongs on the streets, I did not know she had any place to go.

Dean lit up a cigarette and smiled Honey, Donna has family.

Donna, had to leave something came up, and is not going to work for us. Ed, trust me I was surprised at Donna too. Dean thought in more ones than one. .

Well, that's too bad, because the kids seemed to like her, Donna, was just fitting in I thought, Donna never told me about any problems,

Did she mention any too you Dean, No, looking at her husband, you know Donna, never said she was unhappy here, or anything.

But you know some people just don't talk about there problems

. Donna is gone and I found a great replacement, Okle, is a kind woman, I believe she will do a great job,

Ed, said does she have family, yes, Dean, smiled a wonderful sister, her husband passed away, and Okle, raised her husband's children. Okle, has a lot of experience with children Dean said changing the subject I have noticed

Teresa seems to get her way with you Ed, more than the other two children, Oh, no, Ed smiling and shaking his Ed,

There all my children, I would not treat one different than the other.

By the way what happen to Okle's leg, Ed asked Dean.

The same thing happen to Julius, with irritation in her voice, Ed, said look Julius was born that way, was Okle born that way too

All I know Dean said she has a small limp, because of Polio. Ed said in a calm and loving voice the most important part is you like her Dean; you know I put you first. And I love you.

Dean, smiled, the kids they will get used to Okle too. Well Teresa has a puppy to help her keep her mind off of Donna.

Ed knew he had been out smarted by a poor southern girl.

Ed did not like too be outsmarted by anyone much less his wife.

Time and years went by everybody was getting used too Okle, Except Teresa

Teresa asked Okle to come outside,

Okle, thought this little girl wants to show me something, and went on out side to see this high energy little girl, Teresa, threw the ball at Okle and said let's play, Okle, said I can not run and chase the ball,

Why Donna did, said Teresa, you are not fun, and Teresa started screaming at her, Dean, heard yelling come from the front yard, and Dean, put two and two real quick,

Okle, was trying to explain to Teresa, that her leg would not allow her too run and play ball with her, Teresa did not care,

Dean, grabbed Teresa by the arm, look young lady you will not tell Okle what to do, and when, and Teresa, broke loose, and said I want Donna back, you made her go away. You are mean.

Dean, said looking down at Teresa, Okle's job is not to play ball with you, and you march over there and you tell Okle you are sorry, Teresa, would not, and got sent too her room. Dean explained too Okle,

Teresa, just really got attached to Donna that will not happen again, talking about Teresa's little fit about Donna.

Okle, said with sadness, she is so little, Dean, Teresa does not understand, you right Okle, Dean said, but I will not have a rude child. Teresa said I will to play with my puppy.

Dean said little lady you will not, you will to in your bedroom and think about how not to be rude to Okle. Teresa went to her room.

Ed, came walking in like he a ego the size of the earth, Teresa came running out of her bedroom hearing the sound of her Daddy, Teresa running to her Daddy, Daddy, mommy will not let me play with my German Shepherd puppy, she is being mean.

Dean, looked at Ed, I will explain later, Teresa back in your bed room until you can say you are sorry.

Ed said what Teresa has to be sorry for, Ed; I promise I will tell you later, Ed noticed Dean's tone in her voice.

Ed, walking over to Dean, kissing her on the cheek, Dean, smelled another woman's perfume, Ed, said Teresa go ahead and play with your German shepherd puppy. Ed knew what was coming.

Dean, said as she sighed and her voice crackling. you have had some woman hanging on you, I smell the other woman, looking at Ed, do I look like a fool to you, before Ed, could answer Dean, said I guess I have been your fool, with tears in her eyes,

Ed, raised his voice woman you are under a lot of stress Dean, lit a cigarette, A, woman came to the house this morning, a Beautiful Blond, and she said she is pregnant with your child.

With tears rolling down Dean's face, Ed, said, with a stunning look on his face and you believed some stranger who came to our home,

Dean, you are a naive woman, people do things to get money out of people all the time,

Dean was really getting angry now, Dean, walked up close to Ed's face, that same woman who came to house knows the names of our children, she knew my name, she also knew about how we met!

By this time, Dean could not contain her self; she was crying and hurting in away Ed, never saw before.

Alright now, I messed up Dean, Ed had a serious look on his face, my gosh woman try and understand not all of us are perfect.

Ed grabbed Dean's hand,

Baby, please I will take care of what I have done. Dean looks at Ed; you did this, how to you sleep at night, oh my God, what I have married.

Ed, said look I messed up Dean, people do that, I am not perfect, but I do love you and never meant to hurt you, please forgive me, with a kind voice ,

Dean you go around preaching quotes from the bible, what about forgiveness, Can you do that Dean Ed asked. That what you say the bible says, to forgive, if you want to be forgiven.

Dean, knew in her heart forgiving him was the right thing to do, but just looking at him, made Dean , was now running to the bathroom and started throwing up, and crying ,

Okle, came in just for a minute hear Dean, here is a cold towel for you, Okle, went back out to be with the children.

Dean was yelling I can not believe you paid for an abortion. You are heathen Ed; those abortions are not even legal. God help me.

Dean, said in a voice the got Ed's attention, I went to school to specialize in pediatrics. Do you have any idea, what you are doing? As

God as my witness you will deal with this one day. Ed, said look you came from some poor southern little ass town,

Look at all the things you have, look around Dean, Ed, yelled, Open your eyes Dean, Do you see your sister with a house keeper, No Dean, Ed said

You see your sister picking beans, and working at the Egg plant, a factory worker. Ed said you need to be glad what you have.

Dean. Looked at Ed, oh my Gosh you really don't get do you Ed.

Ed, looking at his wife like she is a nut. Educate me Dean, come on college girl tell me

What I do not get in life.

Dean said at the end of your day, it's not about how much money you have, and all the fancy cars,

It's about how you what kindness did you do, and the value of your name. Dean knew she was getting no where with Ed, but upsetting him.

Night time came, Dean, took some pills the doctor had given her, and went to bed. But could not sleep and walked into the kitchen where Okle was. Ed told Okle, that woman is crazy.

Okle said nothing. Dean said nothing. Ed, said I need to check on the dogs in the back yard , Dean was feeling sick and went into the bathroom, Okle heard Dean heaving in the bathroom.

. Okle went and got a ice cold glass of water and a cool towel and walked to Dean's bathroom , Okle knocked on the door, Dean, it's me Okle,

Dean, feeling the pills , come in Okle, Dean, how many pills did you take, two Okle I am just tired of all this, Dean, drink some water please, and here is a cool towel, put that cool towel on your forehead it will make you feel a little better. Okle said do you need anything, Dean, said no. But thank you for asking.

Okle turned around and shut the door behind her.

Dean came out of the bathroom and went and tired to get some sleep.

Later on that night Dean had got back up and was sitting on the kitchen floor her back to the wall, and hitting her head back and forth on the Kitchen wall, staring straight ahead, and shaking.

Okle, called for Ed, Ed came in and could not get Dean to stop, Ed, had sweat on his forehead, Ed said to Okle, keep these kids in there rooms, I need to get a hold of Dean's sister.

Ed was on the phone, the whole time Dean, still hitting her head back and forth on the kitchen wall and hard.

Dean responded to no one. Ed, called Pauline, and said you all need to get up here Dean is having some kind of nervous break down or something,

I can not deal with this and these kids and, I will pay for your plane fair to get up here, Here is the address Pauline, wrote the Dean and Ed's address down, and Pauline and Dade were there quickly.

The cab showed up, Pauline paid the cab driver and Pauline ran to the front door, and let her self and her husband Dade in. Ed, said Oh Thank God, Dean, is gone crazy , Ed said Pauline you do something for Dean, Pauline, said call an ambulance now,

Ed called the ambulance, and was embarrassed by Dean's breakdown. Teresa walked in and said, I want to see mom, Jennifer yelled No, and mom is acting weird.

Teresa opened the door and walked out of her room, not doing what Okle told her. And not listening to her sister.

Teresa, ran out of the bedroom to her mother and stopped quickly and Teresa looked like she seen a ghost, and said screamed Daddy, what is wrong with Mommy,

Ed, yelled Okle get these kids out of here now. Okle said I am doing the best I can; Teresa is the one who I can not get to listen. Ed, Said Teresa gets on in your room. Now. Girl. Teresa , put her head down and went too her room, Jennifer, grabbed Teresa , and said come in here with me, don't be sad, Mom is going to get better,

Aunt Polly is here, she will help. Teresa, crying said what is wrong with mommy. Jennifer lifted her shoulders, I do not know

. Pauline said in horror, the ambulance is here, the EMT people came in gave Dean a shot, calmed her down, and took her too the hospital. Teresa, came running out and said Aunt Polly is my Mother going to die, Pauline looked down at those big blue eyes and blond hair, and said No Teresa. Teresa said, if my mom dies, I want to die with her.

Ed, remember his mother and watching her die from cancer, and he recalled his child hood, and felt the same way. Wanting to go with his Mother.

Ed, walked up too Teresa, look baby girl, I do not want too tell you again get back in your room and go to bed. But Dad, No Ed, said now. With Dean, in the hospital, weeks passed by,

Pauline and Dade stayed a few more days, before Pauline said Ed, I know you are busy, But I need to ask you what happen to my sister, Dean, has never had a breakdown like that? It is none of your business, what happen.

Your place is too be here with your sister, Pauline, could not believe the hardness of Dean's husband. Pauline, said I understand this is not my place, but if I did not love all you I would not be asking, Ed, said your right , It is not your place,

Ed, got pissed off, you need to leave and get on back to Mississippi and pick beans, Dade, said look Ed, I may not have your kind of money, but I do not appreciate you talking to my wife like that, Ed, said to Dade, I do not give a shit what you think. Here is some money, be gone in the morning.

Pauline, and Dade used the phone there were no flights out that night, they had to wait to the next morning, Pauline said to her husband well at least well be back home by 9:00 am tomorrow,

Pauline set her alarm clock in the room she and Dade were staying in. Ed, over heard Pauline saying I can not believe Dean married Ed over Hank. Ed, said nothing and went on too bed.

The next morning Ed, seen Pauline and Dade were gone. Okle said breakfast is ready, Ed said well I am hungry, Okle said here is your coffee, and the news paper is on the table with your breakfast.

Okle took care of the kids, feed and dressed and let them play out side for a while. Now Ed, said to Okle, I am going to pick up Dean, and bring her home today, and I want no stress on her, tell those kids to behave and I mean I want those kids not to bother Dean at all. I want her feel comfortable coming home.

Okle said, I will do that, as she finished cleaning. Ed left to go get Dean, and Okle called Dean's sister , Dean had given Okle a copy of her address book, Okle made the call, and Pauline answered the phone, Hi this Okle calling Dean's house keeper, Hi Okle, how is my sister doing.

Well Ed, just left to go and get her from the Hospital and bring her home today. I just wanted to make a quick call too you, to let you know how your sister Dean is doing.

I will try my best to keep you informed, Okle said, but Ed only really wants long distance calls that involve his business, and Ed does go over the phone bill.

So I need to get off the phone. Pauline said, thank you for your kindness, and for calling me. Dean is blessed to have you. They said Good by to each other, and okle hung the phone, and went back to taking care of the kids and the house.

It was not long before Ed, pulled up and Dean was with him, once in the house, the kids ran too there Mother, mom we missed you, Ed, said now you kids need to go own, go out side , go in your room but get away from your mother for right now.

Okle asked Dean, can I get you anything, no. I ate before I left, but right now I am going to take a shower and maybe lay down for a little while.

Ed, in the mean time hired a dozen workers to take care of his customers.

Ed paid well.

Okle over heard him, I love Dean, but she is not going to let the business I worked so hard on go down hill.

Over a mistake one mistake.

Okle said nothing. Dean, was back home in two weeks and the children missed her so much, Ed, said to everyone in this house, no one is to ask where your mother has been, do not upset her,

Teresa ran up to her Dad, But Daddy you said mommy went on vacation. Ed, looking down at Teresa, that's right you sweet child, your mommy went on a nice vacation. Jennifer, said oh really, that's great Dad, where did mom go?

Ed, new Jennifer was being a smart ass, Jennifer, goes own, go out side or too your rooms do something, but get own away from me right now.

Teresa is starting kindergarten, Jennifer will be in the fifth grade, Ed, known something had to be done about Julius.

Months had gone by, and Dean was feeling for the most part better, no one brought up the vacation that Dean went on.

Okle, said Dean Can you come to the front door, Dean came to the door and

Dean, seen what look like two new Cadillac's being drove up in her drive

, Okle, calling for Dean, I am by the front door, Okle came, in well he sure does try to impress you Dean, with Okle,

, Ed, got out of one white Cadillac, and some strange man got out of the other white Cadillac. Dean, said, I have no idea what Ed is up too know,, Ed, walked in , smiling as if nothing had ever happened, Dean, here is the keys to your new car,

Dean, looked at the keys, well, smile or say something, Dean, said you bought two Cadillac's the same color, why Dean asked Ed,

So people will know we are together, Ed, said most woman would be happy, Dean, looked at Ed, and said I am, I am just very surprised.

Okle, had dinner cooking, the children, were watching TV. The cars are beautiful Ed, "Thank You", Dean said.

Ed said to Dean you and I are going out for dinner tonight, Ed, Dean said Okle is cooking right now, "

That's fine; the kids can eat what ever Okle is cooking,

Ed, said, you and I need to be together, Dean, found it hard to resist Ed, he had slipped in to her heart, Dean, knew in heart Ed, loved her.

Ed took a shower and then Dean, heard the kids wanting to go with them,

Okle, is calming the children down, and getting them focused on the dinner she had cooked for them.

Your parents are just going out; they need to be alone for a little while. All Three kids, did as they were told. Ed and Dean said good by to the kids, and left.

Ed pulled into a new restaurant that was known to be for the rich, Dean, lit up a cigarette; I have never seen or heard of the upper restaurant before,

Ed, said I did not either, but let's see how it is. Ed, said Dean, I really do love you, and I want you to have the best live I can give you, with that Ed, reached in the back seat, and gave her a dozen red roses, with a diamond necklace,

Wow, that is some gifts, Dean, looked in Ed's eyes, she knew he had really been trying to make things work. Ed is becoming so vain, Dean, knew he was a little vain when she met him, but with the business growing, his ego was too much at times.

Once, inside the restaurant, Dean, noticed how beautiful things are, chandeliers, and live music, graceful music, low lighting, in the area of your choice. Ed, gave there name, and was seating quickly. Dean, felt like Ed had been here before.

The recession is over, at least for Ed and Dean, Ed, took Dean's hand and Dean heard a man saying over a microphone, this song is dedicated to Dean Whitehurst.

When a man loves a woman, Dean blushed she was feeling like all the attention was on her, that made Dean Uncomfortable,

Baby, Ed, said, you mean the world to me. Dean, said I love you Ed, I forgive and I know you love me, but a lot of people are looking at me, I do not like all attention, you know that Ed.

Ed smiled, you are the most beautiful and loving woman I have ever met.

The waiter came, Dean and Ed order there drinks, by the way my brother Russell will be staying with us for a little while, until he gets back on his feet, Dean, looked at Ed, why would here want to stay with us,

Well, Dean, Russell needs a little help getting back on his feet, I am his brother I am not going to tell no.

Dean said fine. But you know he has a drinking problem, we can deal with that. Blood is thicker than water, you know that Dean.

The waiter brought there drinks, and handed the Menus to Ed and Dean, and said he would be back in a few minutes. Ed, started taking light sips, of his vodka, and Dean lit up a cigarette, and Ed, said what is on the menu that you would like to have, Ed, said I know what I want, you can order for me as well.

Dean said well we have a spare room your brother Russell can stay in but, the waiter had come back, sir, are you ready to order? Ed had placed his order, and wanted another drink as well.

Ed said another thing I need to tell you I have found a school for Julius, it is far away, and you can visit him any time you want.

Dean, reached for her drink, looking at her husband , with a frantic look on Deans' face, why does a school for Julius have to be so far away, what are you talking about, Dean, asked Ed? Dean starting to drink more, and feeling the alcohol,

Calm down Dean, Ed said, Dean don't cry,

It is a nice school, our son gets beat up, and picked on almost every day, I will not have that now. Ed said now listen hear,

It's a boarding school, and this school does not allow any off the kids to pick on other kids, Dean, said as she lit up a cigarette, you said Ed, we would not make him feel like a handicap child, Dean, stop.

You know it is for the best. Now, I have done told you, when you want you can visit Julius, and Julius will be coming home at Christmas time, and summer time. Dean, took a big drink, and thought how to I look in my son's eyes and tell him, we are sending you away.

Dean, seen the waiter heading towards there table, Dean, said please order me a vodka and said Ed, excuse me I need to go to the ladies room, once in the ladies room, she looked in the mirror, and said how can Ed, send our son off,

Dean, felt like crying, but knew wrong place and time, dean, washed her hands , powder her nose, and walked back to the table, Once back at the table, You know you seemed like you were gone forever,

Dean, tried too smile back. Now here is a toast to you Dean, I want you, and love you. Maybe I am not the best at showing it at times, but you have my heart Dean.

Dean smiled her heart lit back up.

After we leave here us going out dancing. Dean and Ed enjoyed there meals and there time together, Ed paid the bill and left,

Dean and Ed, were now pulling up to a club, bright lights, and city sound, Ed and Dean walked in and Ed smiled at pretty woman,

Dean, said too Ed did we come here to dance or you too smile at every pretty face you see, Ed, said let's dance, not argue.

Dean, wanted to have a good time, Dean looked at Ed, right in his eye's , He loving and gently pulled her close to him as they started to dance, Dean, felt her husbands strong arms around , Ed is holding her close, Dean thought, it feels so safe and wonderful in my husbands arms.

It's out of them, when I get anxious. Dean leaned her head on Ed's shoulders and they both enjoyed the dance and closeness.

Between the drinks and dancing it was almost midnight. Ed, smiling with Dean, time to go baby, it late.

The evening went by great after that, They paid the bill, and a man with a umbrella came up and said , it is raining sir , outside, Ed, said I see, You can hold the umbrella over my wife's head so she does not get wet , but I do not need your service. Ed and Ed and Dean went to the car, Dean thanked the umbrella man, and got in the car with Ed. Ed drove home with Dean's head on his shoulders. Dean thought I want this moment to last forever.

It was not long before Ed was pulling up in the drive way, Ed, said sugar wake up, and were home. Ed and Dean, went in side there house and everything was quite, Ed and Dean went to bed and made love.

The next morning, Ed got up with a singing tone as he said Good Morning Okle and looked out side, Ed said it going to be sunny day today, and Dean was up already taking a shower. Okle got Ed his cup of coffee, and newspaper.

With his breakfast waiting for him. Dean came out looking pretty, and fixed her own cup of coffee, Dean Okle said I would have got your coffee for you, Dean, kind of smiled thanks, but I can get it too, you do a lot around here. Ed, told Dean about the new drivers he had hired and

Ed, and told Dean, she did not have to worry about the drivers, except on Friday's when they would get paid. That Dean would now be taking care the pay checks.

Dean, missed opening accounts and talking with people, not flirting, like Ed. Dean said too Ed, Okle hearing every word. And keeping quite.

.

The phone rang, Okle said Dean, it's your Mother on the phone, and Dean knew it had to be urgent for Mama to make a long distant call. Dean

Grabbed a cigarette and walked fast to the telephone, Hello Mama, Dean You Papa is very ill I wanted to call you the Doctor's have said, he is not gone long, Tears in Mama Voice Dean heard.

Mama, I had no idea papa was sick, why would you not call me sooner?

Child, you Papa just fell from a ladder and I do not know all the Doctors right words are, Except Papa, when he fell, injured his lungs, but too keep him alive , they said it's about almost impossible, Mama ,said as she cried.

I will call you back in about twenty minutes, Mama Dean said.

Dean hung the phone and called Pauline her sister, Pauline answered the phone, Hey there it is Dean, Oh Dean, I was getting ready to call you, Dean, said Mama just called what happened to papa,

Dean, calm down this just happened,

We had no idea Papa was this sick from the fall off a ladder?

And the Doctors don't know one thing from the other, the last Doctor came from Jackson, and said Papa does not have long, a day or two.

Mama wanted to be the one to call you Dean; I love you as my friend and sister,

But I was not going to over step my place; when Mama had made it clear she wanted too call you. I understand, I have not forgotten the respect mama and Papa taught us.

Pauline and Dean told each other they loved each other. And Dean said I am calling Mama back

Dean, called her Mama back with tears in eyes, Mama, I am going to pack some clothes, and start driving now, the airport is over a hour's drive from your town to the airport, and Dade is the only driver,

So I should be down there tonight, I, love you and I am on my way Ed and I both will be. Dean said I love you Mama, I will be there soon. Dean, hung the phone, and

Ed, walked through the front door, smiling and whistling, Ed looked at Dean's face, what now Dean,

We have to leave my Papa is not going to make it, he fell off a ladder, and the Doctor's have told my Mama and Sister , My Papa does not have much time left to live , Dean said

I have talked to my Mama and Pauline, and Papa only has a day or two at best, tears in Dean's eyes.

Dean looked at Ed and said we have too leaved now. Ed, rubbing his eyebrow's Sugar, I am so sorry to hear about your Daddy, I really am, but I can not go with you,

Dean stopped and turned around and why not?

Incase you have not noticed Dean, we have people depending on us for paychecks and money is out there to be made, again, I am so sorry, But you will have to go alone, You will have your sister and your Mama when you get down there, and Dean, did not have the time to deal with the mess of Ed not coming with her.

Dean, could not believe what she was hearing, she grabbed a suite cases, some clothes , shoes, make up and all that would be needed on the trip, Dean, seen a bottle of vodka in the back of the closet and put that in the suitcase too.

Okle, knocked on Dean's bedroom door, it's me Okle, come on in,

Dean, was now sitting on her bed, Okle hugged her and said I will take care of the children. Dean, lit a cigarette, Julius, and Jennifer need to be there Teresa, will just be a hand full; I will leave her here, Ed, walked in. Okle, we need a few minutes, Okle got up and walked out of the bedroom. Dean, found comfort with Okle.

Ed hugged Dean, tightly and said if I could I would go with you, it's not that I do not want to go, but business is business. Ed said

One of us has to stay.

Again, I would love to be there, for you Dean but I can not do this.

Fine, Dean said. No problem.

Okle notice the pain in Dean. But kept quiet.

I am going to take Julius and Jennifer with me to my Papa's funeral. Teresa, is too little and will be too much to deal with and and my Papa's funeral.

Ed said Dean, Julius has to go too the boarding school this Saturday he has to be there to sign in with a parent I was going to tell you later on today,

Dean, looking pale, Dean said that boarding school mess

That can be put off; I want our son to be able to say well by to his Grandpa,

Dean, do not put that boy through no funeral and all that crying and sadness. Ed said no Dean and it's not going to happen, I have already prepaid the money, and with that you can believe Julius will be in that boarding school this Saturday.

And there is no way around it.

Dean could not believe all this at one time. Dean remember

Mama, always said when it rains it pours, she said out loud. Ed, said Dean.

Things happen, look at it this way; I will be here for our family, while you are there for your Mama and sister.

Dean, lit up a cigarette, and said; Jennifer can go with me, unless you plan to send her off too.

Ed, looked at Dean, now I understand you are going through some pain, but do not take it out on me. Jennifer can go, I will take Teresa with me up to the school where Teresa can say Good by to Julius, they play so much, Dean said fine.

You, know you pay more attention to Teresa way more attention than you do the other children,

Dean, said I am not the only one who has noticed that Teresa can do no wrong in your eyes, Dean now raising her voice, the other children , Dean said

You have bought Teresa two ponies, she can only ride one at a time, which made no sense,

Jennifer, feels like you love Teresa more, and Jennifer had to beg for a kitten. I do not want inside my animals in my house. . Ed said a cat. Not at this house.

Those ponies are at the farm, if Jennifer would go to the farm, she can have as many cats, if Jennifer wants a kitten or cat is has to go to the farm. No more of this Dean. ,

Teresa, is an easy child to get along with. Really Dean said.

Well Teresa sure gives Okle a hard time to go.

now and then, and you have seen this, and you say nothing. Ed, said Dean.

You upset right now. I understand it may look like Teresa, gets a little more attention, but you know better Dean, Really Ed,

Dean said when you turn on the radio, you have Teresa, standing on your shoes and dancing and laughing, Dean asked Ed, how do you think Jennifer feels when you will not do the same fun thing of dancing with her? Dean said

When Jennifer asks you to do that, You tell her she is to big, Ed, looked at Dean, and said she is too big, Dean, said I have to get going to Mama's , to see my Papa, I just pray I make it before Papa dies. Ed, said as he held Dean, I do love you and I am sorry I can not be there.

Well, Ed said you and Jennifer will have something to talk about when you drive back to Mississippi, I love all these kids the same.

Yes, Teresa is a high energy child. Dean said. I need to get down to Mississippi quickly time is not on my side.

I have to get on the road as quick as I can, Dean, please do not drive fast, why don't you take a plane, Dean, turned around and said,

Dade Pauline's husband is the only one that drives in the family, besides Papa, and the airport is over an hour away, I am not going too ask them to meet me at the airport, that would take two hours away from the spending time with Papa, Dean said, with tears in her eyes and I refuse to put that burden on my family.

Dean, hugged Julius well by, and told him when she gets back she will come and see him. And that he is in the best school. Dean had convinced Julius that this is really the best thing for him, and when Julius gets there if he is unhappy all he has to do is say so. Julius, had tears filling in eye's , refusing to let them roll down his face, He smiled Mom , I see you when you get back, and I am really sorry about Grandpa getting worse, Dad, said he is going to pass away, and that is why you can not come with us to the school.

Dean, kneeled down, and looked in Julius eyes and said that right, but I will be up there to see you as soon as I can Dean said. And I love you son.

I love you to Mom and I will miss you. Julius reached up and hugged his Mother tightly.

Dean was angry at Ed but Dean is not showing this in front of the kids.

Teresa, ran up with her blond hair flying in the wind, I want to go with you, No, baby , you need to stay here with your Daddy, Okle, came out side, Dean, Jennifer is ready to go , I will take Teresa, Teresa was screaming for her mother all the way back inside the house. Dean and Jennifer had everything packed and in the car and pulled out and went to Mississippi,

Dean, had told Jennifer about Julius going away to school, Jennifer did not understand and no matter what anyone said it did not make sense to send Julius away. Once down in Mississippi, Dean's family could not understand why her husband why not with her.

Everybody seemed to be asking Dean where your husband, Dean felt ashamed, Dean could feel the eyes on her, or it sure seemed that way, why was my own husband who does not show up at my Papa's funeral.

Dean, went to the casket, and started talking Papa, I got myself in a mess, Papa, I need to your advice,

Dean put her hands on the closed casket, Oh Papa, I am going to miss you, But I will talk to you every day, in my heart, Dean, said JESUS please, let Papa in the gates of Heaven, Dean, wiped her tears, and turned around, Papa was gone.

Dean, cried so hard at the funeral, she was crying for some many reasons the hugs were every where, and the sympathy was in every one's eyes there were a lot of people at Papa's funeral. Loving folks that loved him too.

Dean, could not count the times, smiling faces said your Papa had value to his name, and he loved God, Dean, they would say it does not get any better than that.

After the funeral, everyone is back at Mama, house. Every one seemed lost, but Dean knew with her sister Pauline living next door would take care of Mama and Pauline would make sure Mama is in good hands.

Dean gave Pauline money, to help out with everything.

Dean, asked Pauline to keep an eye on Jennifer, she just wanted to take a ride around town and be alone for a little while. Dean knew Mama was taking a nap.

Before Dean, left she made a collect call to home, Okle answered the phone, and how are you Dean asked okle. I will make it by the grace of God.

Is Ed there?

Okle said no him and Teresa and Julius are all gone. Ok, Okle I am just checking in. Dean said you have the number down here if you need to call me for any reason. Okle knew what Dean meant.

Dean hung up the phone. Dean, walked up and hugged Pauline, Pauline, grabbed her sister, and looked her they eye, you and I are to peas in a pod, Dean, gave a half smile, you go own and take your ride.

I understand more than what you think I do Dean. Dean, said, it is a Blessing to have a sister like you. Like wise Pauline said, as she picked up her beans that had to be hand washed. Dean said well I am going to take my ride and try to just clear my mind.

, Dean, left and pulled out of the drive way.

Dean, drove around this same old town, looking at the tall green tree's , wind that blew with a slight breeze, as Dean, was driving around, people still waved, sitting on the porches, kids playing.

It did feel good to be home, tall corn stalks, and green beans growing in the fields, Dean, noticed a tire swing, boy that brought back memories.

Dean thought I wish I could turn back time just for a minute to tell Papa, thank you for raising me with all your love and for being there for me.

Dean, lit up a cigarette, and drove slowly

On down to only the town café,

Dean, got out of her car and walked in and sat down, Mable, came up with a big smile and said in a loud voice, well if it can't Wadena in town,

Mable, reached down with a big smile on her face and hugged Dean, Dean hugged Mable back.

It is so good too see you, but not like this with your well your daddy and all. Wadena hugged Mable back. It is good too see you too.

Again Waudean I am, so sorry to hear about you Daddy, Thank You Mable, Mable grabbed

Dean's hand held her hand up and said Waudean, no one here in this town has a ring like that, with a loud voice, wow, and who did you marry to have a rock like that? Dean looked with a slight smile, Well, he is not from here. Mable, eye's brow's went up, Mable laughed we all know that, Dean, recalling Hank.

How is nursing going for you, and do you have any children? Mable, said listen me question after question I have

for you, I want to know what has been going on with you, ,
Mable Excuse me a man behind Mable said, Dean looked over
Mable's shoulder's and there was Hank.

Mable, said well how are you Hank, you just have you a
seat, and I will bring the both of you coffee on the house,

Hank, nodded as he sat across the booth from Dean,

Hank, grabbed Dean's hands I am so sorry about Daddy
passing away. He sure was a good man. Dean, cleared her
throat, and said Thank You,

Hank, saw Dean had been crying. Dean, I am still your
friend, Dean, had a hard time looking into Hank's eyes; he is
so simple and kind. What you see is what you get. Dean, lit
up a cigarette,

Well Dean, I hear you are doing well and you really look
good, you too Hank. Hank, said you know every now and
then, I wonder how you are doing, I guess when a person
really loves someone, they always care how they are doing and
if there happy, Hank said, I still hear you sweet voice, with
your blue eyes, sometimes

I have dreams that you want me back, Dean, sipping her
coffee, and feeling guilty and wanted at the same time. Dean
said you know I have some thoughts of mine own at times.
But only the Lord will know them.

Hank, and Dean, had the whole town talking in about
ten minutes.

Dean looked out and people were starring at Dean and
Hank, Dean, said this town has not changed. Dean, lit up a
cigarette, Mable, walking over too Dean and Hank and had a
big smile on her face.

Here is you all's coffee, let me know if you want anything
else. Mable, winked at Dean, as she walked away.

Hank, took a drink of his coffee, so I have to ask you
Dean, are you happy with your husband,

Dean, looked down, and said we have days like anybody else,

Dean, asked as she looked out the huge window, Hank how have you been? Hank, said well I been doing pretty good, I bought that land that you and I liked and said one day we would buy that, Dean, looked at Hank

,Dean said you bought all that land, that is great. I know you liked that area as much as I did. Dean asked are you happy? I mean really happy? I, guess I have been still hanging on to yesterday,

Dean, said there are times, I must admit I question my choices that I have made. I love my children, but then Dean stopped. And looked at Hank, you are still a wonderful man to me and you always will be. Dean, reached for another cigarette, you know its funny how a person can plan there lives, and try to be wise. And then out of no where like a puzzle on the table, just pieces every where.

Hank, said I understand you point of view on that. I still you Waudean.

Dean, said Hank I can not do this, Dean, now reaching for her purse I have to go, but I want you to know one thing, what's that Hank said.

You are truly a wonderful man. And I am blessed to have been so much a part of your life at one point. But that fact of the matter is, I am married and have a life far from here. I really do need to get back to Mama's house, But you are more than welcome to stop by anytime.

Hank, stood up, please let me walk you too your car, that's fine Dean said. Well, as Hank and Dean, waved to a couple of folks and said by to Mable as they walked out the door. Mable, walked fast to go and look out the window, saw Hank open the door and kiss Waudean on the cheek. It looked like Waudean is crying. It did not take long for Mable to pick up the telephone and start gossiping.

Waudean's

Car pulled out, Dean stopped the car and looked at Hank for a minute, and said "Thank You again Hank" and Hank just stood there for a minute and walked on too his truck. Dean felt so confused. And missing Papa's advice.

Dean pulled over after she made sure no one was around, and pulled the vodka out of her purse and drank right from the bottle. Just enough to take the edge off.

And then Dean, put the bottle of vodka back in her purse. And put a piece of gum in her mouth. And perfume on. Dean, looked in the revere mirror, Dean, said out loud, I have to have something to take the edge off , looking to see if her eyes , they were not swollen to bad from all the crying.

Dean looked at the bottle of vodka in her purse, I do not have a problem, and anyone would want to have a drink, if they had to bury the Papa.

Dean, drove back home pulled in Mama House, looking at the dirt road, and recalling what Ed had said about dirt roads.

What in God's name have I got myself into? Putting the car into park, Jennifer came running to her Mom, where did you go?

Dean said I Just needed some time Jennifer; it is so hard to loose a parent.

Jennifer, hugged her mother, let's go inside grabbing her mother's hand, Dean felt so close to Jennifer.

Days had gone by and it was time to head on back home.

Dean packed her and Jennifer stuff in the suite cases. Hugged and kissed everyone good by. Dean, said Mama I will send you money to help you,

Child I do not need any money,

Well I would like to send some just in case you would want or need anything, because I love you, Pauline, walked in, grabbing and hugging dean at the same time, It is going to be hard to take care of Mama, with Papa gone.

I wish you could stay Dean, Pauline said. Dean said I do too. Jennifer, stood beside her mother, I love you Mom.

Mama, wiped her face what a loving child you have Dean. Thank You Mama. But it time for us to head back home, Jennifer took the suite cases and put them in the car, and went back in and said Good by to everyone,

Dean, said Jennifer I will be out in a moment or two, Dean, said to Mama and Pauline , I will be back. But if you all need anything, please me call. Pauline hugged her sister with sweat rolling off her body,

Dean, just because you're far away, your still close in our hearts. Dean, had tears in her eyes, "Thank You" that goes three ways for all of us. Dean walked out, wiping her tears. As Dean pulled out of the dirt drive way, Dean looked at his old house, recalling those childhood memories, her papa planting, and painting,

Papa did a wonderful job, no house could compare to the love and value this home has. Dean, looked on the seats, and saw an old bag, what's in the bag, oh Grandma put sandwiches in there, Grandma, said we might get hungry.

Dean could not help but look at Mama's beautiful roses, of all bright colors, huge, and stunning to the eye. And all the years Papa told Mama her roses were the prettiest in town. And off church every Sunday, and prayers,

Dean, thought they had problems like any other marriage, but is sure is amazing when you walk with the Lord, oh Jesus resolves the problems.

And Dean and Jennifer got back in the care and were back on the highway back home.

The drive back home went pretty quick Jennifer kept talking and keeping her Mother's thoughts on Dad, and the farm. And Okle. And everything else, Jennifer was very mature for her age, her kindness was what Dean, needed right now.

Dean did not want to think of Ed right now, Dean knew as well as Ed knew, he had her heart, and the heart decides who you love.

By night fall Dean, head lights on the car was pulling back in her drive way at home. Ed's car was here that was a good sign. Look Dad's home Jennifer said.

Dean, put the car in park and turned off the engine. And her and Jennifer got out and walked in the house, there was Ed sitting at the kitchen table going over paperwork, Hello were our home

Dean said. Baby, I have missed you. Ed got up and hugged and kissed Dean, like she had been gone for a year, But Dean noticed he did not see her or Jennifer when they first walked in the house. But Dean kept quite.

Ed said I have some beautiful flowers for you, one for each day you were gone, I missed you, my best friend and wife.

Dean said that is a nice welcome home. Ed, smiled where is Jennifer, I seen her come in and I think she went back outside she seen one of her friends.

Dean, said she will come in a few minutes Jennifer is tired from the trip, Jennifer is just saying Hello to a couple of friends.

Ed, said to Okle, where is the kids, Teresa is in bed, and Jennifer is outside talking to one of her friends. Ed, said to Okle, tell Jennifer, she has ten minutes outside and then take a shower and get to bed. Yes sir Okle said.

You doing alright Ed asked Dean Yes, I am. Ed said.

Dean , you and I are going to drive down to the farm in the morning, it's suppose to be great weather, Dean said I am so tired of driving,

Ed, said I will do the driving, tomorrow is suppose to be another sunny day, perfect weather. And I need too get down farm and see if the construction has been finished on the lake. Ed said, putting drink down

Beside we need to be alone.

Dean said I want to see Julius, or call him, I miss him. Ed looked at the clock, there are no phone calls at this time I miss my son. Ed said Dean; he is in a good place, Dean, said never the less I want to go see our son.

Do that some other time. We have to get to the farm, I already explained too you why. Dean, too tired too argues. God I sure miss my Papa Dean Said.

Teresa, woke up and came running too her Mommy I missed you.

Dean reached down and hugged Teresa I missed too. Ed, said now little Teresa it's fine to come in and see your Mother, but you were in bed, and it's time to get back in bed. Teresa begged her Daddy, oh please as Teresa climbed on her Daddy's lap; let me stay up for just a couple of minutes. Ed smiled ok Teresa.

But, Teresa climbed down and went and watched TV, Okle, hugged Dean. I am glad your home. Ed said too Okle it's time for Teresa too gets back to bed;

I will get Teresa back in bed Okle said. After that Ed and Dean, I will be in getting to bed myself. But before I go to be

Okle, said can I get you something too eat, Well me and Jennifer made sandwiches before we left mama's house and snacked on them pretty much , But Thank You for asking me Okle Dean said.

.

The next morning beautiful sunny day, the sun shining through the trees , light shinning between the branches, and the wind had a , slight breeze, it feels good out here today.

Ed said with a smile, Dean, fixed her self up, the kids are still sleeping,

Dean, said after we get back from the farm I want to go see Julius at his school.

You mentioned that Dean, last night, Dean you need call Julius now in case something comes up where you can not go see him.

Dean sighed and lit up a cigarette;

Dean called the school and asked to speak to her son by name. Julius, was on the telephone quickly, Mom, when are you coming up here too see me,

Dean said as she held back the tears, Son, I will be up there soon, do you want me to bring you anything. No. but its just strange here, I guess I just have to get used to it. Dean, talked about her Papa, Julius said he was sorry he could not be there for her, Dean, said it's ok, No, it's Dad, said Julius I had to be here so quick he said. , Mom, is Dad ashamed of me because of my fingers being different shapes and sizes, and my feet, Oh No. Dean said, the kids were getting so mean, and you know that Julius.

Dean, said Julius before I let you go, do the kids say anything about your hands or feet to you, No. they do not.

Well Julius, your Dad, is waiting for me to get off the phone, I need to let you know son I love you and miss you I will get up there as soon as I can. Ok Mother, I love you Mom. And Julius with lonlyness in his voice hung up the phone.

Dean fought back the tears. Ed, said, I noticed you are about to cry, Ed looking into Dean's eyes, it's for the best. Dean said I want to go visit our son now. Ed said we will discuss that later.

Dean lit up another cigarette and said why in the world would I have too put off seeing my son at school, I gave birth to him Ed, and I miss him.

Ed, said well that might have to be put off for a day or two, what dean said, with a stunned look on her face, Dean,

Ed said, you kept telling me you miss opening accounts and so I have hired you someone to drive with you, Times are changing, you have watch people these days, and they will take you and hurt you.

The guy I hired will be here tomorrow, Dean said, as she lit a cigarette up , I do not understand, this guy what is his name , his name is Larry, now he knows karate, special in knum chucks, he can help you in case you come up on any trouble,

Dean, with a shocked look on her face, Dean looked at Ed; I have had no trouble in the past why would I now?

Dean, that's a competitive market out there, and territory, you think you and I are the only ones who want to put things in stores?

This is what I am talking about Dean, you are naïve. And innocent. There is a lot of money to be made and when it comes to that type of money, it can be dangerous; People are getting paid off for some areas, wise up Dean. Dean, looked right her husbands eyes, Not as naïve as when you met me. Ed ignored that remark.

You need protection. Dean, thought protection from what.

Fine. Ed. Let's just get going to the farm. Ed reached for Dean's hand, look I love you, I know you would never let me down, and kissed Dean on the cheek.

Dean said it would have been nice if you would have mentioned this man named Larry that I will be with, before now.

Ed and Dean, said by to Okle, and also mention there will be no way to

Reach them.

Okle said ok, and Okle started cleaning. And taking care of the house and kids. And Waved good by as Ed and Dean pulled out of the drive way.

Teresa woke up first asking for her Mother,

Okle said with a warm and kind voice, your Mother and Dad will be gone all day, but I you and I can put a puzzle together if you want, Teresa, smiled that will be fun,

Okle said right now please goes wash your hands before you eat your breakfast, Teresa did as she was told, and Jennifer could sleep to noon. And no one said anything.

Ed and Dean, did not waste any time getting to the farm, once down at there farm, it was really looking good and Ed was impressed the beautiful acres of grass seemed huge, the only thing missing is there needs to be gates on all the entrance too this property, Ed, said to Dean Whitehurst Lake, I like that sound of that,.

Ed, walked as he owned the world.

Dean said to Ed, you know there is an old saying, what is that Ed, said Ed. You reap what you sow,

Dean, don't start on that again. Little did Ed; know that Dean had found another woman's telephone number. While she was at her Papa's funeral. Ed had been to places too.

Ed, said as they got out of the car, look around, fresh country air, Dean said. Ed said, let's take a walk and see what they have done,

Dean walked towards the back of the house, that small pond, is gone.

It is a huge pond with a water fall and lights in it.

, Dean, thought that was odd looking. The men had planted flowers, Ed, walked up, well what do you think, and it looks nice,

Ed is you sure you want that pond that big? Yes, and your flowers the men did a great job, Dean, lit up a cigarette, and looked at Ed with kind eyes, they are beautiful flowers, I would have enjoyed planting the flowers myself.

That's part of garden, Dean said but I was looking forward to planting the garden myself.

. Ed, kept walking I am not going to tell these men to tear out that garden, because you would have enjoyed planting the flowers,

Dean said firmly I did not say that, just next time, would it harm you to ask me if I would like to plant the flowers that are all I am saying.

Ed, said I'll be darn, what dean, said, you know I will have to call Okle, and have her call Larry, I forgot that he was coming today, and he can come tomorrow, Ed, went and made the call , Dean, thought and I could not go and visit my son today. Dean, reached in her purse took a small sip of vodka Dean made sure no one seen her do this.

Dean could not believe she is now hiding a bottle of vodka. Dean thought I came from a family who does not curse or drink.

Dean thought Ed can down right just think of himself. Dean looked around, the garden looked nice, but I need to do that, it takes my mind off all the insanity that seems to be going on in my life.

Ed came back smiling and singing, well, okle is a great person, she will call Larry and he will be there tomorrow.

Ed and. Dean was up by the lake, watching the ripple's on the water, and the nature sounds around the lake, it is breath taking, and the leaves on the trees, was really pretty to watch, all around this big lake, the scenery here Dean, looked at Ed and says it looks as pretty as a post card.

Ed said walking up. Turned out pretty good. Dean, noticed how over bearing Ed had become, more money, more cars, more land, Ed, said now we have to work on the east pasture,

Dean said what do you want to do with that, baby, Teresa loves, riding her ponies over there, spring feed, it's already fenced in,

Dean, said Teresa will have both sides of the highway land to ride on,

Dean, said don't you think Teresa should stay on one side or the other, Ed, said no, I will need to put another barn on that part of the land, since it is across the Highway, Dean, said I really do not want Teresa crossing this highway on her pony, it is dangerous,

Dean, there is also a underpass , It's over there, look to your right, , Dean, walked a little closer , While I be darn, I never noticed that before,

Well, Dean, Do you really think I would let something happen to Teresa, Dean said of course not, and Julius or Jennifer either.

Were there parents, we look out for them and teach them. Dean, though, this man has a heart, but he could sell snow in June to people in Arizona, Dean, thought. Ed said looking at Dean,

Let's go get something for lunch, Dean, said I have done no shopping for this house, I know that Ed said. I mean let's go someplace and get something to eat, there has to be somewhere in this town to get something to eat.

Ed and Dean, got in there car and left and found a burger barn, Ed said I am hungry let's go in here and at least try it.

Dean said it reminds me of that old café back home. Ed said Speaking of your old home; maybe you could invite your family up after we are done fixing up this farm and have them up. I know Ed said we will pay there way.

Dean said that would be nice. Ed and Dean, walked into Burger barn, friendly people, served fast, and Ed placed an order for two hamburgers with every thing, and French fries.

Ed and Dean, sat back in a old faded red booth,

Dean said I know we both are really busy at times, but I really do miss Julius and need to see him soon. Ed said we discussed that matter already, after you meet Larry, and take care of business then you can go see Julius.

Burgers up, a voice called out, and a waitress brought Ed and Dean the food.

Ed and Dean ate, enjoyed the lunch, this was not a bad hamburger. Dean said I thought it was really good.

Ed, and Dean, paid the bill, but Dean, noticed Ed had left a no tip,

Dean, grabbed some cash out her purse and put a couple of dollars and hurried back to put the tip on the table.

Dean, remember how hard she worked and what tips meant.

Dean knew she had not forgotten where she had come from. Too bad Ed had.

Ed, looked back at Dean and said what are you doing Dean, Ed said I paid the bill, Dean said I forgot something on the table,

Dean, had convinced herself she had not laid, she did forget the tip. This really met something in this time of economy, and its tips mean a lot to the person who waits on you. Dean noticed Ed is getting over bearing at times.

Dean and Ed walked back and got back in the Cadillac had drove back to the farm, you know Dean said the scenery down here is just breath taking, and it peaceful,

Ed, said I know it's something, like the fact you and I and the kids can all come down here. Dean touched Ed's shoulder, have you talked to your children in California, no. I have not I have been too busy to do that,

But after we get this farm settled to the way I want it too look, and get back to business I will call Eddie and Jacqueline to see if they would like to come down. Dean, smiled, that is a nice idea,

Maybe we could get Julius out of school to come down too, Ed, said I am not going to take that boy out that school too come see the farm,

He will wait until summer time.

Ed said we will have all the kids down this summer, how does that sound with a smile on Ed's face. That would be nice Dean said.

Ed, said we need too gets some ducks down here and I want that old barn burnt and replaced, that old barn looks like it has had it days. And at the same time I will get a barn built on the other side of the Highway, Teresa, will love it. Ponies on both sides, Ed smiled, Dean, said Jennifer wants a kitten,

Ed, said I guess, cats, around the barn they will serve there purpose, keep the mice away. Ed said you can tell Jennifer, to pick out a couple of kittens,

Ed, said, oh Dean, I will be hiring people on a permante basis to keep up this property,

Dean, said how much is that going to cost, Ed, said, Dean, do not worry about the money part. I am just letting you know; we need people down here to bush hog the land, and look after things,

Dean, lit a cigarette, and thought Ed, is getting too big for his britches.

Ed looking at his watch, Dean, we need to get on back to home. Dean, with her hair swirled around her beautiful face, is it that late already Ed, yes Baby, time to get on the road. Dean, lit a cigarette,

Ed and Dean got back in the car; Ed looked at him self in the rear view mirror, I am a handsome man, Dean, turned and looked at him, yes, you are Ed.

Dean said did you pay the workers at the farm for the garden work,

Ed, looked at Dean like something was wrong with her, Of course I paid the workers.

But going forward Dean, I open a bank account down here in Madison county bank, so them people will always have a paycheck, that way pay checks can not get over looked.

Dean, said before we leave let me go in the house and use the restroom,

Ed was almost out of the drive way, He did a u turn and drove back to the house, I wish you would have used the bathroom before we almost go on the Highway

, Dean, said, Ed I need to use the rest room, Dean, open the door to the two story house

. Dean grabbed her purse and pulled out the bottle of vodka, as Dean looked in the mirror, my Gosh how vain, she said, repeating Ed, I am a good looking man. Dean, took a sip of vodka, my god, this money has changed Ed, and not for the better. Dean went to the first bathroom, and when she was done,

Dean washed her hands, and she took the towel and wiped off the bottom of the sick, Dean noticed there, was one pearl looking ear ring. Dean knew it was not her ear ring.

She grabbed the one ear ring and put in her purse.

And locked the house door behind her. Dean, got in the car, and Ed said well that was fast, Dean, and Ed started down the driveway, Ed, do you let the workers go inside the house, No way Ed said. Why do you ask that?

Well Dean, said with irradiation in her voice, I found this, has she held the one pearl ear ring in her hand, Ed, now on the Highway, I do not know what you have I am driving, it is a woman's ear ring Ed.

Well Dean, I have no idea what you are talking about, Maybe with all the stuff the people left behind when the sold the property one of the lad's ear rings came off. Dean, why are you making such a fuss over nothing?

It was a great day and you have to just stir up something. Dean, you should not be with me if you don't trust me. Ed said Woman what do I have to do to prove that I love only you?

Dean, said holding back the tears, I married you for better or worse, and where I come from , that has meaning and value too it, When we took our vows for better or worse, I meant my vows.

God as my witness I did.

Dean, I love you or I would not be with you, and I love kids. But you can not look at me with any trust every time you get insecure with life. Ed said as he looked in Dean's eyes.

Dean, said with a convincing voice I have forgiven you and God has my witness I have tried to forget some of things you have done in this marriage, but,

But nothing Ed said. I am not talking about this anymore.

If you do not trust me, then get on back to Mississippi. Dean, felt a tears roll down her face, Dean, could not believe how Ed thought so much of his self, and so little of there marriage. Dean, thought to her self, Get on down to Mississippi, Dean, lit up a cigarette.

Dean, said you really do not get it do you; get what Ed said, your blessings that have been given to you by God.

Dean said,

The money how your accounts and money has grown, and the property and all the material things we have.

Dean said you really think you did all this, don't you, Dean, I am not saying you did not help, Dean, for the first time raised her voice, No, Ed. It's God Blessings to us.

Ed said, Woman, what in the world are you talking about, Dean said

When we hired Okle,

Okle thought it was her blessing, But God blessed us two fold. Dean, said, Ed said does not start that preaching with me. It was starting to storm, and Lighting, Ed said a storm in coming are way. Dean said nothing.

Dean turned her head as she lit up a cigarette. I have told our children there is a God and about Jesus. Dean said you know what Teresa told me the other day,

What Dean, Teresa told me that her Daddy told her there was no God; do not say that to our children. Dean, turn on the radio.

Dean knew she was ignored on that conversation, but telling the kids there is no God, was something Ed was not going to do.

Dean did not care what Ed thought or said. Now. Dean, felt better.

Ed and Dean were almost home, Ed pulled his car into a store, and Dean said what do we need from the store?

Ed pulled in the store parking lot and put in park and left the car running, I will be right back, and Ed never answered Dean.

Ed was in the store about ten minutes or so. Dean, patiently waiting. Ed, got back in the car and had vodka and some other alcohol with him.

Dean looked down at the bags. And said nothing.

Ed and Dean, drove home, Dean slept most of the way. Ed pulled up in the drive, and Ed said Dean, wake up were home.

Teresa toy's were all over the place. Ed, said getting out of the car, sweet baby girl, you need to pick up your toys, ok Daddy,, and Teresa was outside playing with her German Shepherd puppy that was getting really big,

Teresa , Hi Mom and Dad, smiling and running to her Dad, Hey there little girl, what have you been doing all day, playing with my toys, and teaching my puppy tricks, Ed, looked down at Teresa , that is nice.

Now do not too forget too pick up your toys, like Daddy asked you too. Teresa picked up every toy. Then

Teresa , walked inside the house , Teresa , found her Dad, and said I walked my puppy and I trained Duke my puppy a couple of tricks Daddy,

Teresa grabbed her Daddy hands, and not letting go, Daddy do you want to see the tricks my puppy knows, Not right Teresa, Dad please, oh please Ed, said for a minute I guess, Teresa ran out side eager to show her Daddy duke the trick's, Teresa waited for he Dad to come out side and Teresa, seen her Dad, coming out side to see the dogs tricks. Teresa

Got her puppy and said watch Daddy, Teresa said sit to the Duke, Teresa, pointed her finger and said Sit, and Duke sat.

Teresa pointed her finger down, and said lay down Duke, and Duke laid down, Daddy, this is a really good trick watch.

Ed looked at the large German shepherd.

Teresa said do your thing to , Duke a large German shepherd jumped towards Ed's throat now showed his teeth, and   growled and gnashing of the teeth and Duke's hair standing straight up on his back , went in attack mode , and Duke was going towards Ed. With full force.

Ed, backed up, and grabbed a rake and put it in front of him and with a surprise look on his face, Call that dog back now. Teresa.

Teresa, noticed her Daddy was not happy, what's wrong Daddy,

Why in the world would you teach that dog to attack? And me at that Ed asked.

Teresa said, looking up at her Daddy and Duke now wagging his tail. And, you put that dog Duke in the cage away from my dogs. Teresa said nothing.

Dad that's what your dogs do that you have, and I can never go around them because you said they will attack me. Teresa looked up and said

I am going to be just you dad. We are pals Dad.

Ed said, looking down at Teresa Do not teach that dog anything else. Do you understand me Teresa, Teresa put her head down and touched her dog, yes Dad.

Ed said you can teach your dog how to fetch a stick or a ball. But no more attacking people. Ed, said Teresa Where is your sister, Jennifer is up the street with her friends. Teresa seen her Dad looked back at her with a odd look.

Well, I am going back in the house, Okle, Ed called out, I am in the kitchen Okle said,

Ed said as he sat down in the kitchen chair , did you know Teresa was teaching that dog how to attack people ? No.

Teresa said she was teaching her dogs some tricks. And how to sit and behave. Ed, said Okle you need to keep a better eye on

Teresa, Okle said ok. And by the way Dinner will be in about ten minutes.

Ed fixed him self a drink, and went into the back living room and used the telephone, Dean, had taken a shower and felt so refreshed, where is Ed asking Okle, he is in the back living room I believe.

Dean, open the door and Ed was getting off the telephone, Dean, went and kissed Ed, who you were talking too, Oh, I called Larry to make sure he would be here tomorrow at nine am sharp. Dean said nothing but she knew she could not see Julius that day either.

Dinner will be will be in about ten minutes okle had said. Dean and Ed went into the kitchen sat down, Jennifer came running through house, sorry I am late for dinner,

Okle, said you are not late you are right on time, everybody sat down and ate. After Dinner,

Ed and Dean talked about old times, Ed turned on the radio, Teresa came running, Daddy let me dance on your feet again, Ed, was so egar to let Teresa, they danced, and danced, Ed, said ok. That's enough. Dean, said it's about that time I am going to get ready for bed. Ed said I am not far behind you.

Tell okle to make sure Teresa gets a bath; she has been playing with the dog. Ok Dean said.

The next morning Ed, smelled ham being cooked, and walked into the kitchen, Okle I must tell you, you're cooking is really good. Ed went and took a shower and came back out ready to eat.

"Thank You" Ed. Breakfast is ready I need to get the kids up. Teresa was the easy one to get up, and Jennifer was like pulling teeth to get out of bed.

The phone rang, Okle answered the phone, Ed, telephone, and it was marlos, out of New Orleans, la. Yea, Ed, this hear territory is getting big, I know I have sent you letters, but I want you too know , the money is really coming in. Ed smiled, glad to hear business is well, I will drop you a post card. The call ended. Dean, walked in, who was that, oh just business Ed said.

Dean paid no attention just another money call Dean thought and another business trip.

It was not long for the kids ate gone outside.

And the door bell Rang, A husky man, with wide shoulders, was at the door, Okle, heard the man asks for Ed and that he was suppose to be here at nine.

Okle let him in, Dean, had told her ahead of time to expect a man named Larry.

Larry came in and Ed told him to have a sit and Ed and Larry talked Ed, went over his job duties, and the free room and board and the pay that went with that. Larry liked that. So far Larry thought Ed seemed like a nice person to work for.

Dean, walked and gave a warm smile and said Hello I am Dean, and you must be Larry, Yes. Glad to meet you too.

Larry, noticed Dean, had a kinder way with her words, and her voice was warmer and friendly.

Ed, said now Dean, I have done told Larry about the pay and the room and board. And his job duties. Dean, lit a cigarette up, that's fine,

The Phone rang, Okle answered the phone, Collect call from a Julius, I will accept the call, Julius was so happy to talk to anyone at home, Hi Okle, is my mom there? Yes I will get her, Dean, okle said Julius is on the telephone.

Dean, said excuse me Larry, I will be right back.

Oh mom, how are you Julius asked? Julius I am glad you called I am fine and you? Its ok, mom when are you coming up too see me? Soon Julius,

Julius do you want me to bring you something when I come up? No mom. How are Jennifer and Teresa? There fine, Julius your Dad is calling me, you dad just hired a guy and you know business is with your dad. Yes, I do. Dean said, Julius, I am sorry to cut this phone call short, but your Dad is calling me.

I will see you soon son, and I miss son and love you more than you know. Julius said I love you too, and it will be nice to see you again mom. Dean heard the hurt in Julius voice.

Dean also heard calling her name louder. Julius I have to say good by right, ok and Dean hung up the phone.

Larry was in his late twenty's going by looks, but Dean knew Ed would fill all the details in later , Ed, had a way of finding a person weak point, Dean, was learning.

Dean, smiled and said if you hungry we have plenty too eat, no thank you Larry said, I have already ate but Thank You for asking.

Well, it's time to get too work, Ed said I will see you two later, and Dean, do not forget , I may have to go out of town this weekend ,

Where to now Ed, back down to Memphis , tn. I am checking on a territory in that area. I need to also go to New Orleans, la. Dean, said is that a new territory, it's one I been dealing with, Ed, said I hope I can get some money out of it. Okle, had heard Ed call with Marlos, Okle kept quite.

Ed, smiled and looked at his gold watch money is to be made. Ed said you have a good day now, and kissed Dean on the cheek,

Larry and Dean left, for the first day of work together, Dean, learned a lot about Larry, in the first week working with him, Larry did not know his Dad, and his Mother, just left him after he graduated, no brothers or sisters.

Dean, learned Larry is a loyal and kind person, Dean, thought how sad, like Julius at school. No family around.

Dean, missing Julius so much, as time went by Dean started treating Larry like a son.   . As time went by Larry and met Julius when he came home from school, Jennifer, and Teresa. And Okle.

Time passed by and

It was summer time again, and everyone including Larry went to the farm, Ed's ego was growing to a point of just plum full of him self, Dean had confided in Okle.

Okle, said Dean, I am here for you, with a smile. Dean, said Ed's kids from his previous marriage are coming down and going to down at the farm too, Everybody was invited, Dean, got Okle off where no one heard her, and said, I want you too know you are more than welcome to join us down at the farm, Oh thank You for the invitation, but I believe my place is here

. It was not long before Ed's children Eddie and Jacqueline were here with Ed and Dean.

. Dean, winked at Okle, enjoy the peace and quite. Days went by and everyone was heading in the cars Ed and the boys in one car, Ed also had Teresa in the car. And Dean had Jennifer and Jacqueline,

Once they all got down at the farm Eddie and Jacqueline saw this beautiful two story house, and Dean, over heard them talking our mom has to work two jobs, and Dad has all this. Jacqueline said, Eddie let's just enjoy this time with dad, and not tell our mother about all what Dad has. Her brother Eddie agreed. And another thing, let's not come back here at all, there living the great life, while we live, mom working two jobs.

But Dean heard Ed asking to many questions about his ex-wife, how does she look, do you all have a recent picture of your Mother, Ed, was smoking a ham, and Teresa was off riding her horse,

Jennifer, playing by the lake with one of her friends that came too.

Dean told Ed at the farm she will be back in a little while she is going too drive up and see Jane, a friend Dean, had made in a small town. Ed said is this a good time for you too leave, the kids and all are here, Dean, said I back you up when you have to leave on business trips , or when ever you have to just go some place by your self. So please show me the same respect.

With that Dean, grabbed her purse got in car and left, dean drove about twenty minutes, admiring the scenery,

Dean pulled up in Jane's drive way and seen she was home. Dean, knocked on Jane's old wooden door, and Jane said, oh my gosh, Dean, it is so good to see you. Come in and have a seat. Dean, sat down on old worn furniture, and hand made old curtains

Dean started talking to Jane, with tears just a rolling down Dean's face, Jane, my gosh grabbed a tissue and gave it too Dean, Jane sitting beside Dean, what happen Dean, for you to be so upset.

, Jane looked and Dean, you know I know you husband is a lot to handle at times, Dean, cried to Jane. Ed is a vain person, Dean, said I just wish my heart could let him go. But I will love Ed always.

Dean said I am angry he thinks I do not know about the telephone numbers of these women he calls.

That man has the emotions of a worm. As

Dean, sipped her vodka, and lit up a cigarette, Dean grabbing Jane's hand, Dean,

Jane said I am saying this because I am you friend, watch your drinking it can become a bad habit. Dean knew Jane had only said that out of respect for dean.

Dean, lit up a cigarette and looked at Jane, and said. Dean, with anger on her face, and crying

My Gosh, we have paid for now two abortions and that's just the one's I know about,

, Jane with a shocked look on her face Dean said. I know there has too been more out woman out there, I am so ashamed, Dean said. Jane said, that's Ed's battle with heaven and hell.

Jane, sat down and said I must admit your husband thinks he is just better than other people at times, and then other times, your husband will do the kindest things for people who have nothing , he will pay there bill of some kind, or just give them money,

Dean, looked at Jane,

What, where did you hear that from, Dean, come on this is a small town, you know how that is, Dean, you grew up in a small town, you can not fart in this town with out knowing who did and when. Dean smiled. That' true.

Jane is Ed helping single woman, Jane, grabbed Dean's hand, no. He helped Mr. Graham, you know the government was going to take his land, your husband Ed found out some how put a stop to that, all we know

Mr. Graham thinks a lot of your husband.

Dean smiled that's nice Ed did that.

Jane, said do not get me wrong. I know how he chases other woman, or looks like he wants too, and woman to woman I know the pain and that how hurts and feels. Dean said, we I come from a person does not get a divorce, for any reason, Dean, looked at Jane I made my bed and now I got lay in it.

Ed put you in a bad position, Dean, come on. After talking for a long while Dean, felt better, and blocked out Ed and his cheating.

Well, the conversation turned in to talking about gardens and kids, Dean, said I better get back. Ed, will think I do not want to be with him, or the family time.

But Dean said to Jane, sometimes I just get tired. And ask God, guide me, I keep falling down, pull me out God. Jane said God is not going to let you down.

Dean gave Jane a big hug and said "Thank You" for being a wonderful friend.

Same here Jane said. Friends are rare. Jane said changing the subject my niece is here, she back in the back spare room I want you to meet her,

Jane, called for Judy, Judy, came in and Jane, said I want you too meet my good friend Dean Whitehurst, they own the Whitehurst farm and lake, Judy's eye lit up,

Dean, said nice to meet you Judy, I have daughter about you size, her name is Teresa, Dean, looked at Jane, and said Jane, would you mind if I took Judy down to the farm, were all down there, infact you come to Jane, you can get out of the house for a little while,

Jane, smiled you know it might do me and Judy some good to come down, Jane looked at Judy, and said, well Judy would you like to go and meet Teresa, Judy , said sure. Dean, notice sadness in Judy

Jane grabbed her purse and all there went and got in the car, Judy, was quite the whole ride, Dean, pulled up too the house, and Ed, was waving and smiling too Dean, Dean, said Jane, Ed's smoking a pork ,

I hope you can join us for dinner , Jane, and Dean and Judy walked in the house, ,

Dean, looked at Jane and said do you all want something to drink, Jane, said ice water sounds good, it's pretty hot outside,

Dean, got her water, Dean, looked at Judy, would you like anything to drink? No thank you Judy said.

Dean, looked out the window, and said Teresa is out side with her horse, let me catch her before she takes off, Judy said which one is Teresa, she is the one standing beside her Dad, that Ed,. Dean, said let's go out side, before Teresa take off riding, Dean said Judy do you see that white horse Teresa is on? Judy, looked out and seen the white horse, Judy said yes Dean, Dean, looked down at Judy, what ever you do child that horse might look beautiful, but it is mean as a snake, and for some odd reason, Teresa is the only one who can ride that horse, Dean said there are other horse that are normal, that you are welcome to ride anytime you want.

All Three walked out, Ed, said how are you Jane, fine Ed, and you, I could not be better. Jane, says what ever you're cooking there, sure smells good.

Ed, said there is plenty of food, who is that you have with you Ed said, this here is my niece Judy, Ed said well nice too met you Judy, and Ed said ,

Teresa, who was about to leave on her horse, come here Teresa, Teresa Yelled back, What Dad, Ed, waived his hand , back and forth as to come back here, Teresa, sighed, turned her horse back and ran the horse fast back towards her Dad, Teresa , slow that horse down, go put your horse up for a minute, I want you too meet someone,

Teresa, not happy , went and tied her horse up, walking fast, yes, what is so important , that I had to stop riding my horse, it's a nice day Dad, I want to get ridding my Prince.

Ed, said, this here is Judy, Teresa, said Hi Judy, Judy, made eye contact with Teresa,

Teresa, smiled Hey Judy do you like horses, Judy said yes,

Teresa , come on, let's walk to the barn , Judy said I have done some riding but I really am not that good, Teresa, said that's ok, I will be you out a slow horse,

Teresa and Judy went into the huge barn, and Judy, said wow, are all these your horses, Teresa, said yes, as she went and got Tasha, a apple gray quarter horse, ,Judy said this horse is really pretty, Teresa said, you will like riding her ,

Tasha, is a really calm horse, I could put a two year old child on her, and she would not get ski dish or anything, and Tasha does not kick or bite,

Teresa , saddle up Tasha for Judy, and Teresa and Judy walking with Tasha, went back and got Prince, Teresa horse,

Jane, turned around and said , well I see you too girls hit if off, Jane, Judy said Teresa has invited me to go horse back riding, do you mind if I go, Jane, said not at all you and Teresa ride and have some fun, Teresa said I do not know when I will be back ,

But we will be back by dinner time. Teresa and Judy, rode up too the lake, Judy, stopped her horse, and Teresa noticed, and stopped her horse,

Teresa said anything wrong Judy, no this lake is beautiful, the tree's and my gosh this lake is huge, do you ride them boats,? The wind was blowing, just right, Prince's mane was blowing in the wind, Teresa, said is prince not the best looking horse, Judy, looked at Prince, he is pretty, but your mom, said he is mean, Teresa, said yea, Prince for some reason does not like a lot of people, Teresa, said kind of like me. I guess. But Judy, Teresa, said, you are a cool person. Judy said thanks Teresa,

Teresa said sometimes, Judy said my Aunt Jane said your Dad had this lake built , is that true?

Teresa said yes I think my Dad calls it Whitehurst Lake, Teresa, said come on let's getting riding we can look at that lake later,

Teresa and Judy rode on the damn of the lake and went into the woods, on trail rides, and Teresa and Judy, talking as there riding became good friends, Judy was glad. Teresa asked so are you living with your Aunt Jane?

Judy said I wish I could, Judy, looked like she was holding back tears, but I have a step dad, and he is so mean, Teresa, stopped her horse, and how is he mean? Well, you know he is just mean, and really no one can do any thing about him , Teresa, said does your step Dad beat you or something, Judy, said I wish, that's all he did. Judy, put her hand over her mouth, and said, look I know I just met you Teresa, but you can not say any thing I just said to any one, I will pay a dear price if my step dad finds out. Teresa, said calm down, I have no desire to say anything to anyone.

Judy, said I call him red, Teresa, said that's a weird name, Judy said yea I know, Teresa noticed how said and the tears Judy was trying to hold back,

Teresa said do you want to talk about your step dad any more, Judy said no.

Ok, time went by and the sun was going down, Teresa and Judy were pretty wore out from riding all day, riding back towards the barn , Teresa put her horse away, and Judy unsaddle her horse, and said Teresa by the way I had a lot of fun today.

Teresa said me too. Judy said Aunt Jane said you had a sister, Teresa, said oh yea her name is Jennifer, and she does not like riding horses at all, she thinks she is a walking Barbie doll, Judy, me and my sister are so different how we have the same parents I will never know.

Teresa and Judy, went into house and washed up, Teresa said I am going to take a shower before we eat, you look like the same size of me , try on some off my clothes, that way you can take a shower and a fresh clothes.

Judy, did try on Teresa clothes while Teresa was in the shower, and sure enough they fit,

Teresa came out, hey they clothes fit you perfect. Teresa, said after your shower, and you get dressed come on out side and we eat on the back patio. Judy said ok.

Teresa, got to the table, and everybody and mostly eaten already, Jane, said where is Judy, oh, she taking a shower and I gave her some fresh clothes, so we did not smell horses, Jane, smiled good idea, Judy came out and fixed her self a plate and Teresa and Judy became really close.

Night fall had came , and it was time for Jane and Judy to go home,

Teresa and Judy switched phone numbers, but Judy said you will have to call me my Aunt Jane can not really afford any long distance calls.

Teresa said ok. Hey, I will ride back with my mom, when she takes you and your Aunt home. Teresa, Judy, Aunt Jane, and Dean, headed back to Jane's house,

Well Dean, Jane said, I sure had a nice time, and so did Judy, we will get those clothes back to you, Teresa, said that's ok she can have them.

Judy, surprised, said are you sure, yea, kept the clothes.

Teresa and her mother waved well by, as the got in the car and headed back home.

Once back at the farm every one had a good time, but the weekend went too fast, for everyone and Dean was ready to go home.

Ed, said alright everyone let's load up and get on back home, Larry, you make sure, Everybody's luggage is packed and put in the cars.

With a stern voice. Larry Ed said did you hear me? Yes I did, I am going to get on that now, Larry had everyone's stuffed packed and ready to go with Dean's help, the kids pitched in very little. Ed, said let's hurry up on this. Dean, said Ed in a hurry because,

Ed's children had to be on a plane back to California. Once back home, Teresa went and called Judy, they wrote each other, and Teresa learned more about Judy, and Teresa was getting very angry about Judy step dad.

Larry unloaded the van and cars, Eddie and Jacqueline took there showers cleaned up and Dean, got Ed's children on the plane Dean said Eddie and Jacqueline here is a check I want you to give this too your Mother, Please I am asking you both and too tell your mother, not too let Your Dad know about this money.

Eddie looked at the check, oh my gosh, my mom, will be so happy, Eddie, showed Jacqueline the check, they both hugged Dean;

Dean said please call too let us know you made it back safe. Well, Jacqueline said, Thanks for a great time, tell my Dad, we liked seeing everyone for me. Dean smiled at the boarded the plane.

Dean, came back home, Okle was cooking something that smelled really good, Dean, said to Okle do you know where Ed is? I believe he is taking a shower. Dean sat down.

Dean, told Okle that Ed, still paid more attention too Teresa, than the other children, It was nice he gave Teresa attention

Dean , as she looked at Okle , but the other kids need the same amount of attention and love.

Ed, acts like Teresa is only child and Okle said excuse me but why does Ed do that? All I know is Teresa looks like Ed's mother, Ed's mother died when he was seven years old, and his dad passed away before his Mother. And long story short Teresa looks like Ed's Mother.

Well, Okle said maybe that has something to do with it, because I see where Ed does not tell Teresa no on to many things
. Anything as far as wanting ponies, or dogs, you know material things. Teresa has her Daddy over a barrel. Okle, said Dean, Teresa is a lot like her Daddy

. Okle said that's a shame he did not see his children off at the airport. Dean, said that's ok, I made sure there ok and safe, they should be calling to let us know there home safe. Dean, told Okle about the check to Ed's ex-wife.

Okle sat down and said Dean, you know how Ed is with giving her anything extra, I do not care,

Dean said I felt sad for Eddie and Jacqueline , they live on hard times, and they come down here and see there Dad having a lot. , Dean, said a lot there not a part of. And that breaks my heart.

Okle said I agree.

Ed, walked in and the conversation changed quickly too Okle do we need anything from the store? Because I am going to get some cigarettes. No we are good on everything. Ed kissed Dean on the lips, leaving right now are you? Dean said just to the store.

Dean went to the store and she got her cigarettes and a couple bottles of wine and vodka.

Dean, pulled back in the drive way, everyone was at the dinner table eating, Dean, joined them, .This was a great dinner Okle, Dean and Ed said. Now with summer over, you can take Julius to school, I have another business trip, a short one, to Chicago, I will be back in a few days, but I do not have time to take that boy to that school. It was time for Julius to go back to school, Julius had sadness on his face , Julius asked his Mother and Dad, could he go to school and live at home,

Ed said no way. Julius walked away, with his head down, and started packing his suite case. .

Okle heard Julius crying, Okle knocked on Julius bedroom door, and it's me Okle. Come in Julius said. As Julius wiped his eyes

. Okle, said, I want you to know I am proud of you, and you are a really smart kid, do not let people get you down, and your parents they do love you, and miss you, they may not show it all the time, but they do.

Okle got up and walked over to Julius and said I love you and I will miss you. Julius said Thanks okle. Okle shut the door behind her.

Dean, was in her room now and getting ready to take Julius to school, Dean came out, and Teresa and Jennifer was waiting, Can I go Teresa asked, Julius said sure, you can even have your own room there,

Dean, looked at Julius and said take your suite cases to the car, Dean, looked at the girls, this trip I want it to be special for Julius, he has to go back, and he is sad.

Jennifer said, a lot of parents keep there children and let them go too school and live at home, Dean, said stop it Jennifer,

Jennifer, knew right then, her mother was hurting, Jennifer said Mom, I am sorry. Dean said it's ok. Take care of your sister; Okle has a lot to do today. I will be back later on today.

Dean and Julius got in the car, and drove off, once they arrived at the Boarding school, pulling through the black iron gates,, Dean noticed Julius looked so unhappy, Dean, put her hand on Julius shoulder, son, life does get easier, this way being here no kids hold you down or make fun of you,

Please look at it that way, As a Mother I am trying to protect you. Julius, reached for his suite cases, and gave his Mother a tight hug. I know it's not you, its dad. And Julius walked away not looking back. Julius was getting stronger with this boarding school.

Dean, got back in her car, with tears in rolling down her face, and drove passed the iron gates, and headed home. Dean thought I just left my son, and I miss him already.

Dean felt the rain drops starting and got in the car. As Dean lit a cigarette, the rain can be so pretty at times, with a rainbow, showing up later. But it only rained harder all the way home.

Dean lit a cigarette, it was raining hard, so hard it was hard to see and drive, Dean slowed down.

When Dean pulled in the drive way, the front door was open and Dean seen Ed was yelling at Jennifer, Dean ran in the house to get out of the rain and to see what is going on, Ed, really did not yell a lot.

As Dean, walked in the house Jennifer, had just thrown a glass and missed her Dad's head, about two inches Ed was so upset , The . Glass is broken all over the floor, Jennifer is still yelling. Dean, walked in hearing

That's is it for you, Dean, tried to get answers out of Ed, but he was getting phone numbers of boarding schools, and Dean, went into Jennifer room what is going on here? Jennifer, was crying, that man is crazy, He has no right to tell me there is no God, he is out of place.

Dean, put her head down, is this what this disagreement is about? Or is there more to the story, Yes, Dad's been drinking mom, and he was making fun of Okle's limp, and then he was making fun of Larry,

, Jennifer, said you know when Larry gets up set he will sometimes stutter, you know that mom, Dean told Jennifer to calm down , Jennifer was so upset she started crying , I am that angry, is why I am crying Mother. Dean, hugged Jennifer, looked in to Jennifer eyes and said Please calm down, Jennifer looked at her dad he should not make fun of people, God sees what you do.

And another thing mother as Jennifer threw up hair back, and looked her Mother right in the eye, Teresa heard all the screaming and yelling Teresa shut her door and called Judy, one day you can come up here where I live, Judy said I do not know if my step dad would allow that, Teresa said and one day, I have to meet your step dad. Teresa said I have to get off the phone, my dad is yelling about something, talk to you later. Teresa over heard. Jennifer saying

I do not need anybody too tell me there is not a God, and

You think I do not know about the cheating, the other woman mom, Stop Jennifer, you have no idea what a marriage takes, it is about give and take Jennifer, and all marriages can be hard.

Teresa, shut her door and went to sleep.

As the years went by and the bank accounts grew, Dean, sent money to her Mama and Pauline, Ed, never noticed the money gone. .

Dean had started her own bank account with out Ed on it. And Dean hid money in the house that Ed did not know about.

Ed and Dean had money to buy new cars every year, trips to where ever they felt like going, and Ed's brother Russell came and went, like the seasons.

Okle was great, stable and a wonderful person. Dean, had told Okle, God had to send you too our home, you are a blessing. Okle, said Blessing go both ways. Dean was growing founder of Okle by the day.

Everything was falling into place, Dean went down to see her family in Mississippi, every July with out Ed. Teresa her best friend besides her horse, prince, was Judy l, and of course she still played a lot with the twins.

Mama and Pauline did not even ask why Ed did not come with her anymore.

Ed, pulling in the drive way, Dean was watching TV. Ed had been drinking and Dean was unhappy about taking Julius to that school.

As Dean, walked in the house Jennifer, had just thrown a glass and missed her Dad's head, about two inches Ed was so upset , Dean, looked down at the floor and seen The . Glass is broken all over the floor, Jennifer is still yelling.

Dean walked in hearing broken glass, and the yelling got louder. Dean heard

That's it for you, Dad, Jennifer yelled.

Dean, tried to get answers out of Ed, but he was getting phone getting numbers of boarding schools, and Dean, went into Jennifer room what is going on here? Jennifer, was crying, pounding fist down on the bed, that man is crazy,

He has no right to tell me there is no God, he is out of place.

Dean, put her head down, touching Jennifer gently is what this disagreement is about? Or is there more to the story,

Yes, Dad's been drinking mom, and he was making fun of Okle's limp, and then he was making fun of Larry,

, Jennifer, said with hurt in her voice Mother you know when Larry gets up set he will sometimes stutter, you know that mom,

Dean told Jennifer to calm down, Jennifer was so upset she started crying harder, I am that angry, that is why I am crying Mother.

Dean, hugged Jennifer, looked in to Jennifer eyes and said Please calm down, Jennifer said dad he should not make fun of people,

God sees what you do.

And another thing mother as Jennifer threw up hair back, and looked her Mother right in the eye,

I do not need anybody too tell me there is not a God, and Jennifer getting more upset, Jennifer yelling Mother

You think I do not know about Dad cheating you, and the other woman mom, Dean, said Stop it Jennifer, you have no idea what a marriage takes, it is about give and take Jennifer, and all marriages can be hard. Jennifer grabbed her Mother's hand, Mom, which is why he tries to say there is no God, Because Dad can not live by his rules and face God.

Dad thinks he wrote book on life.

, as Dean tried too help Jennifer understand life sometimes is unfair.

Jennifer yelled it a good marriage when you have a man, that cheats on you, and lies to your face.

Dad is so good at opening accounts and making money, but Dad has no spine. Dean, gently grabbed her daughter and said Jennifer, calm down right now, before this argument gets any worse.

Ed, walked in Jennifer's bedroom

, Ed walked in Jennifer bed room with a angry voice and pointed his finger right at Jennifer face, get your stuff packed you are going to a school far away from here, Ed, then shut the door behind him as he left.

Jennifer, grabbed her Mother's hand, Mom, with tears in her eyes, this is unfair I did not to anything to be sent away, and you know it Mom.

Jennifer, calm down, stay right here, Dean, said Ed, I want to speak with you for a minute,

Dean walked out of the Jennifer bedroom to the kitchen, where Okle was cooking, and Okle heard everything.

. Ed, sitting at the kitchen table, Ed said as he pointed his finger at Jennifer bedroom

Dean, that girl has a smart mouth on her; I will not deal with that.

Dean, said, please Ed do not send Jennifer away, she is a teenager, and she is on her period, and Jennifer gets moody at the time of the month.

Ed said not my problem. Ed said I do not care what her problem is; tomorrow she is on the first plane out of here.

Ed, think for a minute that is no reason to send our other child off. Ed, poured himself a drink,

Ed said woman are you forgetting I am doing all I can do make money and keep this family, and I will no deal with a crazy teenager, Jennifer is leaving. That is the end of this conversation Dean. Ed went to the bath room while he was gone,

Dean, had tears in her eyes, and feeling sick to her stomach, Okle, came up and said, Dean, it not my place but I don't think Ed is thinking right; sending your children off is not the answer.

Dean, said Okle I agree. And Jennifer is so sensitive.

Dean, lit up a cigarette and walked away to the bathroom, Dean, was taking another valium, Dean waited a few minutes, wiped the tears away, Ed, walked fast back in the kitchen,

Dean, walked to her bedroom got the pill bottle and took a valium,

Dean, looked in mirror, God, this is not the life I planned. I can not fix this God.

Dean, walked back to Ed, and. Dean said please Ed do not send Jennifer away.

As, Ed. Took another sip of his vodka, do not test me with that child. Jennifer is lucky I do not send her out of this country.

Jennifer has crossed the line with me; Jennifer will learn what life is about.

And as Ed sat back Jennifer, will learn the hard way not to burn her bridges.

.

Dean, was now chain smoking, Ed walked out of the kitchen,

Okle, with a stern look on her face, but warm eyes, Dean, again it's none of my business I do want to cross the line, But Jennifer and Ed, they might need a break.

Jennifer will not keep her mouth shut,

Jennifer will just keep on disagreeing with her Daddy, and keep making him angry,

Okle said I love all your children, but Jennifer says what is on her mind.

Okle said, has she hugged Dean

I do not agree with Ed, sending these children off, I am just the housekeeper, Dean, grabbed Okle, this is not how I planned my life, my God,

As she looked at Okle, Dean said I feel like I am walking in a maze , with no ending, Dean, stood up and hugged Okle, I have got to lay down , all this yelling is making me sick. Dean, seen Ed in the hall way and said

Teresa,

is the one who voices her thoughts,

Teresa walks and talks and acts like she pays the bills around here and all you do is go out and buy her what ever her little heart desires.

Dean said Jennifer see's that. Maybe Ed if you paid the same amount of love and attention to Jennifer as you do Teresa, we would not have this problem.

With that

Dean walked back in the kitchen and sat down with Ed. I want too tell you Ed, with tears rolling down Dean's face, you are making a mistake sending Jennifer away. You think our son is happy?

Ed, with a serious look on his face, that boy is happy and taken care of. Dean, turned around how would you know?

Dean said you have not called him one time; I can not handle this turmoil anymore I have to lay down. Dean said.

Before you go lay down, Tell Jennifer to be packed and ready to get out of here by nine o'clock in the morning.

Dean went her daughter's and Open Jennifer bedroom door, Jennifer, your Dad wants you to be ready in by nine o'clock am. Jennifer shook her head. And said fine. Dean laid down and with Jennifer for a few minutes, Mom, why can't you say no to Dad,

Dean, lying down, I have tried Jennifer, it does not work.

Dean, got up, and said looking at Jennifer, and feeling sorry for her, Jennifer I have to go to bed. Dean tried to sleep.

Dean laid there talking to God, give me advice God,

Jennifer, came out her bedroom walked into the kitchen and said Hey Dad, let me save you some money, let me go live with Aunt Polly in Mississippi, let me do you a favor, you need one.

Ed, said that is fine with me, they have if they have an academy school down there, then get on down there. Jennifer, with tears in voice, said I am calling Aunt Polly, Jennifer picked up the phone and called her Aunt Polly and told her what was going on,

Okle, went woke up Dean, Okle said I thought you might want to be up for this phone call,

, Dean, with a surprise look on her face, what? Jennifer is calling your sister in Mississippi,

Dean hurried up and went into the Kitchen where Jennifer was with Ed. and then Dean got on the phone, talked to her Pauline and said it would be best for Jennifer to maybe try and live down there

If not Ed, was going to send her off to a boarding school. Pauline said I will let Jennifer stay here and go to the academy but you know that cost lot's of money, Pauline, I will pay you too help me with this ordeal.

Pauline, said I can not image sending your children off Dean, Dean, tried to hold back the tears, Pauline, said let me know what time, and Dade and I will be at Jackson, Ms. Airport to pick her up. Thank You Pauline your welcome,

I will send money weekly for her. Dean, said if you need extra money please let me know, I know you are doing for my child what I can not do.

Dean said well by and hung up the phone. Dean went back to bed, and cried until she feels asleep and did not hear Ed come too bed.

And the next day , Jennifer had her stuffed packed in her suite cases, lot's of hugs from Okle, and Larry, Teresa, and her Mother, Ed, with his coffee in his hand, said Look, maybe that school can teach you some sense about life,

Get your self together, maybe you can come back when you know how to talk to me. As your Dad. And not like one of you're pissed off friends.

Jennifer said. I love you Mom. , and Jennifer said I will try and learn to understand why you choose to have kids.

As Jennifer enter the cab. Jennifer did not look back as the cab left. Jennifer cried to the airport. Hurt and angry.

Jennifer thought to her self at least Dad did not get the last word in. Dean called Pauline and told her what time Jennifer flight would be in Jackson, Ms. Pauline, said we will get her and try to make her as comfortable as possible, Thanks you. Sis. Dean and Pauline said there Good By's and hung the phone.

Larry came up and gently put his and on Dean's shoulder please do not cry, you are not a bad mother, Ed, is a mean man, as Larry stuttered his words,

Dean knew Larry was upset, Larry only stutters his words when he was upset.

Dean, said Larry, that's Ed, when he good he is great, but him and Jennifer for what ever reason clash. On every level. Ed, over heard Larry, and walked in, and said if you do not stay out of family, you will not have a job, you got me. As Ed walked off. Dean, grabbed Larry arm, Ed's got a lot on his mind, do not let him get you up set Larry. Dean, said

Well, this day is not starting out the best. Larry, I will be ready to go to work in about an hour. Dean, with her kind eyes, please makes sure we have the entire inventory that is needed for the accounts today.

Dean said Okle Larry and I are getting ready to leave, to check on accounts, and other business stuff. Okle please tell Ed, he is going to feed those dogs. Dean, looked at

Larry,

Dean said never go near those German shepherd dogs in the very back of the yard, those dogs are caged up for a reason, they can not get out, but Lord knows they will try, and Dean, said Larry if they ever get out those dogs will eat you alive. Please, always remember to stay away from those dogs.

Okle said I know I said very little about those dogs, Ed takes care of them, and when he is out of town, I just toss the food over, never get close to them. Ed, just now put in a automatic feeder for those dogs, we will now use it all the time, you are I can pour the dog food in this steel looking tunnel and it goes right in the food bowls, the same with the water.. With that being said

Larry, said Dean, why would you and Ed have such mean German shepherds around at all, and your children. Larry, seen the expression on Dean's face,

Look Larry said, I will make sure the dogs are feed and the inventory is ready. I will take Okle's place to toss the food too the dogs, so Okle does not have too. Okle, said Larry, I just want to thank you for doing that. I know those dogs are trained and very mean.

Dean, nodded ok as she went to take a shower, once in the shower, and the water made her body feel far away, Dean closed her eyes for a couple seconds and Dean, could see Hank's face, and heard Hank's warm voice, call me if you need me, and when Hank was angry, Dean remember Hank said You will reap what you sow. Dean, wiped her eyes,

Dean, leaning into the tile wall, letting the shower water washes the soap off her body and her tears down the drain.

Dean, got out of the shower, looked in the mirror, God help me, let me have a good day.

Help me get strength, Dean, heard Ed's voice, Dean, are you alright in there it sounds like you are talking too someone/

Dean, sighed to herself, I am thinking out loud that's all; I will be out in a few minutes.

Dean thought why is it so hard to pray in this house,

Dean, talking too her self, God help me with my marriage and life.

I am trying everything I know how. Dean, fixed her hair, and make up, it was not too much longer Dean, came out looking the way Ed, fell in love with her.

Ed, walked up as to Dean, Did I ever tell you how much you mean too me?

Dean, looked up and smiled, you mean the world too me too. No, Dean, I love you and Thank You for standing behind me,

Ed grabbed Dean's hand, you a wonderful friend and woman, you preach Dean about God and Jesus, well all I know is, you might be right,

He sent me you. Dean, felt comfort in Ed's voice and heart and he hugged her.

Dean had goose bumps from Ed being so kind. Dean hugged Ed. And said Life is hard, but please do not think money is the answer to all or any problems.

The phone rang, Okle answered the telephone, Yes, I will accept the collect call, as Okle is holding the red phone with the long cord on it, Dean, it is Jennifer, I am coming , just a second Okle, Ed, said did you tell

Okle never to accept collect calls from Julius and Jennifer or do I need to do that, Okle over heard that, Dean, grabbed that telephone from Okle, and said I am so glad you called, Jennifer I love you and I am glad you called. . School will be fine it will just be a little adjustment. That's all.

And you will come home and I will drive you back myself in the summer. I love you, and I will talk too you later, Dean hung up the telephone. Dean over heard

Okle telling Ed, I will not refuse a collect call from those children Ed, and another thing you have no idea if they need help, or if something is wrong, I know I am out of my place, but I love your children as if they were my own, now if you want to fire me, Please let me know now, as Okle looked at Ed.

Ed said you have a point there, but do not accept all calls; those kids will try and call every day.

Okle wiped her apron, and said Ed, I am an honest woman, and I work hard for you. And you know that, but

I will not refuse a collect call from your children. Now do you want me to leave or stay? Ed, said Okle you're a good woman, I am glad you love those kids, Now you use your best Judgment Okle, when to accept collect calls from those kids, they will call every day. Okle said ok went back to her housework. And Dean and Larry left for work. Dean

Months went by, Dean, thinking of her sister Pauline had called a while back, but Dean, could not really talk with Ed right there.

, Dean was home and Ed was out of town, Dean, told Okle, you know at least I can talk with out Ed, getting up set over long distance calls,

Dean said he spends so much money on this and that, Dean, said with the house quite and Teresa in bed. This would be a good time to call my sister Pauline.

Dean, lit up a cigarette and had a little glass of wine, and made the call to her sister.

The phone rang about three or four times,

Pauline answered the phone, Hey Dean , I am glad I called me back, Dean, flipped her ashes of course I am going to call you back , How is everything going? Well fine,

Dean, said Pauline you sound like you have something heavy on your mind, what's wrong? Well mama is doing fine, and misses you.

Pauline said, I really do not know how to tell you this, except just to come out and say it, Dean said, just tell me, Pauline said

Jennifer has met Hank Jr.

Dean, grabbed her drink, I know it's a small town, but how did that happen,

Well, Pauline said you know my husband Dade works on people lawn mowers and such, and Hank came over with his

131

son, and you know Jennifer is just as pretty as she can be, and Hank Jr. has eyes for Jennifer.

Hank Jr. has asked me and Dade, if he can take Jennifer too the movies. I said I would have to ask you. Dean.

Dean, said oh Pauline, I really do not think that is the best idea,

Dean, said I don't want my family business known, and I do not know what will come out of Jennifer's mouth. Pauline said Dean you have put me in the middle of raising Jennifer, and she has been so sad, most of the time she has been here. And Jennifer is old enough to date.

That is why I am thinking it is best for her too gets out and see a movie, what harm can it cause Dean? Pauline Dean said I guess,

Dean said Pauline I need to know does Hank senior know Jennifer is my daughter, Pauline, hesitated for a minute,

Yes Dean, he does. And I am just going to tell you, Hank Jr. Looks the same way at Jennifer as Hank senior looked at you. I am just being honest with you.

Dean reached for her drink. Feeling the alcohol ,

Pauline said is everything alright with you, your voice sounds odd, almost like a person who has been drinking, Pauline said I know you do not drink, I did not mean to insult if that came out wrong,

Dean, said no, I had a cold, and taking medication is makes me drowsy sometimes. Well that makes sense. Dean, shut eyes, God forgive me for lying.

Dean, lit up another cigarette, well I guess it is good for her too get out; staying in all the time is not good for anyone.

Pauline said, I need to tell you something else, you know Jennifer said she was going to ride her bike and me and Dade, thought that would be fine, but Dean, I have to tell you , Jennifer crossed the tracks you know Dean ,where the colored folks stay. Pauline said we can't be having that. Pauline said to

Dean, you have to remember blacks on one side of this town and white folks on the other. Dean said of course I remember that. Dean, thought how could any normal person forget that, But Dean kept her thoughts too her self.

Dean, said what, oh my gosh. Dean, said between Hank Jr. and crossing the tracks, Hank Senior, must have a bad thought on my family, Dean, thought I know how people can be down there , with there silent rules. And judgmental ways.

Pauline said, Dean, Hank would never say anything bad about you or your children, Dean, said, oh Pauline I want to tell Jennifer the history of Hank senior and I, but I can not do it. At least not now.

. Dean said I still feel like I let Hank down, if you recall Pauline I gave Hank my word I would be back to marry him, Pauline said Dean, I do remember, the whole town remembers. Pauline said

Daddy raised us upon faith, loving God, and he taught us when we give our word, we back it up.

Dean said, that's I what I am talking about, Now here is my daughter dating his son. And it sounds like it is going pretty well as far as dating goes.

Pauline said there young. Dean said how is Mama doing? Just fine, sit's on her porch swing, reading her Bible,

Mama, has done went a got a little kitten for her self, and she keeps this little kitten in the house, Dean, said Mama, has a kitten in her house, Mama , just loves that little Kitten Pauline said. Dean said I just never thought I would see the day Mama had an animal in the house.

Jennifer, goes and see's Mama all the time Pauline said.

And Jennifer just loves her. Jennifer is adjusting; Pauline said Jennifer will be ok.

Pauline said Jennifer is walking in now would you like to talk too her,

Dean, said Oh yes.

Jennifer, came in Pauline handed her the phone, it's your Mother, Jennifer smiled, Hi Mom, How are you? I am fine, and you Jennifer really good, mom I like it down here better than I thought,

they eat a lot of beans down here though, lima beans, green beans, red beans, black eye peas, and corn bread.

I know mom by the time I am 18 years old, I know I will never want too see another bean in my life. Dean giggled.

Mom, I am seeing a really cool guy, his name is Hank, and he has a cool car. He is a lot of fun to be around. Dean said that is great.

Dean said how long have you been seeing this boy, Jennifer said a pretty long time, when you come down you can meet him,

Dean, lit a cigarette, and starting biting he lip a little, Well, What is his name? Jennifer said Hank

I am glad you are happy Jennifer, Mom, Hank told me I am the most beautiful girl he has ever seen, and he treats me so well, he opens the car door for me. Hank is tall dark and handsome,

Hank even told me Mom, if he can't be with me, he would not want to be with anyone. Else Jennifer said, that is so sweet. Dean said yes it is.

Dean asked Jennifer have you met Hank's parents, Jennifer said oh, yes, they are real nice people.

Hank's dad is really a cool person, and his mom is so nice. Quite by nice.

Mom, I have a question for you, why does Hank's Dad, have a picture of you?

Dean, said what, has Dean almost dropped her drink,

Well me and hank was going through the cellar, at his house,

And the were a bunch of pictures, me and hank started going through them and his Dad has a picture of you. Jennifer said I thought that is so weird.

Because when I seen that picture, I told Hank jr. that is my mother. Hank said wow, how weird. My Dad has never talked about her. Yet my dad has a picture of your mother.

Dean, said Jennifer, one day you and I will talk, right now I am really concerned if you are happy down there, Mom I am, happier than living around Dad, your right mom, me and Dad just argue all the time.

Well, Jennifer said to her Mom I love you I hope you come down soon, I know you will come down in July 10th for you and grandma's birthday.

Dean said I will see if I might be able to come sooner, Jennifer I need to talk to your Aunt Polly, ok mom hold and I will get her for you. Oh, mom one more thing, what Jennifer, thank you for the money. You are welcome, Aunt Polly, dean heard Jennifer scream, at the top of her lungs for her aunt. Pauline got back on the telephone, Pauline said to Dean, I just want you to know, Jennifer crossed the tracks, Dean, said oh my Gosh

Pauline said, calm down, Dean,

Jennifer I think at the time was just riding and riding and ended over there, Jennifer came back and told me she had down rode her bike across the tracks on the colored side of town.

Lord has mercy, Pauline said. Calm down Dean,

Dade sat Jennifer down and explained to her down here, white's folks live on one side and colored live on the other, and we do not cross over the tracks.

Dean, paused I understand that, and I am glad you told Jennifer how it is down there, But Jennifer makes friends of all colors.

Dean said you know Ed likes people of colors, and back grounds,

Dean, said we have taught our children never dislike someone because of the color there skin. Pauline said I understand. But Jennifer is living in Mississippi now.

Pauline I have nothing against any one, but Dean you know how it is here, you do remember Canton, Ms. Dean, said yes but Pauline, and people are people. There is good and bad in every race.

Pauline said Dade has cleared that up. It will not happen again. Jennifer promised. Jennifer understands the rules and our culture down here.

And Jennifer said she did not want to disappoint her Uncle or me, and Hank jr. is making a big impression on Jennifer. Pauline said. Before I go and check on Mama, I need to tell you Jennifer

, Pauline said to her sister Dean, I just do not know how to tell you , tell me what Dean said, I guess I am just going to come out with it and tell, you. Jennifer, told Mama, that Ed does not treat you or the children well, and that he has well you know been with other women, behind your back,

OH my God, Mama knows all this, hold on Dean, Jennifer was crying , and Mama just happen to be the one to see her on the porch , poor girl was crying her eyes out , and Mama asked her what could be so bad to make Jennifer cry, and Jennifer, spilled the beans,

Jennifer told Mama, about Ed giving you some type of a disease , and you had to go to the doctor for it, Jennifer , said she misses her brother and sister a lot, but she does not miss her daddy, Mama told her to pray for her you all and her daddy, Because Satan, will take you a person down no matter how much they have or don't have.

Pray to God to protect you all. You know Mama,

Dean, said, well Thank God, Mama has never brought it up too me. Pauline said

Well, I got to get on back to check on Mama, Pauline, said and I will tell Jennifer she can go to the movies,

I will let you know how it all turns out. Pauline, said

Dean said to Pauline Thank You for all what you are doing, and please tell Mama, and Jennifer I do love them.

Pauline said, I will do that. Good by for now. Dean hung the phone. Up.

Larry, walked in and told Dean, everything is done for today, Larry, was in and out. Doing all types of chores.

Dean had noticed Ed was really working Larry hard, here and at the farm,

Dean, thinking to her self, it does not make sense, there are folks Ed has hired to take care of the farm.

Okle, said well Dean it is time for me to go to bed.

Dean said I am getting ready for bed myself, Dean, checked on Teresa, sleeping peaceful.

Dean, lay down on the bed, thoughts of Hank knowing how messed up her life is, Dean, closed her eyes. Dean thought of all the time she could have spent with Julius and Jennifer.

She would be there for Teresa. Dean laid there thinking But Teresa is very close to her Daddy.

About a week later,

Teresa came in and told okle me and my Dad will not be here for dinner, Okle asked why is that Teresa, We are going shopping and out to eat.

My Dad said so. That's why Okle.

Larry, walked passed by, and told Teresa you should be kinder with your words. Teresa, looked at Larry, and did not say anything.

Teresa thought Larry is right, I was rude.

Teresa and her Dad left, Ed, said Teresa, I need to get some gas ,

Ed pulled into a gas station, Teresa seen her Dad flirting with some woman at the counter, Teresa put her face closer to the car window, and Teresa, got out of the car, and went into the gas station, and screamed Dad as loud as she could as she quickly grabbed a candy bar,

Ed, has just paid for the gasoline,

Teresa, waving and running towards her Dad, said I am starving so bad I have to eat this candy bar right now.

Ed, was embarrsed threw an extra fifty cents down on the counter and walked out with Teresa,

Teresa tour open the wrapper like she had not ate in days, Teresa, said to beautiful looking counter lady that her Dad was talking too, Hey, did my Dad tell you I have eight brothers and five sisters?

The beautiful red head , said no, and Teresa thought you look pissed off.

The lady said , is that is your Dad?

Teresa took another huge bite out of the candy bar and tried to be as messy as possible, Yep, that my Dad,

The lady, said give him this piece of paper back. Teresa open the paper, it had Ed's phone number on it.

Teresa, said, Ok. And took the piece of paper and threw it in the trash in front of the pretty woman,

Teresa, said you could have done that much,

Teresa told the lady, this is my family and you , will not break up.

The lady said I have no intention of breaking up a family girl?

Teresa, said how stupid you , you see a man with a kid, and you can't figure it out.

Teresa said talking loudly

oh I get it you are retarded, and walked out.

Teresa, went and got back in the car, and Ed, said my why did you do that Teresa, screaming and running in the store, while I am trying to pay for gasoline,

Teresa looked at her Dad, and said Dad, it's weird, I was so hungry, my stomach was hurting.

Teresa, said, that lady, had pimples all over her face,

Teresa, looked at her Dad, and said gross, and said I bet you she got pimples and black heads on places on her body that would make you sick.

. Teresa, turned on the radio, and looked at her Dad, I am glad mom does not look like that.

Teresa and her dad went and ate. Once back home, Ed took Teresa shopping, Ed, said I will stay out here in the car , Ed pointed his finger and said here is my charge card go on and get you self something. , Teresa, took the charge card, and went into the store, Teresa, thinking about her dad, flirting with that woman at the gas station, Teresa, walked in to the Diamond store, and looked around and said , I will take that diamond watch, the man said, this here watch, Teresa, said yes, that is the one I am pointing too. I want that one, the man said this watch is over a thousand dollars, Teresa, said to the man behind the counter, do I look like I care? In fact throw some diamond ear rings in with it. Teresa, gave the charge card and grabbed the recipt, and Teresa walked back to the car . Ed, said well baby girl , did you find anything you liked, Teresa, said you know for once I had no problem, Teresa grabbed the bag and pulled out the diamond watch and diamond ear rings , Teresa, said thanks Dad. Ed, looked at the reciept, and said Teresa,

Teresa went to Okle and said, Hey Okle I did not mean to talk to you that way. Okle said smiled, good to see you growing up. Teresa

Ed and Dean's life style as the time went by, it was time for Julius to Graduate, Ed and Dean were looking forward to that, so proud there son is going to graduate.

Dean, was talking one day to Ed, and said I believe a colored family has moved in the neighborhood, Ed, said really, Well I hope they like it here, and people are nice to them.

It's the 70's, after time is changing. Dean, said I agree,

The telephone rang, and it was the boarding school, the President Marshall King of the school said, I need to speak to Edward, Whitehurst, Ed, came to the phone, Hello, I am the President of the school you son Julius attends, Ed, said , is there something wrong, I know in two weeks Julius will be graduated.

Well, Mr. Whitehurst, your son Julius and some other kids at this school, broke in a soda machine and stole the money, and we the school found pot on Julius and in his room.

Ed said you have got to be mistaken. This your fault, not mine, I pay you to well, for you to try and tell me my son is smoking pot and stealing,

Well Mr. Whitehurst, that's not all, your son will get a diploma from this school, but we will mail it too you.

Your son will not be allowed to walk across the stage to get his diploma, along with others who were involved.

Ed, rubbed his forehead, Ed said my

Boy has been at that school for over six or seven years, and you are telling me, Julius can not be allowed to get his diploma at your school.

Marshall King said the school is sending Julius home tomorrow. Ed said that's fine. I will look into this matter, for your sake I hope your right Mr. King.

Ed hung up the telephone. Ed, told okle, I will be in the back living room, I need to make a private call

Okle over heard him talking to some man in New Orleans, la. And something about money, and the word kick backs.

Okle, had ears of a dolphin. Okle kept quite.

Ed came back in the kitchen calling Dean.

Okle heard it all again, as Ed called Dean's name, and told her the story with Julius, Dean, shocked our son would not do drugs, and we have money so, that makes no sense him stealing.

Ed said Julius will be home tomorrow, both of us will be here, to get his side of the story. Julius will call, and both of us will pick him up. Dean, changing the subject did I tell you

That a colored family Mr. Nixon was part of the head police quarters and is going to chief of police,

The Nixon family had adopted twins two little colored boys , small for there age, and Teresa, was always playing with them, Ed told Dean

Ed, said I have notice Teresa really does not play with any little girls, if she does I have not seen, Ed, turned around Okle, have you?

Yes, Teresa plays with everyone, not just the colored twins,

Teresa, walked in, and joined the conversation much older now and blond eye and blue eyes, and small and petite.

Ed, said Teresa, what are those twins names that you play with, Ronald and Donald, why Dad, I did not know there names,

Ed asked Teresa, do you play with the girls around here, not a whole lot , I like playing with Ronald and Donald better,

Teresa looked at her Dad and said what girls are around here are stuck up ,and to boring. And talk about how pretty they are.

Dean, lit up a cigarette,

Ed, said that's fine, but you should play with maybe with other people too, you don't want to limit you fun, Ed, said come here Teresa,

Teresa came closer, I do not care if you play with the colored twins, Teresa you are getting to an age, where you have to wise with the choices you make.

And the company you keep.

Dean, thought Ed you need to follow your own advice.

Dad, are you worried I might kiss one of the twins?

Ed, raised his eye brows, I do not want you kissing any boys right now you are not old enough for that.

And Teresa, I raised you to be able to have a open mind, not to hate any race , that if you have a problem with that person, take it up with that person, not the race. Teresa said so what's the problem,

Well Whites and Blacks do not, never mind child your too immature to understand what I am saying even when you do get old enough to date, you know what I am saying Teresa, Teresa said I do.

Now, can I go back outside and play, Ed sure. Go ahead. Dean said Teresa is growing up fast Ed, times are different.

Dean, said Ed why didn't you ask Teresa who she is going out side to play with, Ed, crossed his legs and said in about five minutes or so, I am going to go out side and see for my self who she picks to play with, Ed, said I am curious, after I just told Teresa, she should play with all kinds of kids. Okle, kept quite, and turned around and just gave Dean a look, the look that says here comes problems.

Ed, said Okle what are we having for Dinner, Okle said Leg of lamb, and the sides that goes with it, Ed, said Okle you make sure Teresa does not know we are having Leg of Lamb, Okle turned around and said I do not understand,

Ed said I had a lamb down at the farm and you know how Teresa is with animals, she makes best friends out of animals.

And that girl will have a fit, because the lamb we are eating for dinner, Teresa named it Amy, is going to be on the dinner table.

Okle said I understand. Ed got up and went out side,

Ed seen Teresa playing base ball right in the middle of the street with the colored twins. Ed came back in the house. Ed said nothing. Ed, thought Teresa would not go out her way not to listen to , Teresa had to have forgotten what I said.

Dean, thought Ed, would have never been this kind to the other children.

Dean said time is really flying by.

Dinner time came, and everyone was at the table, except Julius and Jennifer,

Teresa, sat down next too her dad, and looked at her plate of food, it smelled funny, Teresa said, Okle what did you make for dinner, it looks and smells weird,

Okle did not answer, Teresa, yelled Okle you are two feet from me, what are we having for dinner,

Dean, spoke up Teresa, you do not have to yell, maybe Okle did not hear you, and we are having veal for dinner,

Teresa, touched the meat on the plate, and looked across the dinner table to her mother

And said what it veal? Dean said a baby calf.

Teresa, looked at her Dad, amy is missing tell me Dad you did you do not have my pet on this dinner table, Ed, said to Teresa, no way, Dean, said Teresa, again it is veal.

Teresa, went into a fit, pushed the plate away, and said, that is mean, who would kill a baby cow, Teresa said to Okle,

I want a peanut butter and Jelly sandwich for dinner, The door bang rang Teresa, got up and said oh I will get it, it was Ronald and Donald, wanting to know if Teresa could come out , Teresa whispered something in there ears, and Ronald Donald came behind Teresa, as the three of them walked into the kitchen,

Teresa, looked at her Dad, and said, Dad Ronald and Donald said they really like the taste of veal,

Teresa, looking at Okle and said can Ronald and Donald stay for dinner, ?

Ed, turned to Ronald and Donald and said, you boys can have dinner with us some other time, Ed, said Teresa, you are going to eat something, Ed, told the twins Teresa is going to eat , she might be out later, Ronald and Donald left.

Okle fixed Teresa a peanut butter and Jelly sandwich. Teresa ate it, and said I am done, ate fast. Teresa, ok I am done. And I am going outside too see my friends. Teresa, said as she is walking out the front door , I have friends who don't eat there pets. Ed just shook his head. Dean, said I tied with the veal story, Ed said forget about, let's eat. Teresa, thought of all the times I played with that Lamb amy, and brushed the lambs hair, How does my parents then eat her. Teresa, said I just have to forget about this, or it will drive me nuts.

,

Ed and Dean and the rest finished there meal. Ed got up and told Okle you cooked a great meal. Okle, said Thank You,

Dean, stayed seated, Ed, looked at Dean, and said I will be right back, Ed went out the front door and came back in a few minutes later, seeing the weather, look like it was going to start raining.

Ed, came back in Dean, is talking to Okle, Ed, said what are you all talking about, Dean, said it was how good the Leg of Lamb was, Ed, said I see, That .

Teresa went outside and started playing with the twins, Ed, said I need a drink, Ed said I will get it myself, Dean said why do you seem mad? Dean, followed Ed into the back living room, Teresa needs to learn to play with little girls, not boys all the time, Dean, lit a cigarette, and Ed picked up his vodka, there is something about Teresa , the girl does not understand , playing kick ball , Ed, rubbing his forehead, That girl does not have a clue.

Dean, said well she is getting older now, Dean, said Ed, I think you are just closer to Teresa, take for instance you take

Teresa down at the farm, you and Teresa go fishing together, and horse back riding together, you take Teresa and drive to the ice cream parlor, that's over ten minutes to get too, and when you not out of town on the weekends,

Then is almost every weekend, you and Teresa ride horses across the east pasture and that's both of you crossing the Highway on horses.

Dean said as she smoked her cigarette, Ed you did not do any of those things with the other kids.

Teresa, came in Dad, you left your car window down and it's raining, Ed, tossed his car keys to Teresa, he said start it up and then push the button and the windows will go up. Teresa, said got it Dad,

Teresa ran in back in the house , it was getting late and raining, in for the night, Ed, was on about his third drink and he was calling for Larry,

Larry came up, Yes Mr. Whitehurst, take the trash out, I did already to that, and then you go feed them dogs out in the back,

Larry, looked at Dean, with help in his eyes, Dean, said I do not think that is a good idea, Ed those mean German shepherds will eat Larry alive, what are you thinking?

Dean said I believe you have had too much too drink if you really are insisting Larry goes and feeds those mean dogs.

Ed, said I will go out there with him, it's about time those dogs get used to Larry feeding them,

Ed, put on his rain coat, and told Larry to come as he is, Larry said I am in a t-shirt and jean, it will only take a second too get a rain coat, Ed, looked at Dean, I guess, Larry, ran and got a rain coat,

Dean, watched out the back picture window , smoking another cigarette, as Ed and Larry went to the shed first to get the dog food, and the Larry and Ed walked towards the dogs, all four dogs, were biting the fence and pulling the fence back and forth with the gnashing teeth, and trying to get towards Larry,

Now the dogs, jumping up and down trying to get to Larry, with snarling teeth, and growling, and Dean, went out side and said Larry, come in, Ed said no, he is getting used to these dogs,

Ed, reached for the gate, Larry backed up, and said that dog in the front is going to get out, before Larry could move, Ed shut the gate,

The first dog got out and started biting Larry, Ed, called the dog off right away, but there was blood on the ground and Larry's pants were ripped and his hands were bitten so badly, Ed got the dog off and put in back in the cage.

Larry, running in the house, Dean, said Oh My God, get the car I will take you to the hospital, you are going to need stitches , on they way to the hospital Larry said Ed, did that on purpose , Dean, said no Ed, would not do that Larry,

Ed, came hey Larry, one out four dogs, it is going to take time, for these dogs to get used too you,

Ed, looked around he seen Okle, Ed said Okle where is Larry at,

Dean rushed larry to the Hospital, Ed, Larry will need stitches, Okle, said I am just now down getting the blood off the floors, Ed, said to Okle, I am sure it was not that much blood. Okle said nothing. Teresa heard all of this and watched from her bedroom window.

My God, that woman, over reacts to everything.

Ed, grabbed his drink, Teresa, came in where and said Dad I want to go out with you and try and feed the dogs,

Ed, looked down at Teresa, girl you will not,

Teresa, holding her Dad's hand and pulling him back out side, yes, or I will go out there by my self,

Ed, said, Ed did not notice what Teresa had put in her pocket. Teresa had distracted her Dad.

Well, they will not do the same thing, Teresa went out there,

Teresa got right by the fence and the dogs were showing there teeth, and doing every thing dogs could do to eat through a fence.

Teresa pulled out hot sauce and poured as much as she could in each dog she could get too.

And those mean dogs showing there teeth, Teresa threw what was left in the hot sauce bottle right in those evil dogs eyes. .

While the dogs, were gasping, for water, and stumbling over each other to the water bowls, Teresa took a stick and hit them on there nose,

Ed said what is wrong with you, Teresa? Those dogs are meant to be guard dogs.

Teresa said nothing is wrong with me, those dogs, are not going to growl at me, and try and bite me. Teresa, looked at her Dad, and through the stick to the side of the dogs, fence

Teresa, said now look at your dogs, all four dogs, were drinking water, and the dogs did not look who was at the fence.

Ed said, where did you get the idea, to do that, as

Teresa and Ed walked back into the house, pulling off there wet rain coats, and dropping them on the floor

, Ed, said Teresa, I am going to ask you one more time, where did you get that idea to do that, Teresa, said, you made me put hot sauce on my finger nails so I would not bite my nails.

Teresa, smiled I guess it works on dogs too.

Ed said to Okle I really wish I would have just shown Larry the auto feeder for those dogs, but he still needs to see them and try and get used to being around them. Those dogs are important to me. Okle said nothing back to Ed.

Teresa said Dad, I will feed your dogs, Teresa said hey Okle, and do we have any left over so called Veal?

Okle said Teresa it is time for you too take your bath and get ready for bed, Teresa did as she was told, and Teresa was feeling pretty good about herself.

Okle finished cleaning up the kitchen, and about two hours later.

Dean and Larry came back, Dean, walked in the house first, holding the door open for Larry, Dean, said Ed, Larry needed eleven stitches on his right leg, seven stiches on the other leg, and his hands are tour up, I can believe you had Larry go out and feed those dogs, Larry, just looked at Ed,, Ed poured him self another drink,

Larry said to Ed I do not like working for you, I stay here and work because of the respect I have for Dean, so I have been now honest with you, Ed, said you need to recall who hired you boy, and you will do what I tell you if you want a job. Larry, walked passed everyone and went to bed.

Dean, said to Ed you act like you could care less what happen to Larry, How could you? He works hard; he is a good person,

Ed, took a drink of his vodka, and started stuttering, and making fun of Larry, Larry heard him, but did not say a word.

Dean said I have had enough of this, I am going to bed. Dean, asked Okle where is Teresa, she should be done taking her bath, and in bed by now. Dean, open Teresa bedroom door, and Teresa was talking on the phone to Judy, Dean, said Teresa, it's time for bed, tell Judy you will talk to her some time, Teresa, did so, and went to sleep.

Dean, got ready for bed, took a valium and went to sleep. Dean, drifted off to sleep, thinking God intervene, I have tried all I know

. Dean said Ed is changing the money and his pride, Dean fell asleep, and dreamed of a man once who once loved her so much, Dean dreaming of that small town with the Southern breeze, and Mama hanging out the laundry.

Morning came to fast, Dean woke up, thinking to her self, boy that was some dream, and walked in the kitchen for some coffee, and Okle said, well good morning Dean, here some coffee, Okle leaned down, did you sleep ok?

Dean, looked as she lit a cigarette yes, I just slept so hard, and so deep.

This coffee will get me going thank you, Dean, sipped her coffee, Thank You Okle for the coffee,

Ed, went to the store, he told me to tell if you wake up, Dean, said how long has he been gone? Okle said maybe ten minutes or so.

Okle was almost done cleaning. Dean said with it being Friday and all, something about you all going to the farm.

The phone rang it was a man with a deep southern accent, Yes, is Mr. Whitehurst there? Okle said no sir he is not, May I take message, and when Mr. Whitehurst get back I will give him the message. Tell him Max Bishop called.

Tell him to call me; Mr. Whitehurst has my phone number.

Okle Yes Sir. And hung up the telephone.

Dean, asked who was that, some man name Max Bishop, Dean, Lit a cigarette and said Julius is suppose to be coming home today, Okle, said I heard as she was cleaning.

Well, Dean, said I thought about joining a bowling league or team , what ever they call it, I could make some friends, and spend time for myself, I need that, I miss having friends, Dean, said I have already checked into , Bowling Tigers has leagues I can join, they have a few openings, but they would be every Monday nights,

I would start around 6:00 pm and more than likely be back home the latest by 9:30 pm, Okle , said with a smile, that would do you good, to get out, and have some fun, Have you ever bowled before,

Dean, turned red, and kind of put her head down, no, but lifting her head back up, I want too at least try it. Okle said I think you would have a grand time.

Dean said you know Ed travels and go here and there, and takes Teresa a lot places, and I realize Teresa is getting older, and I think it would be ok with Ed if I did that, when Ed gets back that's what I plan to discuss with him today.

Okle, and Dean, heard the front door open and shut and Ed was smiling and whistling a tune, Good Morning to you beautiful Ladies, and kissed Dean on the cheek, Dean, realized this was her time to talk about bowling,

Honey, Dean said to Ed, would you mind if I joined a bowling team. Ed, turned around and said why would you want to do that, you have the farm and, Dean, said I miss having friends Ed. I am a Woman

And women like to have Woman friends. Well, Ed said how many time would it take you away from home, Dean, said only on Monday nights, and I have checked into , and the bowling alley called Bowling Tigers, has openings for a few more bowlers,

Ed, laughed Dean you have never bowled a day in your life,

Dean said well how it can hurt to try and learn and maybe make some friends. Ed said fine.

Ed, said maybe it is a good idea, if you get some friends, you will see other wife's not getting upset so much when there husband's go out of town.

Dean, said nothing, but thought, you mean get woman pregnant.

Okle said, Ed, a Max Bishop called. And he said you have his number to please call him when you get in.

Ed, poured him self a glass of ice tea, and said I will be making a call in the back living room, oh Dean, Ed said how is Larry, Dean, looked at Ed with disgust in her eyes,

Larry is still sleeping he will need the next week off for sure, Ed, said Dean I did not mean for him to get bitten.

Ed, shut the back door to the back living room behind him to make his call, Well Okle said, is Larry pretty bad I did not want to check on him, I was afraid I would wake him up,

Dean, said he is hurting with those stitches, but he really has no respect for Ed, and I understand, my heart hurts for Larry, he has no family, no friends.

And Ed takes advantage of that, I heard Ed making fun of Larry when Larry stuttered his words as he came running in from the back yard.

I tell you Okle, I have a friend in you, so please know that, I just want to get out that's all. Okle hugged Dean, you go make you some friends, and I bet you will be a great bowler. Dean said who you said called Ed, some man with a deep southern accent he said his name is Max Bishop.

Dean, seen Teresa coming down the hall way, Okle said , Teresa, wash your hands before you come eat your breakfast, Teresa, rubbing her eye's and trying to wake up, washed her hands, and came in the kitchen, Good morning, Mom, and Okle.

Good Morning, Okle said here are your eggs and bacon, and orange juice,

Teresa ate and her breakfast, hearing her mother talks about the bowling team. Teresa finished her meal and went and got dressed. And went out side to be with her fiends.

. Okle asked Dean, you think Ed will send Teresa to a boarding school, I guess he will, but then there so close , I have no idea , sometimes I think yes, that Ed is just waiting for Teresa to make a mistake, and then other times, he let's Teresa get by with anything.

The front door open and shut, Dean and Okle seen Julius walking in with suite cases and looking scared to death

Dean, got and rushed over and hugged him, Julius looked surprised, Mom, I know school called you, I know honey , but Julius you were suppose to call us to come and get you, that's ok I paid the cab. J

Julius said Mom, Okle, came up and hugged Julius, and said I am so glad to see you, and kissed him on the cheek, Julius said, Thank You Okle I missed you and I am glad to be home, but Mom we have too talk, sit down Julius,

Julius said let me put my suite cases in my bed room, and I will be right back out, Okle and Dean, looked at each,

Dean, said in a whisper, I hope Ed stays on the phone a little longer,

Okle said I hope so too. Julius came in, Okle handed Julius an ice cold glass of sweet tea, Julius said,

Okle you did not forget, Julius said, looking surprised you even put the lemon in there, Thanks Okle. Julius sat down, Dean, lit a cigarette,

Now Julius please tell what happen, Mom, me and about 5 other boys were out side, and one of my friends busted into the soda machine at the boarding school and stole all the money, Dean, eyes got wide open, But mom I do not do drugs.

Julius, that school has a rule that we as parents must keep a minim of 300.00 dollars just for you do to stuff on the weekends,

You had money, and that is the school policy to have that much money, so I know Dean, said that you all had money, why would your friends do that?

Julius said, we were all messing around, and it just got out of hand, and we were pulled in one by one, and I would not tell who did it Mom, and I do still not want to say it. Well, Dean, said, you know you will be mailed your diploma, and you can not walk across the stage.

Julius said Mother I never wanted to disappoint you or Dad, I feel really bad and I have no idea how Dad is going to handle this.

Well, here came Ed walking in and seen Julius and, Ed asked Dean and Okle to leave the kitchen he wanted to talk to his son,

Dean, said Okle I am going out side, I need some fresh air and check on Teresa, that girl is always some where doing something,

Okle said I will be cleaning Teresa's room, and getting I noticed the plants need to be water.

Dean sat out side on the porch, she noticed Teresa riding bikes with the colored twins, so what have fun kid, Dean thought.

Dean, was trying everything to keep her mind off Ed and Julius, , Dean, thought of the farm and the beautiful two story house, any woman would want, then Dean realized ,

Papa right, Satan will bring you down if he can. And Ed needs to be careful how he treats people, Dean holding her hands together , God, she thought save me , I love my husband, by my heart will not let go , Make Ed a loving person like he used to be.

Teresa is growing up so fast, and Ed treats her like a little queen, why couldn't all the kids be treated equal, the bible tells you not to have favorites. Dean, looked down at her watch,

Dean, got up and went in the house, and Ed passed Dean and said I need to go to the bank I will be back after that, Julius is fine, he is in his bed room,

Ed, said , Dean, said I am going to talk to Julius, and then I will be leaving myself I am going to the bowling alley to see if I can join a league.

Ed kissed Dean Good by. Dean went and told Okle keep an eye on Teresa, a big eye. Dean, went into Julius's bedroom and Julius looked lost, Dean, said Julius how did it go with your Dad? Julius said ,

Dad told me some time in the future he will be working me around the other drivers, and maybe I could earn money , like the drives the delivery for you . Dean, put her hand on Julius should, it's going to be ok. Julius looked at his mother, no way.

And Dean left,

Okle over heard Julius talking in his room on the phone, his Dad deserved him getting kicked out of school,

My Dad told me all the money he spent on me, I am glad my Dad did not get to see me get my diploma on stage, my Dad is ashamed of my fingers, he will not admit, but I see it in his eyes, and I can see him staring at my fingers, and my little sister used to write me letters, on how My dad would get drunk and make fun of people, that are not perfect.

My parents sent me away, they said for my education, bull shit; it was because of my fingers, they think I am stupid. I am glad I got kicked out, it was worth too me.

, Okle walked away with a tear in her eye. Okle never said a word. Okle knew how it felt when people stared and looked so hard, at not a perfect looking person. And how bad it felt.

The phone rang, it was Aunt Polly and Okle answered the phone, No Pauline, your sister is not here but I will tell her too call you, is it an emergency, Oh, no Pauline said, but I do need to talk too Dean.

Okle said when she gets back I will give her the message. Okle hung the phone, and checked on Teresa, Okle noticed Teresa was getting big, not the little bitty girl when she first came. And Okle knew Ed thought Teresa could say no wrong or do no wrong. Okle shook her head, as she went back to cleaning.

Dean, made it back before Ed, which Dean, thought was odd, he just was going to the bank, Dean, knocked on Julius door, are you Ok? Yes, mom. Just down. I just want to lay here, will you shut the door, yes son. Okle, said your back so soon, wow what a quick trip. What happen, Okle said.

Dean, eye's had happiness in them, I am on a league ,and I will be on this league for months, every Monday , and I met this wonderful lady name Fay smith, she is so funny, out spoken but ever so funny.

She married too. I think I am really going to like her, she helped fill out forms, and she will be on my team,

God is wonderful. As Dean kissed Okle.

Dean, walked down stairs with some medication and a ice glass of water, she gently woke Larry up,

Larry oh my legs and hand hurt mom, I mean Dean,

Dean, said I also have some muffins I want you to eat Larry before you take this medicine,

Larry took a couple of bites, but he said his hand really hurts, Dean said Larry I want you too take this two pills and drink this water with, and I want you to stay in bed all day. If Ed says anything to you, please let me know, I will be staying home today, Julius came home.

Larry, smiled he is nice how is he? Dean, smiled Julius is going to be fine.

Larry, I know you have no family Dean said,

But I hope you know in your heart, you are family here, Larry, said I don't think Ed knows what family is.

Dean, said your still family and do not forget that. Larry, said them pills you gave me are making me sleepy,

Dean, covered Larry back up, and said that's what they are suppose to do, Larry you know there is a intercom system in this house , I showed you before, so if you need me, or Okle you push that button. Larry drifted to sleep.

Dean, looked at Larry, and realized her son was hurting as bad has Larry.

Dean walked back up to go to her room and Okle stopped her, your sister called while you were gone, I meant to tell you as soon as you walked in, but you were busy.

Okle, if you don't mind would you please check on Larry during the day, Okle said I will do that, Dean, said I will be checking on him to. Okle, said then I think we make a pretty darn good team.

Dean, smiled, as she made the call back to her sister in Mississippi, the rang for ever it seemed like, Dade answered the phone, Hey there Dade, how are you , fine, Dean, said is Pauline around ,

 Hold on I will get her, Dean, lit a cigarette , first time Dade seemed cold. Dean, thought, Pauline, said, Hey there Dean, sorry I was out side when you called, Dean, said is something wrong?

Pauline said, well Dean, yes and no.

Dean, sat down and said please just tell me , Hank jr. has asked Jennifer to get married, Dean voice crackled , Well, that is silly and you know that Pauline , my daughter as not even graduated.

Pauline said, Jennifer is pregnant, and she is going to get married, Jennifer has asked her Uncle Dade to walk her down the isle.

 Dean's heart is beating, oh my Lord, Dean, said Ed, will not allow either one of these actions to take place Pauline,

Pauline said maybe up there where he could have had control over his daughter and raised her,

But down here, things are like they are. Pauline said, how in the world can Ed, stop this girl from having her baby, my lord,

Dean thought of the abortions Ed had paid for, the women he got pregnant. Dean, put her head down, with a tear rolling down, Pauline said, I just letting you know Jennifer and Hank will be getting married , and soon.

Dean, said is Jennifer there I want to talk to her, she is hold on Dean I will get Jennifer on the phone for you, Jennifer, got on the phone, and said Mother I did not plan this, I am sorry that I have hurt you and let you down, Dean, said wait a minute, you were to go down there for an Education, not learn how to have a family at a young at age, Jennifer, argued back,

Look mom, I am going to have a baby, I will get married first. I do not care if Dad comes or not, he will not walk me down the church isle to get married I have already asked Uncle Dade, Dean, said, with tears in her voice, listen to what you are saying, you will have no education, you will be stuck in a small town, have you thought of the long run with Hank Jr. Jennifer, said, Mother, I would like you at my wedding. Dean, sighed the room felt like it was going in circles.

Jennifer, said yes, all I am going to say Mother is I love you, I am going to say it again, I never meant too hurt you,

Mother my heart I followed and I had about as much control over that as you had letting Dad sending your kids away from you.

And letting Dad treat you like you are the other woman, instead of his wife. At least Hank treats me like a queen.

Mom, I am not trying to be mean, but there is more too life than new fancy cars every year, and trips to here and there, Jennifer said, Mom, I want you to tell Dad, he did me a favor and he had to open his wallet to send me down here , ask him if he is happy now?

Dean realized Jennifer had made up her mind. Jennifer, Well I guess it is best to say congratulations. Jennifer could hear her Mother did not mean it.

Well, Mother I am going to get off the phone and call you later, think about what I said, about is here for the wedding.

Mom, you know you could always get away from Dad and come back to your home town.

Dean said I love you and I am going to hang up, I will call you back later on this week sometime.

Jennifer said Mom I love you too, please tell everyone I said hello, and give Okle a kiss for me.

Dean, hung the phone and just put her head down, and Okle came up too her, you know Dean, once children grow up; they have to make there own choices, like the rest of us.

Okle handed Dean a tissue, as Dean cried.

Okle, heard most of the conversation, Dean, looked at Okle, I believe Jennifer may have done this to get even with her Daddy,

Jennifer is going to have a baby and now getting married Hank jr.

Dean. Looked at Okle, well you have heard it all in this house, but you know what, I was going to Marry Hank Senior, at one time. Okle, eye's got big. Oh my.

Dean, said I do not know what to do,

Ed, came walking in the house he seen the look on Dean's face, Ed, said now what Dean, did you not get on the bowling league., Dean, looked at Ed, no, its not that simple. Please sit down, Ed sat down,

Dean, told Ed almost everything, Hank Senior did not come up.

Ed said you know I tried too giving Jennifer the best Education she would need, we both know Dean, with out

Education, and life is a dead end street. Dean, said Ed, we have made mistakes sending these children away, Bull shit Ed said, our children made there own mistakes, Ed, said and I refuse to pay for some small poor town wedding, That girl is on her own. Jennifer can have ten kids, but Jennifer has burnt her bridge with me.

Teresa, came running in almost knocking okle down, Hey Dad, you are home, don't forget we get to look at cars pretty soon,

Dean, thought how quick bikes to cars.

The baby was now all grown up enough to drive. They grew up so fast; Teresa said I get my permit soon Dean, thought with all that's been going on, Teresa is getting ready to drive. Dean, thought wow my kids are all grown up. Dean heard Teresa saying

Daddy, I know Ed said, look baby girl you pick out the car you want and we will look at it, Oh, Daddy, I already found one,

Ed, said really, and what did you pick out for your first car? I picked out a White corvette. It has t tops, and a spoiler rack, so cool Dad.

Dean, raised her eyebrows, I think that is a little much for a first car. Ed, said Dean I done told Teresa she could have a car with in reason, and I find that a corvette is in reason,

Teresa, smiled as she gave her Dad a hug, you will have your corvette they day you get your car, Ed, said there is no reason to rub this in your sister face. Teresa said ok , Dad Thanks Teresa said to her dad, you never let any one down;

Okle, thought as long as it is material things you are right Teresa, Ed Whitehurst thinks love is material things. , Back to cleaning the house okle went. Teresa said

I am going back out side. Ed said ok baby girl. Ed, said, speaking of letting people down Where is Julius?

Dean said he is sleeping him sick, that boy gets kicked out of boarding school and all he can do is sleep.

Dean said Teresa is not your baby girl any more she will be driving soon. Ed, said well

Tomorrow Julius will get up and work with the rest of the drivers and work just has hard as they do, if he wants to live here. His pay will be a little under the rest of the drivers Dean,

Dean, look at Ed and said, to Ed, don't you think it should be equal pay for our son,

Ed, said when Julius can do the same amount of work like the other drivers on the routes, then that will be the day Julius gets paid the same, Ed said Julius is lucky I am paying him at all, he should be paying me, for all that money I invested in his Education, and Julius just wasted it.

Ed said with a look on his face that said trouble to okle, Now Dean I will be going out of town this weekend, Dean, maybe you can take Teresa down to the farm and let her ride her horses.

Dean, thought with everything going on, that's all Ed can think about is Teresa riding her horses.

Dean, said yes Ed. I will try and do that,

Ed, said baby I promised her that Teresa and I would do some horse back riding together and maybe some fishing, but something as come up , there is a territory I need to go down to New Orleans, and I really do not know how long I am going to be gone,

Dean, I am not going to be the one to tell Teresa , that I could not keep my promise to her, so you Dean, will need to tell her after I am gone, that something came up and I had to go own a business trip,

Dean said why you can't tell Teresa, Ed said to Dean, it will break her heart, just do what I ask you to do,

Dean, said I think you should be honest and tell Teresa your self,

Ed got angry and said. Look I give you the best life style , you see you are driving a new car every year, you have a live in house keeper, and diamonds, and a second home

, Ed said I have given you a lot, Nothing you would have got as a nurse, or living in Mississippi. Okle turned around and walked out.

Dean said with tears money has changed you Ed, you have no feelings for anyone but your self, and you only think of Teresa, Dean said in the Bible Ed, it tell you not to have favorites and you should know that,

Dean said Your daughter Jennifer wants nothing to do with you, and your son, look at him Julius is depressed,

Ed, said if Julius is depressed , then do not steal, tell Julius that, and if Jennifer wants nothing to do with me , wait and see, how she likes being poor. Ed said small ass town. Ed, said when it comes to needing something Jennifer will need me before I need her, Dean , with hurt in her voice , how can you say that Ed about you own flesh and Blood.?

Ed said to Dean, You out of all people should know realize love can not pay the bills. . Ed, said as got up in Dean's face Ed voice even louder you do recall being poor.

Dean, Ed is just waiting for Dean to answer him.

Dean said it that why you think I married you, Ed, said of course not Dean, I am just saying life is easier with money, and you did not have a penny in your pocket when I met you. Ed said this conversation is over.

Dean, said well then who is Max Bishop, Ed said he is a business partner down in New Orleans, I had planned to go down there and leave tomorrow night, but It's best if I leave tonight and get down there.

Ed said tell Larry I need my car loaded up. Dean said no.

Ed, I will not, Larry was bitten by your mean dogs, and he needs rest I told you that.

Teresa, came walking in, it's starting to rain out side. Okle do you know what we having for dinner, Okle said yes Chicken,

Teresa, started yelling at Okle, and said I hate chicken why you would cook chicken when you know I hate the smell of it.

Dean, looked at Teresa, my gosh Teresa, you can eat something else, Teresa said ok and turned around and walked out. Teresa, thinking to her self my family is stupid, they do not know by now I do not like chicken, and do not want too even smell it cooking.

Ed, came back in, what in the world is Teresa upset about, Okle said Teresa is moody that time of the month,

Ed said I did not know she was going though perorids already.

Dean, said yes Ed Teresa is not a little baby girl, she is a woman by Gods plans.

Ed, said well poor girl that's what's wrong with her.

Dean, shook her Ed, said Teresa, come here, Teresa came in and said what? How do you feel, I feel fine, why,

Well I was just asking that's all. Teresa was embarrassed and mad now everyone new Teresa had started her monthly period

Teresa, said with a loud voice looking at everyone and said is everyone in this room feeling ok?

No one in the room said any thing. After Teresa walked out Ed said Teresa acts nuts sometimes, I mean really like a funny crazy.

Ed thought that was funny, Dean, said it not funny. Teresa walked out. Okle finished cooking dinner.

Ed, called Teresa back, hey baby girl, you know you are growing up, yes dad, and you want that white corvette right?

Teresa, stopped , and said of course, Ed, said baby girl, sit down, Teresa sat, down , and looked at her dad, What Dad, are you sad?

Yes, Teresa, said don't be sad, I love you Dad. Ed, said Teresa, I have bad news, what is that Dad, I am so sorry baby girl, but we can not go horse back riding this weekend, Teresa, mouth dropped open, and said why? Baby girl, if you want Daddy to buy you cars, and horses, then,

Well Teresa, I have to go out of town this weekend, Dad, let me go with you please, Teresa said. Ed, said not this trip, but the next trip to you can go, I promise.

Now, your Mother is going to take you to the farm , so you can go ahead and ride your horses, Teresa, looked up , Dad it won't be the same and you know that, mom does not like horses, Mom, just likes gardens.

Well, baby girl I would put the trip off if I could, but this trip I can not. Teresa, I love you and you will have lots of fun. Teresa said. Ok. Dad

. Ed, said you know your mother is nice she taking you down there, tell her thank you. Teresa said ok. Dad. Ed said wait a minute T

Teresa, would you mind taking my suite cases too the car for me, I have too leave tonight, Ok Dad, Ed, said it looks like it has stopped raining.

Teresa took the suite cases out to the car. Hugged her Dad by, oh, Dad, don't forget to bring me something back from your trip,

Ed looked at Teresa, have I ever forgot, No Dad you have not.

Dean and Okle could not believe the extreme kindness Ed had for only one of his children. Okle said Dean changing the subject are you still going to join that bowling league?

Dean, look at Okle and Dean said, I wish I could but with all the insanity in my life and kids life's, There is now way.

Teresa went and took a bath and got ready for bed. Dean, kissed and hugged Ed good by , and to please call her , when he gets there, Ed said Dean, have you forgotten I have put phone in my car, Dean, eyes wide open, it's the 70's how do they put phones in cars.

Ed, said I paid them, that's how. Here is the number baby, call me any time.

Dean, said I want too see what a phone inside a car looks like before you leave,

Ed smiled, and said ok come on outside, Dean noticed Ed as they walked to the car, that

Ed walked like he invented the phone it self.

Dean, got inside the car, picked up the phone and called the house phone, Okle answered. Dean said it's just me. Ed, put a phone in his car, and I wanted to see it and if I could hear off this car phone like a house phone Okle.

And I will be back in the house in few minutes. Okle said ok and hung up the phone.

Ed, said do you like it? Dean, said yes, but why would you need a phone in the car? Dean, I travel a lot and you know it,

Dean, I was also thinking of you when I got this installed.

Dean said how much something likes that cost. Ed, said do not worry about, I pay the bills. Ed said I am not being mean when I say that, but you worry about money, and we have plenty.

Ed said as he looked ad Dean, sometimes I do not understand you , Ed said you have seen the bank accounts ,

Ed, leaned over and kissed Dean, this way I will not miss you so much if I can hear your voice.

Dean's heart did not beat as fast, as it used too,

When Ed said those kind of things too her. Dean, opened the car door to get out,

Ed said baby I am going to go ahead and leave now, Dean, said with a hurt voice right now, I thought you said tonight. Ed, seen the hurt in his wife's eyes.

Dean, don't cry, its business,

Ed, started the car, and threw Dean a kiss.

Dean was crying for her children, and everything that was going on.

Dean could hear her mama and papa voice when it rains it pours.

Dean walked back inside the house.

Okle said I took some food to Larry, and gave him so more medicine;

Larry got up and walked up to Dean, Dean, said Hello Larry are you feeling a lit bit better,

Larry said yes, but he said he was going to eat and go back to bed.

Dean went and checked on Julius, he is on the phone,

I believe with a girl, Dean Thought to her self, and going by the conversation what part Dean did hear it sounded like love, young love. Dean, thought just please be careful with your heart son.

Dean though what else can this day hold?

Dean, went into Julius room, and he said Mom, um can you come back I am talking on the phone, Dean, said no Julius I need to talk to you now.

I am sorry but please tell who ever you are talking too, you will call them back.

Julius did what he was told, and Dean. Said Your Dad wants you starting tomorrow to learn the route like the other drivers do, you will get paid.

Julius, your dad is starting you at the bottom so one day you can have the business, Julius said, did Dad said that,

Julius that is what is going to happen,

Dean, said with any company you start at the bottom and learn your way to the top, then looking at her Julius, then Dean said you will know the business from top to bottom. Dean said

Now you are still getting your car for your graduation, Julius said I am, but. Dean said no buts.

Tomorrow I am taking Teresa down to the farm to ride her horses, but I want you to find a car you want, you deserve and your were promised a car. Julius, said mom, that is really nice of you, are you sure Dad is not going to get upset over this.

Dean, said Julius do not worry about your dad, Julius said it that what you wanted to talk to me about, yes, I have already made the call , you will ride with Marvin tomorrow, and learn from him, He is really good, Julius said ok.

Dean, said Julius you will need to be ready by seven am Julius ok,

Dean, said Julius was that any one special on the phone, Julius said well mother, I met this girl at boarding school,

Dean, said really how did you meet this girl, Julius said her name is sandy, and it was a Saturday night, and me and some the other boys all went to the movies, and walking back, she smiled and me I smiled back and any way I have been seeing sandy for about seven months, sandy is a real nice girl mother, you will like her.

Dean, said do you feel like you have to get married right away, Julius said , Mother no, of course not , Julius looked at his Mother, and said Sandy is not pregnant . Julius said; feel like I have fallen in love with her Mother.

Julius said I know I have strong feelings for her but I really would live with her before I married her, Dean, said oh my Lord, Julius, have you ever heard the expression, why buy the cow , when the milk is free?

Julius, said laughing Mom you are too funny, Dean, said , let me put it to you like this, If I put a open soda, on the table, and then a unopened soda right next too each other,

Dean, looking at her son, Dean asked Julius which soda you would take.

Julius said the one that has not been opened. Of course.

Dean, said why? Julius said because I do not know who drank out of the other soda mother; Julius said this is a strange conversation we are having,

Dean, looking at her Julius, I can see it in your eyes. I believe you love this girl Sandra, and I believe you at one point will be having her move down here with you.

Julius said, well mom, I do want my own apartment, and since I am working for you, I should be able to afford it, and yes mom, I was talking to Sandy, about moving down here and getting an apartment.

Julius said Sandy was always there for me mom, when I had to live at the school Dean asked her Julius, why would sandy or you Julius play house?

Julius said I would not call it that, I just want to make sure we can be living together , before we get married,

Dean, said to Julius, God did not make you a soul mate, to see if you might change your mind. Dean said you need to think about what you are doing. God see it

Julius looked at his mother with hope she would understand,

Mom, living and working for Dad would just be too much on me, Dad never lets up. Dean said I know your Dad as always been aggressive when it came to business.

Julius, said what do you think? I mean about sandy moving down here, I respect you thoughts Mom. ,

Dean, grabbed Julius's hands and held them, I think you should be wise and make sure you do not get the opened soda.

And if you play with Satan by playing house, how do you expect God to bless you?

Julius said. Mom. I am going to tell you, I love sandy, and she is not used. Julius said just try and understand my point of view,

Mom, I will be ready in the morning to go to work, but I want to go back and call sandy,

And Julius left and went and shut his bedroom door.

Okle went to bed, and Teresa was sleeping,

Dean , sat at the kitchen table thinking how did my life get so out of control, I had plans, of being nurse.

Dean, poured herself a drink, and lit a cigarette,

Dean picked up the phone and called Jane, there was no answer and then Dean realized the time and quickly hung the phone. Almost midnight, where does the time go. Dean, finished her drink, and called Ed on his car phone,

Ed, answered hey baby I am glad you called me, I was just thinking about you, and when we met, Ed, asked Dean, are you still happy as the day we got married?

Dean, feeling the vodka, of course I do. I miss you and love you even more.

Ed said well Dean, you are my partner and best friend, I may not have the best way of showing it at times, but I want you to know Dean that you have my heart. Dean got Goosebumps feeling the love all over again.

Dean, said to Ed, Honey I wanted a call to you, where are you at, I am heading towards Memphis, TN. I will get a motel in a couple of hours, and get into New Orleans tomorrow.

Dean, said well I am tired and going to bed, I love you Ed, I love you too Dean, Ed and Dean said good by to each other.

Dean , pulled back the cover , and laid down on the silk sheets, Dean, rubbed her hands across the silk sheets, and thought , Silk sheets are over rated, I want white cotton regular sheets, and with Ed gone tomorrow I will ask Okle to put them .

Dean, thinking to her self, oh yes, that's right those old cotton sheets are packed away, they can be washed. As Dean, faded off in a deep sleep.

The next morning Larry was up and feeling better, Okle cooked a big breakfast, trying to please everyone in this house was not easy, Okle knew that.

Dean, saw the coffee already made and waiting for her, Dean, poured a cup of coffee, and lit up a cigarette,

Dean said good morning Larry, Larry said Dean, Good morning and thank you for taking care of me over those dog bites.

Dean, put her hand on Larry shoulder, and said Larry that's what family is about, but I am glad to see up and feeling better.

Dean, looked at the time, nine o'clock, Dean, walked too Julius room, and open the door and he was gone. Dean, called okle , and asked okle what time did Julius get up, Oh, he was up and waiting for the drivers early, he seemed excited, he left with Marvin.

Dean said I hope he has a good day.

Dean asked Larry, would you like to go to the farm with me and Teresa today, Larry, said sure. Okle, can you get Teresa up and ready to go for me,

I want to go and get those old white cotton sheets and wash them and put them on the bed, Okle, said I will get Teresa up for you and have her ready to go to the farm

, But Dean, Ed gave me strict orders not to have those old white cotton sheets on your bed. Dean, said well Ed is not here, and I want to sleep on something, that I do not feel like

169

I am going to slide off, Okle smiled, so you do care for silk sheets?

No, Ed thinks he is above cotton sheets, Lord, Okle, Said, I do not know if you know it, but, he said he only wanted silk sheets on Teresa bed. And I best have Teresa sleeping on cotton sheets and Dean, why do I have to powder Teresa's sheets every day.

Dean, said, what do you mean you, Okle said, Ed told me to put fresh baby powder on Teresa's sheets every day when I make her bed.

Dean, said I have no idea, but I plan to ask Ed about that, Okle said, now Dean, I do not want to be causing any problems between you all.

Dean, said Okle you could not possible cause any problems, God sent you to this house, angel in need. Dean walked up too Okle, Did Ed ever ask you to powder Jennifer sheets when Jennifer was here. No Dean he did not.

Dean walked away, God, Ed all I wanted to do is love you, and how did things get so messed up. Dean, walked to those old cotton sheets, held them up, Dean, talking out loud; there is nothing wrong with these sheets, no tears, and no rips, what is Ed's problem.

Then Dean, remember, Donna, the first house keeper was on these sheets, with her husband behind her back.

Dean, looked hard at the white cotton sheets, Dean, said I forgive you Donna, where ever you at, Jesus I know I have to forgive if I want to be forgiven.

Dean, put the sheets in the washer, and went and got Okle,

Okle, said here is Teresa, Larry said Dean I am ready when you are. Teresa said I already ate, I am ready too. Teresa, said I can not wait to go ride my horse,

Southern Rain

Dean, looked at Teresa, which one are you going to ride, Teresa, said Prince, he is the solid white one, Dean, said that horse is mean, Teresa, said Mother, Prince can tell who is not a good person, that's all. Horse have a sense , kind of like a dog has a sense of a person that may fear them.

No Mom prince is not mean,. Teresa, that horse prince has thrown every one off him and tried to bite people, Mother, Teresa you mean every one but me. Prince, is picky, and he is moody that's all.

Dean said nothing as they all got in the car. The ride to the farm went quick, Teresa, said mom. You can ride one of the other horses and we could go riding together, Dean, said Teresa I would love to go riding with you, but I am very scared of horses and you know that,

Mom, you are scared to death of water, and then you and Dad have a huge lake private lake for us, but you will not swim, Teresa, said Mom just try and not be afraid of things.

Dean thought she had a female Ed in the car with her.

Once down at the farm, Teresa rode all day, Dean, said hello to Nadine, who took care of the house down at the farm,

And went and worked in her garden. Larry went fishing.

By sunset Teresa came riding back on Prince, Dean, was done with her garden, Teresa, put Prince away, Clifford asked do you want me to bath your horse,

Teresa said if you want, but I took prince swimming in the creek, so I really do not think he needs it. Teresa , said hey Clifford how long have you been working for my Dad, Well, a long time now,

Do you like my Dad, Clifford looked at Teresa, yes. Your Dad is a good person to work for. Teresa said I was just wandering if you liked my Dad.

Teresa, went to the house and Larry and her Mother were almost done eating, Dean, said there your plate of food Teresa, Teresa sat down and ate, Mom, I am tired when are we going home, Dean, said as soon as you are done with eating. I done mom,

Teresa walked out, and said I will meet you in the car. A few minutes later Larry and Dean came to the car, and they all got in and they headed back home.

Teresa, fell asleep, and Larry said when will I be back on the route,

Dean, said Larry, Julius is on the route for right now, and you can ride with the other drivers, but Larry I could sure use your help, just being at the house, mow the lawn, clean out the gutters, clean the screens on the windows, stuff like that.

Larry said but Ed did not hire me for that.

Dean, said Larry you let me worry about Ed, not you.

Dean, once back home and late, Teresa went in and took a bath and went too bed, Larry was also tired and did the same,

Dean, notice Julius in his room, Dean, knocked on the door, and said it your mother, as she walked in, Julius was on the phone to sandy,

Julius, I need to ask you, how was your first day of work with Marvin? Julius, told sandy to hold on, Ugh, mom, it went fine.

I will like it more, when I get to know the people like Marvin does, and the inventory. But I am talking to sandy; Ok Dean shut the bedroom door.

Dean, said hello to okle, as she sat down and smoked a cigarette,

Okle said Dean I put those sheets on your bed, like you asked. Dean, Thanked Okle,

Are you hungry Dean, oh no Okle but thanks for asking. Dean said I am going to give Ed a quick call before I get ready for bed; it's been a long day.

Dean, called Ed, and Ed was in a really good mood, but he had bad news he would not be back as soon as he wanted. Dean said oh I understand its business.

Ed, said it is horrible humid down here, the swamp waters, I down run over what looked like a armadillos,

Dean said I thought you said you were in New Orleans, I would not think that animals like that would be in a city,

Ed, said you are right Dean, but there are some side roads , I had take because of construction work , and that put me on black top roads , and next to swamps and bayou'

Dean, said well when do you plan to come home?

Baby I would be home now if I could. But to answer your question, I really can not say right now.

Dean, I going to a business deal, call me later, Ed hung up the phone.

Dean, looked at the phone, hearing a dial tone, I can not believe he closed the conversation like that, Dean hung up the phone.

Weeks went by and Dean, seen that Teresa had now had her drivers license, Dean, said how did you get that own your own? You need a birth certificate.

Okle gave me the stuff I needed, because I told her that you were ok with her giving me my birth certificate.

Teresa, Dean said you down right lied Teresa

I never said that, mom, it's a white lie, Dad does it all the time and you do not get half this upset.

Teresa, said Mother, you think you would ask me how I did on my drivers test, Dean, looked with a stern look on her face, Dean sighed and said Teresa how did you do on the test, I did great. Guess what mom,

173

what Dean said, Ronald and Donald aunt works at the drivers place where you get your license, and I did not even have to take the written part, is that not cool or what/?

Dean, said you did not take the written part at all? Nope, well what car did you take, Teresa, said I took your car, you were sleeping,

Dean raised her voice, Teresa you just do not go around taking my car with out asking. Mom, you were sleeping I was back before you ever woke up, what is the big deal.

Dean, said respect Teresa, something you need to have.

Dean, said Teresa I want you to go to you room and think about what you did and why you think it was wrong,

Teresa, said go to my room, I did not do anything wrong,

Teresa, said oh, I see Julius got his car. Great graduation gift mom. Before I go to my room Julius steals and you believe he did not, and Julius does smoke pot.

And mom I will go to my room, but do you even know Dad put a private phone line in my room, so I can talk to my friends, and I have TV.

Dean, with a shocked look on her face and said no. I had no idea your Dad did all that?

Teresa, you go to your room do not use that phone and do not watch TV, Think about taking my car while I was sleeping and why it was wrong, fine as Teresa slammed her bedroom door.

Teresa, heard her Mother and Okle talking,

Teresa, has no right to have her own private telephone line, my gosh, Ed had made her spoiled.

Dean, said and he never can just tell Teresa no. Dean lit up a cigarette. Okle, goes I know Teresa pretty well, and he best watch that girl. Okle, said Dean to me Teresa acts just like her Daddy, she walks like him and thinks like him. Dean said I hope not.

Dean, called Ed, Ed answered Dean asked why does okle have to put powder on Teresa bed sheets, because I told Okle that's what I wanted, Ed said if you want powder sheets, then tell okle. Ed, why in the world would you get Teresa a private phone number, and put a TV in her room,

Ed said, Dean, look here, I am always on the home phone that I use for business and Teresa is always waiting for me to get off the phone, so I solved the problem.

Dean, said you turning her into a brat.

Ed said Dean I will be home I hope soon, but this is a petty conversation,

Ed asked, Dean, do you want your own private phone , Dean, said Ed , you know you did not do any of these things for the other kids,

Ed, said I am hanging up now, love you, but got to go make money. Dean heard the dial tone again in her ear.

Dean, was up set, dean called Jennifer in Mississippi, Pauline answered the phone, Hey there Pauline it' me Dean, how are you?

Dean asked has Jennifer picked out a wedding date, Pauline said soon.

Jennifer, wants to get married in two weeks, are you coming Dean? Pauline I will be there for my daughters wedding is Ed coming. I do not know Ed is out of town now, and the traveling takes a lot out of him.

I will go to the post office in the morning and over night you a cashiers check, and that will pay for Jennifer's wedding, and I will be down there, maybe even sooner.

I just wanted to give you a call, Pauline said I will call you and let you know when I get the check, so you will not have to worry about if it made it down here or not.

That's fine Dean said.

Dean, poured her self a drink and thought of Jennifer's wedding, how beautiful is will be for her, and seeing Hank Senior,

Dean, remember the sound of his voice, and how faithful he is, that feeling of that small town would feel great. Dean, prayed God give me wisdom; show me how to deal with this. Dean, thought I am leaving in the morning,

Dean went to bed, and got up early she asked Julius if he would like to go to Jennifer's wedding,

Julius was shocked he did not know his sister is getting married and going to have a baby, Julius said no mom, it best if I stay here and still learn the business, you dad is going to expect me to have this down, and mom sandy is coming down for a visit.

But tell Jennifer, I said congratulation, Dean, said you can call your sister if you want. Ok Mom. Teresa, up early too,

Dean, said why you are up so early, Teresa said I do not know I just woke up early. Well you sister is getting married ,

I know you knew that , but your Dad did not want Jennifer's wedding discussed, so I am asking you Teresa would you like to go to the wedding,

Mom, I do not want to go,

Dean said well that's what I figured. Dean said Teresa you know sisters should be there for each other, Teresa said Dad might come home and I want to be here when if he does, I want to get my corvette. Dean, packed her suite cases and asked okle to come in her bedroom, dean, said okle I am leaving you with house money,

Dean, handed Okle a lot of cash,

This should keep Julius and Teresa happy, there both wanting things and well at least this money will take care of that. And okle, Thank you so much for being here for me and my children. Dean said this is going to be a long trip I can feel, and I have not even left yet.

Dean, finished packing and went hugged Julius and Teresa good by, asked Okle please tell Larry good by for me. , and told them she loved them, and walked to car and left to Mississippi. Okle, stared out the window, Lord please let her make Dean make it safe. Give her peace of mind.

.

Larry came in later on and asked okle, is Dean. , Okle said she told me to tell you , to tell you good by for her, Dean, had to leave to go down to Jennifer

'S wedding, Larry, said that is sad that Dean has to go by her self. Okle, said to Larry

, and Dean, knows you will take care of the chores. And check the tires and oil on the driver's truck.

Larry went by Dean's and Ed office space and cleaned out the trash cans, and what needed to be done.

Teresa, turned on her radio, and okle noticed Teresa is listening to what sounds like Motown music, odd, okle thought, Julius listens to that hard rock and roll, Jennifer liked country, and rock and roll.

Teresa, is dancing her room and does not care what any one thinks. Okle noticed someone knocking at the front door, Okle wiping her hands off, walks to see who it, and there is Ronald, one of the colored twins, is Teresa here? Okle said yes, but she is in her room, I will go and get her, Okle, knocked on Teresa door, and said your friend is outside waiting for you;

Teresa went outside and sat on the front porch just talking to Ronald, and how things are. Friends talking. Ronald said, I do chores a lot, but I am taking a quick break, just wanted to come down and say Hi, Okle watching the whole time.

Teresa, said come by any time you want. Ronald said I have to go, as foster kid, I really like my foster parents and any way I just need to get back home, Teresa waved by as she came back in the front door.

Okle, said Teresa, I know you have friends of all kinds, and Ronald is a nice kid. Teresa, looked at Okle and said, what are you trying to say, Okle said well you know how people can talk, one rumor turns into another, and next thing rumors are out of control,

Teresa, said I have a couple of black friends, and I do not care what people think. Teresa said to Okle this is not 1922 in Mississippi.

As Teresa went back in her bedroom, and Smokey Robinson was on the radio. Later on

Teresa walked up to Larry and said where the van keys are, Larry said there put up, why? Teresa said Larry I have my license and I want to go drive,

Larry said your mother did not tell me that you were allowed to drive that van. Teresa, looked at Larry, and said look I am doing something good here,

Larry, I am going to take it to the van to get it wash, and clean up. Teresa said I am going to make this van so clean you can see your self in it. Larry smiled.

Oh Larry said in that case here are the keys.

Larry said your Mother would be so proud of you. Teresa, looked back at Larry, Teresa said, yea my mom would.

Larry, seen Teresa walking and putting things in the van, but it was too far to see what Teresa was putting in the van, Larry, thought, things to clean the van with.

Oh Larry said, watching Teresa, walked to where the safe was, Teresa said

Hey Larry said what you are doing,

Nothing Larry, Teresa said Larry I think Okle wanted you, something about my mom. Okle wanted to tell you.

Larry, walked away and left Teresa around the safe Ed and Dean, kept money in to go see Okle, about Dean.

Teresa, knew Larry, was close too her mother.

Teresa, knew the combination to the safe, Teresa watched her Dad too many times not to remember the combination.

Teresa, quickly and with no problems open the locked safe and, Teresa looked inside, wow, not that is a lot of money,

Teresa took a hand full, and put it in her pocket. Teresa thought this should be enough. Teresa, closed the safe, and noticed the company check book on top of the safe,

Teresa, got a pen a practiced her Dad's hand writing, and grabbed a check, and took went towards her room, passing by Larry, Larry said,

Teresa Okle did not want me. And Okle did not want to talk to me about your mother Teresa, Larry said Teresa why did you say that?

Teresa shrugged her shoulders, oh, I guess I misunderstood,

Teresa walked into her bed room and practiced one more time writing her dad's signature, one more time.

Teresa, thought my Dad's has horrible hand writing, he needs to go to a school that teaches out to write you name beyond a third grade level.

Teresa made out the check, Teresa took one last look at the check held it up in the light and said this is perfect.

Teresa drove up to it to one of her Dads' accounts, mba stores.

Teresa walked in, and notices a familiar face and said Hi Mr. Marvin, who was at the counter, well hello Teresa, how are you fine, I am fine, Teresa said

But my Dad's wants you to cash this check,

Oh, we do that for your Dad all the time, Teresa, thought I know that are I would not be here.

Teresa handed Mr. Marvin the check and he gave her the money.

Mr. Marvin said smiling tell your parents I said Hello, you bet I will, as Teresa walked out the store. Teresa drove back home and called Judy.

I am driving down to see you Judy, wow, that would be great, but I don't know about my Step Dad letting me go,

Teresa told Judy, have some clothes packed, we can go horse back riding. My Dad mentioned to your step Dad a while back, and Fred said he would see not problem, Judy you go horse back riding.

Teresa said so your step Dad Fred will let you go.

Teresa went and told Okle, I am going to the farm to ride my horse, Okle, said I do not think that is a good idea, Teresa waited for Okle, and to get the ok. Teresa, said I wonder who you will get a hold of? Okle said Teresa just stop right now

I, need to call your Mother and see if that's all right,

Okle with her stern voice said No I mean this

Teresa , you wait until I talk to your Mother, Okle , called Dean, and Dean , told Okle ,

Call Ed, on his car phone,

I am dealing with a wedding and Jennifer's upset that her dad is not here, and, trying to get everything together down here, and as much as I can, after all Jennifer is my daughter, so please call Ed.

Okle said ok, hung up the telephone, and called Ed, Ed, did answer the phone to Okle's surprise,

Okle, said Ed I hate to bother you, but Teresa, has her driver license and she wants to go to the farm and ride her horses, Ed, are you there?

Ed said Okle, yes I am here I am very busy, and let Teresa go to the farm, she enjoys riding those horses.

Ok Ed, and Okle hung up the phone, Teresa standing there, Well Okle what did my Dad say, Okle said your Dad said go ahead and go down to the farm,

Okle, my dad is not going to say no, on something I want.

Okle said on some things your Dad should.

Teresa, said I am leaving I might stay the night down there, I will call you Okle, so do not worry, Teresa, gave Okle a hug and see yaw.

Teresa drove all the way to the farm listening to music, feeling like an adult. Teresa, finally reached Judy's house,

Teresa got out of the van , and knocked Judy's front door, and Judy answered the door, hey Judy said come on in, her step Dad was there,

Teresa said Hi, Fred the step dad, said with his mean voice I don't want Judy gone all day, that girl has chores, Teresa could smell the booze in the house.

Teresa, said sure, were just going to ride around for awhile, me and Judy just , feel the wind as we ride, it's a lot of fun.

Judy, said Teresa I will be back in few minutes as Judy walked to back room,

Teresa I will be out in just a few minutes, Teresa, said ok. I will wait out here with Fred, until your ready.

Teresa, sat down and said Fred what are you doing to day,

Well, with Judy gone I am going to get some peace, and lay down and sleep,

Teresa, said, you must be really tired to sleep during the day.

Teresa noticed the whiskey bottle on the side of the couch and Fred chain smoking.

But my Dad does take a nap now and then too. It must be really hard to be an adult and worry about bills,

Fred, snapped at Teresa, how would you know?

Your dad spoils you and the second Judy starts acting like you Teresa, is the day I end your friendship.

Judy, needs to respect me more any way, Fred, chain smoking, I am raising that girl. And getting no money for it. Teresa, looked at Fred said yea Fred you are just so right on everything,

Judy feels lucky to have you as a step dad, Fred, did not say any thing, Teresa, thought yea, keep that smirk.

Judy, came walking out, with no smile, and said Judy said Fred are you sure it's ok that I go riding with Teresa,

Fred said in a angry voice girl I done told you once, I said you could, but you will be scrubbing these floors, when you get back,

And another thing, that wood I want you to chop it up in back. And then stack it they way I showed you. Fred is now screaming.

Judy said ok. Can I do half of my chores when I get back and half tomorrow, Fred, with a stone look, said I will surprise you? Judy said nothing.

Teresa, got up and said let's go Judy, and Teresa and Judy left to go riding horses, once at the farm

Teresa, got the horses and saddles them up, Judy, said Teresa you seem like you are in a really big rush to get riding ,

Teresa ,said I am, because after were done ,

I will need to get you home fast, Judy, said, Teresa, did you ever tell any one about what my step Dad has been doing to me ?

Teresa, said as she put her hand on Judy' s shoulder, Fred is evil, this is not your fault , and I know small towns do a whole on anything Teresa said. Teresa, said Judy, I will not tell any one that your step Dad molested you. Teresa said I have told you that trust me. Teresa said Judy, I have known for quite a while now, and no body knows.

Teresa and Judy now riding the horses, they had been riding about twenty minutes; Teresa noticed as Judy was riding, Judy looked as free as a bird.

Teresa, stopped her horse quickly and said to Judy oh, my Gosh, Teresa told

Judy I told my Dad, that I would give that man that lives up the road, some money to fix my Dad's boat motors, I have to do that right now.

Teresa said I forgot his name, but I know where he lives, and he fixes boat motors and law mowers,,

My Dad, told me I had to tell him and too stop there before I go riding,,, Teresa said I forgot, and Teresa, said, I love my Dad, and I messed up and I can not believe I forgot to do the one thing my Dad asked me to do.

Teresa said to Judy I have to leave now Judy,

Judy, looking stunned said ok I will come with you,

No Judy, Teresa said I know you never get time to just breathe, and look around with some type of crap,

Teresa said Judy you enjoy riding, you never get too do it, so enjoy it, Teresa said I promise I will not be long, Teresa said if you get hungry go in the house and fix your self something too eat,

Judy, said, well ok, but how long will you be gone, Teresa, said not long, infact I am going to just tie my horse up, Teresa, said I will be back soon,

Teresa, rode her horse as fast as she could , tied prince up in the shade, and walked and got the keys to the van, and drove off, and first thing Teresa did, she drove fast to the man up the street, .

Teresa said out loud, gosh I wish could remember his name,

Teresa, pulled in the old dirty drive way, this man had so much junk around his house , Teresa looking around at all the junky cars, Teresa thought , Gosh how to you even find your way to your own car that you drive.

This looks more like a junk yard than it does a home.

Teresa pulled up as close she could trying not to run over some metal looking junk, and parts all around this house. Teresa thought I am not getting out of this van, this place is gross. Teresa,

Honked the horn loud three times, the old man came out, with an odd look on his face, Teresa did not give the man a chance to say anything.

Teresa, said can you come down and check my Dad's boat motors? You remember my Dad Mr. Whitehurst right, the man nodded his head yes. Teresa said

, my Dad wanted me ask you if you would fix the boat motors.

Teresa pulled out one hundred dollars,

Teresa said I am not trying to be rude, but what is your name I forgot it, Ernie,

Teresa shoved the one hundred dollars Ernie's in his hands,

Ernie counted the money as Teresa looked at her watch, Ernie said this is way to much money to fix a couple boat motors, Teresa, said my Dad said keep the money.

Ernie shook his head, for this kind of money I will be there soon, Ernie said are you sure your Dad wants me too keep all this money,

Teresa said yes, because he wants it down quickly, Teresa, said but my Dad wants y you down there today in about a hour,

Teresa said my Dad told me too tell you sorry for the short notice. Again,

Ernie, said for this kind of money, I will be down there in a hour,

Teresa said Great, and pulled out, of the Ernie's driveway and Teresa drove fast past the farm to Judy's house,

Teresa pulled along side of the road and not in the drive way,

Teresa walked up and knocked on the door no one answered. Teresa knocked even harder. Still no answer.

Teresa looked in side the window, and seen a whiskeys bottle and Fred passed out, and cigarettes that filled up the ash tray.

Teresa ran too the van, Teresa quickly got out the gasoline out and ran to the house Fred was passed out in and took the gasoline poured it around the house, a lot around the windows and doors,

Teresa went back and started the van, got back out of the van and went and looked in the windows again.

Teresa seen Fred still passed out, Fred had not moved at all.

Teresa, grabbed some matches, lit the one, and threw the lit match right on the ground, and the entire house went up in flames, the heat was so intense , Teresa backed away.

Teresa, jumped back in the Van, the van slowing rolling away from Fred's burning house Teresa looking at her watch,

Teresa, stopped the van for a minute,

Teresa looked back at the house that was burning to the ground,

Teresa thought no way a rat would make out of that house alive.

Teresa, yelled out loud you sorry bastard, you will not live to molest Judy any more. No more sadness. It's gone.

Teresa thought she heard Fred screaming for help.

Teresa thought no way, old man Fred, you will not make out of that house alive.

Teresa thought and Judy will not feel liking killing herself anymore or feel like a piece dog shit any more all because of you Fred.

Teresa, screamed one more time, don't forget the wood, Fred. You might need it to burn something.

Teresa, looked at the rear view mirror, and noticed the angry look on her face, and the smell of gasoline strongly on her hands,

Teresa, told her self, calm down, you did the right thing, that mean Fred forcing Judy, to have sex with him, made Teresa sick.

Teresa thought Fred as been doing this since Judy Mother died at five years old.

Teresa never told any one, the secrets Judy's life to any one. Teresa, said no human being should do this evil crap to any one,

Teresa looked at the time, and back at the burning house, well the house it was now almost to the ground.

Teresa, thought I am not going to feel bad, over a child molesting freak, and this stupid town let's this drunk raise a kid.

Teresa thought I wonder if Fred was inbred. Teresa, thinking, you Fred were Satan, and I can not feel bad, over stopping you from hurting Judy any more. I can not take it.

Teresa drove fast back to the farm and , pulled in the drive way to the farm ,

Teresa rushed out of the van and into the house and , washed the gas smell off her hands   , grabbed some of her Mother's perfume, and went back outside,

Teresa seen Judy horse was tied up too her horse prince.

And. Teresa thought that's odd, Judy loves riding, where could she be? Teresa looked around and did not see Judy any where.

Teresa went back in the house, looked all around, Teresa went into the spare bedroom and there was Judy, sleeping. Teresa, notice the smell of her Mother's perfume was to strong,

Teresa, knew Judy was dead asleep, ran to the bath room grabbed the soap and water and washed most of the perfume off.

Teresa, looked in the mirror, and noticed her hair was a mess, Teresa grabbed the hair brush combed her hair, brushed her teeth, and went back in the spare bedroom where Judy, was sleeping.

Teresa, woke up Judy, with a gentle nudge, Judy woke up with a scared look on her face, oh as Judy looked around, and Judy said there for a second I thought I was back at my step dad's.

Judy, get up let's I am hungry let's get something to eat.

Teresa and Judy went in side, the kitchen

Teresa washed there hands and Teresa fixed her self a sandwich, and Judy did not seem hungry,

Teresa asked Judy did you eat already? Judy said no, I was just tired and came in a laid down, I guess I fell asleep, Judy, said I am sorry,

Teresa, said no big deal, when you tired your tired,

But Judy, split this sandwich with me,

Judy said ok, Judy, said that sandwich really looks good, Judy got washed her hands and took half of the sandwich. Judy looked so sad, Teresa thought.

Judy said I am dreading going back to my step Dad's house, Fred really looked mad knowing I taking off with you.

Teresa, looked at Judy, Fred is evil and, Fred said something about sleeping, oh that's right you were in the other room, I asked your step Dad, what he was going to do while we me and you are horse back riding,

Fred said he might take a nap, Judy, said good, maybe that will put him in a good mood when I get home.

Teresa, took a bite out of her sandwich, and said yea, I hope it does, Judy, finished her sandwich before Teresa.

Teresa and Judy, heard a know at the door, it was Ernie, well I did not see nothing wrong with the boat motors,

Teresa said all I know is my Dad, said to have you fix them, when you run the motors, they make funny noises sometimes, not all the time but sometimes.

Teresa said, and the motors stop running, and then were stuck on in the middle of the lake,

Ernie said, I know Mr. Whitehurst is not happy with that, well I guess I will look at them again, to make sure.

Teresa said I may not be here when you're done with fixing the boat motors, but, keep the money

, My Dad really wanted you too fix the motors and have the hundred dollars. Teresa, said see you later Ernie, by Teresa and Judy as Ernie shut the door.

Teresa, looked at her watch, trying not to show the anxiety , Teresa said Judy I hate to tell you but it that's time for you too go home, Judy, had tears in her eyes, Teresa said where did I put those keys, Judy said oh, there are your keys, on the counter table and pointed over here, Judy got up picked up the keys, and wiped her eyes,

Well, here is your keys , Judy, said I might as well get it over with. So let's go, Teresa said to Judy, I have to get back home, after I take you home,

Judy said, Teresa, before   you shut the door turn off the light, Judy turned off the kitchen light, and Teresa and Judy got in the van, Teresa started the van and looked over at Judy, Teresa said your hands are shaking,

Judy, said I know I wish my hands would not do that, I just wish I did not have to go back to my step Dad's house. Judy looking at Teresa, but if I run away my step dad would find me and things would be so bad. I have tried it before.

Teresa said. Pulling out of the drive way, turn on the radio Judy, see if there some song you like,

Judy, played around with the radio, the closer to Judy's house , the more Judy's hands would shake, and Judy would try to hold back the tears,

Judy ,said Teresa promise me you will never tell anyone , What my step Dad does to me, this is a small town, Fred would kill me.

, Teresa said I have told you I will not tell that your Step Dad Fred is molesting you, I will not tell Judy, Teresa, thought, this will be over soon.

Judy, wiping the tears, if this ever got out in this town, I know these kids around here, and they would say that I could have fought back, and I could have done this or that, with Fred he would kill me first.

Getting closer to Judy's house, Judy said stop the van now Teresa,

Teresa said why?

There is smoke coming from my house, Teresa, acted stunned and said ok,

I will stop the van, Judy, opened the van door, and before Teresa had come to a stop. Judy got of the van, Teresa said I need to, put the van in park, but Judy and kept running towards the burned up house.

Teresa, caught up with Judy, Teresa, grabbed Judy's hand, Judy said, I bet you Teresa Fred got drunk and passed out with them cigarettes, he always did that, I was scared, of this happening and me being dead in a burnt up house, like Fred as not done enough to me. One more thing from Fred,

Judy, said Fred has to be dead, Judy, with sweat rolling over and not crying are shaking, said the house is to the ground, and everything is gone.

Teresa, looked at Judy, Teresa, I am sorry your house is gone, but not Fred.

Judy, said me and you both, Judy, just stood there,

And said Teresa, it's over, all the mean stuff Fred made me do with having sex with him, it's over, Fred can never touch me again. Judy hugged Teresa. Judy said I am free of that evil man.

Teresa, said well now what, do you want too go do, I mean Teresa said do you want me to take your Aunt Jane's

, Judy said yes, My Aunt Jane, she is so nice to me. I do not have to chop wood at all, and there is a bathroom in her house, and well you know Teresa, that out house is nasty, it's the 70's, every body seems to have a bath room in there house.

Teresa drove off as Judy was flipping off the burnt house,

Teresa, well I have to get home after I drop you off, Judy, look at you ,

Judy said what do you want me too look at? Teresa said your hands, there not shaking, and you're not holding back tears.

Teresa, said well this is your Aunt drive way right, yes, pull in. Teresa and Judy pulled the van in the drive way and got out, Judy walked in first and Teresa followed, Judy, told her Aunt about what happen,

Aunt Jane said, that is horrible, and Aunt Jane was crying, Teresa, gently pushed Judy, While Aunt Jane was on the phone, Teresa said, Judy start crying, are there going to know that you do not miss Fred and then there going to ask questions.

Teresa waited for a while. Aunt Jane said yes I will be waiting here with my niece, Judy. To the police. Teresa said to Judy I will call you tonight. ,

Teresa said Jane and Judy I am really sorry this happen, my mom says you never know when a person is going to go, and life is short

But, this is a real eye opener.

Teresa hugged Judy and Jane good by. And left.

Teresa , drove home and by the time she got home, there was her Dad's car in the drive way, Teresa , said out loud shit my Dad was suppose to be out of town for awhile, This was not planned.

Teresa walked in and looked and said Hi to Okle, Okle, looked at Teresa,

Teresa, said what are we having for dinner Okle, Teresa, were are having meatloaf and mashed potatoes and gravy,

Okle said But Teresa, your Dad wants too see you; he has been waiting for you.

Teresa, with her heart beating faster, Okle how long as my Dad been waiting for me, Your Dad got home, and oh going by the time , I say he has been waiting for you about a half hour after you left to go to the farm.

Teresa said ok. Teresa open the back door, and there sat her Dad, Hi Dad, glad your home. Ed, said sit down Teresa I want to talk to you,

Ed said,

First of all you stole money out of my safe, then you stupid ass goes and forges a check on me; you act like stealing is nothing to you Teresa. Ed, and the reason I know that, you stole from your Dad, I trusted you Teresa.

Ed, looked at Teresa and said, I can not believe out all the people in this world you Teresa, would be the very one to steal from you own Dad. Ed, with an angry face.

Teresa, holding back the tears, Ed, said I do want the too see you damn tears, I want too know why you stole from me. And I want the honest truth and I want to hear now.

Teresa said I can not tell you, Dad.

Ed, said what are you saying you can not tell me where you spent my money, which you stole from me?

Teresa, seen her Dad getting more angry by the second,

Ed, said you are a damn thief, and you do not have the spine to tell me the damn truth,

Ed said I will give you one more time to tell me the truth, Teresa, said with tears in her eyes, I can not do that. One day Dad I can tell but not now.

Ed said you stay your stealing stupid self right here,

I will be back, and Ed walked out with angry slamming the door behind him.

Teresa, thought shit I am going to be sent to fucking Guam.

And live off goat meat, as Teresa sighed.

Ed, walked back in with a tape recorder, and set the recorder on the table Ed, played the tape and it's was Teresa and Judy talking on the phone,

Ed played the tape, Teresa did not move. Teresa and her Dad listened to Judy crying over being raped and molested and. Teresa, could not believe her Dad had been recording me.

Ed, reached over and turned off the tape player, and said Teresa You should have come to me, I would have helped the girl my self.

Teresa, got pissed off, and said Dad, you knew this whole time, that Fred was doing this and you sat back and did nothing,

Ed said I have not know that long you idiot,

Teresa said how you Dad you are in New Orleans, or Georgia could, or some where, and I would have never caught up with you, to ask you too help Judy.

Teresa said you are too busy for any thing but making money, Have you noticed that Dad?

Teresa, said and as long as we are getting our cards on the table, all those times you told me,

Mother was on vacation alone. Which by the way was a lot?

Teresa, said Mother was in a fucking nut house, for another nervous breakdown, and not on vacation.

Teresa said loudly Dad, I seen a picture of my half sister,

I went through your wallet one day when you were in the shower, and my half sister is half Mexican, Lolita or something like that, with her age and her phone number, on the back of her picture.

, Teresa looking at her Dad, I called her, my half sister Lolita and she knows my mother is alive and Dad, your daughter Lolita told me that, you Dad had told Lolita, and her Mother that my Mother, your wife Dean, and Julius and Jennifer had died in a plane wreck.

And you want to play the honest and ethics crap with me. Teresa said.

Ed said

Teresa, did you tell your Mother?

Teresa, starring out the picture window, Teresa said no. as she sighed.

Teresa sat down and looked at her Dad and said Dad don't you think Mother has had enough? Teresa said I know for a fact Dad, that

Mother has been in a nut ward, because of illegal abortions, and the diseases you gave her, and all woman y you have been with. Dad.

Ed, was pissed no one calls him on anything, not even Teresa.

Teresa, said how many more are out there, do I have more half sisters or brothers? Teresa said Dad, never mind do not answer my question. Teresa said I will throw up right here if I heard the truth.

Teresa said,

Hey Dad, there is a new family up the street, they have a son and a daughter, are the related too me?

Teresa, was so angry, Teresa said you know

Dad, you would not tell me if they were. I can not believe you told Lolita and her Mother, that my Mother and brother and sister died in a fucking air plane wreck.

Teresa said I guess I was the fucking good kid, because you did not tell Lolita I died, she knew about me.

Teresa said screaming how you can be pissed off at me, with all the shit you have done. Ed had a dead stare at Teresa.

Teresa started biting her lips and fingernails, and crying, because Teresa was so angry.

Okle, said as she opened the door where Ed and Teresa were, and said

Ed, the Madison county Police Department is on the phone,

Ed, said, shook his head; I will take the call back here. Okle shut the door and waited for Ed to pick up the other telephone, Ed, pointed his finger at Teresa, stay put,

Teresa stayed sitting down. Okle heard it all again. And kept quite.

Yes, this is Mr. Whitehurst speaking, Ed, it's Tom with the Madison county police department, I am sure sorry to call you at home, Ed, said what can I do for you Tom? Tom said well

Mr. Whitehurst, we have a couple of questions for your daughter Teresa, said Tom,

Tom said I know you well Ed, Tom said so I will just talk too you first, was your daughter Teresa, with Judy Smith today at your farm?

Ed said Judy smith, Yes, that's the girl that lives with her step dad, Ed, said I believe his name is Fred.

Tom, said let's say Judy used to live with Fred, Ed, said what do you mean used to live with Fred, tom?

Tom said Fred's house was burnt down to the ground with him in it, so Fred is dead, Tom said I went to Fred's burnt down house myself, and there is still a gasoline smell.

Mr. Whitehurst said, so why do you have questions for my daughter Teresa,

Tom, said Mr. Whitehurst, I know you donate a lot of money to this here town, but Fred's house was burnt down to the ground, and, I can not tell you who told me as the town Sheriff, but this person said they thought they seen your van, and Teresa driving it,

Ed, said Tom, I know you are doing your job. Ed started a light laugh, Tom,

Teresa would not do any thing, like you, are trying to insinuate,

Ed said I know my daughter, like you know the back of your hand, and Tom, if my daughter had something to do with Fred's house burning down, believe me I would be calling you, not the other way around. Ed, said how did the last charity go?

Tom said Mr. Whitehurst it went well, your large donation helped our town. Ed said to Tom

But let me get a hold of Teresa, and I will call you back, Tom, said Mr. Whitehurst I know a wealthy man like your self, and a good man, with a good family.

I just have to do my Job, Tom said with a sincere voice, Mr. Whitehurst; you have a wonderful family,

Again the reason I am calling I have to do my job.

Mr. Whitehurst said, oh Tom, Ed kind of laughing, I will call you back, and I have your home number. Good by Tom, as Ed hung the phone.

Ed, looking at Teresa, Ed said now Teresa I have put your little secret puzzle together, Ed said you drove down there , and you got Judy out of the house , or you did this together, Teresa, said looking her Dad eye to eye

Dad, I am telling you the truth, I promised Judy I would never tell anyone, but you recorded me, so you know about Fred.

I had promised Judy I would never tell any one, Teresa said I did not tell you, any thing about what Fred did too Judy, that part I kept my word on.

Teresa said to her Dad,

Dad you and I are close, Ed said. Teresa said I am just going to tell you Dad because I felt Judy had no choice, and no help,

Teresa, said I do not know how much you heard on the your recorder machine but a lot went on , that Judy on told me in person. Teresa looking at her Dad, and said so you do not have the whole story. Teresa said Dad

I am going to tell you something, Fred, was raping Judy almost every night, she had no one to help her,

Dad, Judy tried running away, and Fred made her do things that would make a pig puke.

Ed, looking at Teresa, did you do what I think you did?

Ed said look at me in the eye,

Teresa, lifted her head up and said, and looked her Dad right in the eye , did I burn the house down with a drunk step dad that rapes his step daughter who is Judy every chance he had, is that you question to me Dad,?

Ed said, Yes or no. Teresa looked right in her Dad's eyes, and said yes.

Julius, opened the door where Ed and Teresa were talking, Ed said shut the damn door. Julius shut the door quickly and Julius said to Okle, what is Teresa in trouble for?

Okle said I have no idea.

Julius said well I guess this is not a good time to tell Dad, me and Sandy got married at the justice of the peace.

And I got us an apartment. Okle said the way things are going, Julius you might want to wait on that one, at least for a little while. Okle heard all what Ed and Teresa were saying, Okle thought I can ignore screaming.

Okle said where Larry is; oh he is outside doing something, on the driver's trucks. I think checking the tires and the oil.

Well when you see Larry tell Larry dinner is not far away. Julius went out side and told Larry, and Julius went in his room and smoked a joint, and opens his window, and spayed air freshener,

Julius being high did not realize he used the whole can. Julius trying to image his parents face, he is married and is moving out. Julius thought I hope I still have a job.

Ed, said Teresa, I think you need some help, you had choices, and you did wrong, all the way around.

Ed, said I do not know where the hell to send you, Ed shaking his head, and looking at Teresa,

Teresa, said now standing up,

well I know about the body they found on your farm, I did not record you, with a tape recorder like you did me,

But I know a lot about you Dad, and I know mother does not know about that body being found on the farm. Because Mother was in the nut ward, at the time. Teresa said I know you had a bad business deal go down , and there was a dead person, with your business card on the dead man on top of it , on your Farm Dad, and the Madison County Police know about and it, they police turned there head to that one. Didn't they Dad.

Ed raised his eye brows.

Teresa, you know too much. Are you thinking you do?

Ed said Teresa I am selling your horses all of them, which includes Prince.

Teresa, busted into tears no, do not sell prince, that horse is the only thing that means a lot to me,

Ed raised his voice at Teresa, and said you will not be in this state to see them are ride them anymore. Do you get that girl?

Ed, said Teresa you think you are going to keep your little world you live in, after what you did, Teresa, looked at her Dad, and said you did.

Ed, said as he grabbed the phone book what state would you like to go to school in? Teresa, said just let me live with my Grandma,

Ed said oh, so you want to go live with your Grandma in Mississippi, Ed said I can only image the bull shit you pull down there.

Ed said I can see Teresa now living in a poor southern little town, you deserve it. Ed said why would I give you a choice on where I should send you?

Teresa, said dad just be fair, please, you let Jennifer go live with Aunt Polly and no boarding school,

Just let me try it and if you do not like me grades or anything,

Then Dad you can send me any where you want.

I will not go kicking and fighting to the boarding school, just please give me a chance to go to the same school that Jennifer went. Too.

Ed said now that I think about it you know your Grandma is a good Christian woman, she raised you Mother, and so you can go down there. Maybe your Grandma can fix you, Ed said one mistake, and Teresa stopped her Dad and said Dad I promise I will not mess up. Teresa knew she had a lot of money, her dad was so pissed off over Fred's house burning down he did not bring up what Teresa had done with the cash taken out of the safe.

Ed, said I am calling tom back he is with police department back and then you're Mother, get in there and eat dinner, if you can.

Teresa turned back around Dad, do you remember when I was little and I said I want to be just like you,

Ed said as he chewed on his fancy cigar, Yes, Teresa said no disrespect by, and there was where I went wrong. And shut the door.

Ed, said Teresa, get back in here, Teresa said what, if tom the sheriff ask you anything you paid Ernie like I told you too and you picked up Judy and you two rode horses. Teresa said how do you know about Ernie?

Ed, said you stupid girl, Ernie called me to tell me he could not keep the one hundred dollars when all that needed to be done , was a spark plug to be cleaned and that was only on one boat.

Teresa, walked out, but before Teresa shut the door, Dad I am really sorry I hurt you, no because your sending me away, but because I really hurt you, but because of what I have done. And Teresa shut the door behind her.

Teresa, went in and ate very little, Teresa, said Julius your are eating enough for ten people , Okle said Julius you sure must have worked hard to day, you are really hungry, Teresa, said, looking up hey Julius, there is visine in the bathroom cabinet,

Julius said nothing.

Teresa said to Julius and by the way your eyes look like a road map, Teresa, got up, Okle I am going to my room. Julius said to Okle, what is wrong with Teresa, she never acts like that, Okle said Teresa does too , you just have not been here too hear it or see it. Julius just shook his head.

Teresa, picked up her phone called Judy, and told all what went on.

Judy was shocked in one way, and relieved in another.

Teresa, said look I am sorry about everything, but Judy I have to go.

Judy said I had no idea , you did that, Teresa said Judy if I would have told you, Teresa said I just could not do that, because Judy, you remind me of my Mother, in away, Judy said how do I remind you of your Mother, Teresa said let's just say, I do not think my mother can take any more of my Dad's bull shit, and by the way Judy my Dad knows everything, not because I told him Judy,

Teresa said I kept my word, But Judy my sneaky ass Dad, has been recording my conversations on my private line. Teresa said you do not have to worry about anything. Judy one more thing, my Dad is sending me to live with my Grandma,

I will try and write if I can. Judy, was crying Teresa said don't cry we will always be the best of friends. And Teresa hung up the phone.

Teresa started grabbing clothes and packing clothes on top of clothes, and snow globes and her little statue that looked like prince. Teresa, walked out and went and told Julius and Okle, she would be leaving in the morning, Okle cried, Julius said, I know how you feel. Teresa said I think I have everything packed. Okle said what ever you may have forgotten to pack, you just call me Teresa, Okle said and I will make sure you get it.

Teresa, still very angry walked out and went back where her Dad is , and said, look you and I know what I did was wrong,

But you are not so innocent you're self; I will wait until you get old and send you to a nursing home with your money if you sell my horse prince.

Ed, said, Teresa I am selling your horses. Now get out of here and shut the door, I calling your mother to let her know, of course not the truth, that would break her heart,

Teresa, said you have broke mom's heart so many times , I can even believe she still has any breath of life left in her.

Ed said I am calling your mother and I am going to tell her you forged a check, and you need to be sent off, that is all that will be said. Now get out of here so I can make this call.

Teresa slammed the door behind her. Ed called Tom and said my daughter Teresa was down there and Teresa did me a favor she dropped off some money to old man Ernie, to fix my boat motors.

Ed said infact Ernie called me he felt I was giving him too much money,

Ed said that man does not have a pot to piss in, and he complains about too much money. Tom Said, Well Ernie is an honest man

. Ed said to Tom, to finish what I was saying then Teresa, then went and got Judy and rode horses

Tom said yes, but Ed, we all know Fred Judy's step dad was a town drunk, but he was still a person,

Ed said I feel horrible that man is gone. Down right tragedy, I tell you. Ed said so what do you think about this ordeal Tom?

Tom, said well by the way it looks Fred, got drunk passed out, and was smoking them cigarettes and burned down his own house with him in it.

Ed, said, Sad. That is just horrible.

Tom said I talked to Judy, she said that her and Teresa rode horses and went home and that's when they found, the house burnt up.

I tell you Judy is really crying that girl is taking it hard.

Tom, said Mr. Whitehurst just to let you know, Judy will be staying I guess with her Aunt Jane, Tom said that woman does not drink. Ed, said, that good. Tom, said at least she will have her Aunt Jane, other than that, that girl does not have any one.

Tom and Mr. Whitehurst hung up the phone, and called Dean, in Mississippi, and told Dean, about the forged check Teresa had wrote.

And that Teresa will need to be picked up at the airport tomorrow at seven o'clock. And Teresa will be going to school in Mississippi

Dean, said crying God I just do not think I can take it anymore. Dean said Ed we find a reason to send every child off, God help us.

Dean, trying to change the subject

Dean said Jennifer wedding was beautiful today, I am sorry you were not here. Ed said, you tell Jennifer we will give her a down payment on a house down there.

Dean shocked, Dean, said what did you say

, I said I will give her a down payment on a house Dean, not a big down payment , but we will give Jennifer some type of down payment.

Dean said it's starting to rain; I need to get in there with the rest of the family and friends.

Dean, was crying, Dean knew Ed had been drinking by the tone of his voice, and he would not send Jennifer the time of day, much less any money.

Dean, went back and Joined the reception, and had a couple glasses of wine, Hank Sr. walked up to Dean, and said , as he sat down , Dean who would have ever thought our children would grow one day and be married?

Dean, lit a cigarette and said, as she looked in Hanks eyes, life is funny you know, a person can have all the plans they want, but life's choices can really help a person or hurt them.

Hank gently grabbed Dean's hands and said I could not agree with you more.

Hank said, it's a shame your husband is not here, I know Dean said. As she picked up he wine glass.

Dean, looked at Hank and said where your wife is, Hank said she left me a while back, Dean said why, if you do not mind me asking,

Dean, my wife rose, was a wonderful woman, but Rose told me, she would not compete with a woman over five hundred miles away, and Rose said she had been doing it too long, at Rose said, my heart was with Dean Whitehurst, Rose, packed her bags and left, that is why you do not see her here.

Hank said I told her to come to her son's wedding, Hank said I left word with her sister, but her sister told me, Hank , Rose will not show up , in the middle of you and Dean a love flame that never died, Hank said that last thing Rose said to me is

Hank, go get Dean Whitehurst because you won't allow your heart to love any woman but her.

Rose said I am leaving you for good Hank, But Dean Whitehurst has a lot of money, Dean Whitehurst left this small town for a reason, she wanted more than this little southern town had to offer. Hank said then Rose grabbed her suite case and walked out, Hank said I wanted to go and get Rose, and he looked at Dean,

Hank said but then it dawned on me , really dawned on this time hearing out loud, Rose is right, Dean, I never stopped loving you, I just tried to go own.

Hank changing the subject seeing Dean about to cry,

How about Ed, does he treat you right Hank said. Yes Hank, Dean, did not look Hank in the eyes. Hank knew Dean, could not tell a lie, and if she did she would not look you in the eye.

Dean, said I got a call from Ed, and my other daughter Teresa will be coming down and staying with my Mama, her Grandma, and go to school down here,

Hank, said has he put his hand on the table,

Dean, I do have another son, a little older than your daughter Teresa,

Hank, said with a smile, now that would that is something, if they got married. Dean, smiled and said, yes it would.

Dean, said as she looked around this is about the prettiest gazebo I have ever seen, the lighting and the music, the flowers this wedding turned out so well Dean said.

Hank said, yes it.   , I just wish it would not rain right now.

Hank said I would like to ask you for one dance, since my son is married to your daughter now, I think it would be ok.

Hank, Dean, said one dance, can change a person life.

Hank said Dean, it's just a dance. Dean, remembering the one dances with Ed. A long time ago.

Hanks, I think I will sit right here and watch you all dance and have a good time. Dean said you know I did not like to dance, I do not dance well.

Hank said, as he heard the rain pouring down, well I am sorry, for you not having one dance with me at our kid's wedding Dean said Hank I do want to Thank You for asking me to dance, that was kind of you.

Dean said I hope you understand why I can not just dance with you.

, But, Hank said, too Dean, changing the subject as Hank got up, Southern rain, has the most beautiful smell,

I know Dean said. I am not trying to be rude, please forgive, I am just so tired. Hank got up and started to walk away, Dean, said Hank,

Hank turned quickly around, Dean said would you have coffee with me at the old café' in the morning?

Say around six o'clock am, I have to be at the airport to pick up my daughter Teresa. At seven in the morning.

Hank said, with the big smile, that lit Dean's heart up, I will meet you there, Hank said us being in the same car together ,

Well you know how is down here, it will be in the entertainment section in the news papere the Hank and Dean, had breakfast together. Dean, laughed,

Dean, realized it had been a long time since she had laughed and smiled. And if felt good.

After the reception Dean , and Mama drove back to the house and on the way, Dean asked her Mama, Mama I have something important to ask of you, Mama, smiled what child, Mama, can Teresa live with you?

Mama said why sure, but why would Teresa want to live down here, Dean, lit up a cigarette, Mama Teresa has got to the age she is getting wild, and she will not listen to her Daddy, Mama, Teresa is a Daddy's girl, and if Teresa is not going to listen to Ed, then Ed will send her too a boarding school, Teresa, wants to be down here, with you Mama, Mama, said I would love for Teresa to come live with me.

Dean, I am your Mama, and I know those are you children, but forgive for not understanding why Ed and you just send your children off,

I reckon I am getting old, Dean, said Mama, Thank You for letting Teresa come down here, I will pick her up early in the morning.

Dean knew her Mama would never say no about Teresa living with her, kind Christian woman. Dean thought I want that way with God to like Mama has, Dean, thought I used to be like that.

Dean pulled up in the drive way, and got out of the car and opened her Mama's door, and the both walked in and went to bed. Dean set her alarm to 5:30 am then

Dean, fell fast asleep

Then next day came quick, Dean, rolling over and shutting off the alarm clock, Dean got out of bed, and walked into the kitchen to fix her self a cup of coffee.

And lit up a cigarette, Dean, looked around and seen the most beautiful sunrise, Dean thought I wish I could just stop this moment, it is that beautiful.

Dean, looked at the time, and walked to her old Bed room and got dressed , fix her hair and make up, Dean, grabbed her purse and pulled out her car keys, and quietly shut the door and got in her car and pulled out of the dirt drive way and went to met Hank for coffee.

Dean, pulled up to the old town café's and Hank was already in there waiting for her, Dean, walked in and Mable came over with a very loud voice, Now just look at you two, Hank and Dean having breakfast, Hank , gave Mable a look

, and Mable said oh, I am just a kidding around, Dean, and Hank , what would you all like to have ?

Dean, said just coffee for me, Hank said I want the house special, eggs, ham, hash browns, and grits, Hank said hey Mable extra butter on those grits. Mable smiled, sure thing Hank, Mable walked away.

Dean, lit up a cigarette, Hank said so you thing your daughter will like it down here Dean? Mable brought over two coffees and Hanks breakfast; Hank gave grace to the Lord before he ate,

Dean, said that is nice that you give thanks to the Lord, Hank said Dean I have not changed, Mable said Hank, you did not order coffee, but I knew you wanted some, Mable walked away with a grin on her face, Mable, told the cook, I bet they get back together, the cook said how much you want to bet Mable,

Mable said two stalks of corn, for your butter beans, my did not grow this year.

Dean and Hank heard Mable's loud conversation. Hank, said anyway you think your daughter will like it down here? Dean said I hope so. Hank said is Teresa like Jennifer?

Dean said no, they are complete opposites, Jennifer is my sensitive child, and Teresa, well, and Teresa has a hard time showing her love to people.

Hank said, well after Teresa is here for a while, maybe she will like it and want to stay.

Dean, said I hope Teresa will not cause my Mama any problems,

Hank said you know your Mama, she is so kind and loving the, lord is always with her, Hank said what church does Teresa go to right now, Dean, said I am sad to say none.

Hank, looked at Dean, and said none; your daughter does not go to church at all? Dean, grabbed her cigarettes and lit one, and said Hank, No. Hank said Dean,

I did not mean to upset you, Dean, said looking at her watch, it's not that. I enjoyed meeting you for coffee Dean, said, but I have to leave now to meet Teresa at the airport.

Hank said Dean, I sure enjoyed your company,

Dean, smiled and waved well by, and Dean grabbed her car keys, and got in her Cadillac Dean, drove all the way Jackson, Ms, where the only airport Dean knew of in that state, Dean, pulled up into a parking spot, got out and went inside Jackson Airport, and waited on Teresa,

Dean, noticed the plane seemed to be running late, and Dean got up and asked the lady and the customer service desk, about Teresa's flight, coming in from Saint Louis , mo.

The lady, just as friendly as she could be said, well you just have your self a seat, and I will see , as of right now there as been no delays.

The lady walked away, and Dean stared at the terminal Teresa was suppose to come out of, The lady walked back with a smile on her face, and said , that plane landed a few minutes ago, who ever you are waiting for should be coming through in a short time. Dean, thanked the lady, and went back and sat down.

Dean thought Thank God, the plane did not wreck.

And Dean took a deep breath of relief. Dean, thinking about Hank, his smile, his kind heart, and his wife that left him.

Then Dean started thinking, How can Ed be with other women, I do not understand he does not want to leave me, But Ed can not stop getting with other woman, Dean, remembering her Papa's funeral, How Ed put the business in front of her dieing Papa, Dean, was not crying, but Dean, realized Ed, has a heart, but most of the time it could be cold. Dean, heard Mom, Dean got up and walked quickly to Teresa, Dean, said I am so glad you made it safe. I love you Teresa, Teresa, said I love you too mom.

Dean, said let's go get your luggage, the luggage pick is over there, and Dean, led the way, Teresa followed. Dean, said, how everyone back home, Teresa is, said Okle said she misses you and can't wait for you too come home,

Mom, that's what they all said, just in different ways.

Dean, grabbed one of the two suite cases, Teresa grabbed the other one, Dean, said well I am parked up pretty close, Dean said as she looked back at Teresa,

Teresa did not say anything.

Dean and Teresa , put the luggage inside the trunk of the car, and Dean and Teresa, got in the car, Dean, started the car ,

Teresa said my gosh it is retarded hot down here, Dean, said yes it is Teresa, and your Grandmother does not have air conditioner , Teresa, said loudly what, Grandma never got an air conditioner , Teresa, threw her head back on the head rest, Teresa, said look mom you are going to have to go and buy me a window air condition unit, I know they exist, I have seen them. Dean, said as she was driving back to canton, ms.

Teresa, things and people are different down here, Dean, said Teresa slow down and quite being in such a rush to make a point.

Dean lit up a cigarette, Teresa said mom crack your window, the cigarette smoke stinks. Teresa looked out the window, and seen hot and muggy fields with nothing around for miles. Not even a gas station.

Dean, said I thought we would stop by Jennifer's house, and you can meet her husband, Teresa, with an angry face said does Jennifer have air conditioner?

, Gosh Mother Teresa said, I bet the dead people are sweating,

Dean, sighed to her self,

Dean, said Teresa, stop complaining, Dean, said I know its a little adjustment, but you will like it Teresa,

Dean reached over and grabbed Teresa hand, try and give this place a chance. Teresa, said looking at her Mother, or Dad can send me to Guam Mother right mother?

Teresa, do not be over dramatic. Dean, said your dad would not send you out of the country, Dean said

Teresa, your dad does not show his feelings as well as I would like him too,

But he does love his family,

Teresa , thought he loves us, really, Teresa remembering Lolita her half sister, telling her that, Lolita was so sorry to hear about

t Teresa's who had died , mother and sister and brother dieing in a plane wreck. Teresa, said Yep, Dad really loves us, I am getting goose bumps just feeling the warmth of Dad's love. Teresa said I want to get a bumper sticker that said Daddy's girl. ,

Dean, lit up another cigarette, Teresa turned on the radio
And Dean noticed it was colored folks singing, Dean said what kind of music is that Teresa? Teresa said Mother it is called Disco

. People dance to it; Teresa said it kind of what Elvis did for the music, only now there is black people singing. Teresa said I like it a lot.

I like all kinds of music mother, except for country music, Teresa said Mother have ever noticed that country music is depressing,

Teresa said I mean the words are some body is leaving some body all the time, and some body is in a bar, Teresa, said I would have to be on drugs to listen to the crap.

Dean, thought my gosh Teresa acts and talks like Ed. Teresa said how much farther do we have to drive, well Dean said your sister house is at this exit coming up, Dean said to Teresa, try and be kinder with your words, your sister is pregnant and sensitive, Teresa, said Jennifer has always cried over everything,

Mother are telling me that I should walk in with a tissue, I, do not want to deal with Jennifer and her crying.

Dean, said Teresa I have had about enough, stop it acting this way, Dean, said you know forging that check was not a nice thing to do. It is illegal,

Dean said Teresa your Dad is only trying to teach you a lesson, and make you have respected. Teresa said Mother Dad and respect in the same sentence, is one crazy conversation. Dean said well here is your sister's house, Teresa seen an old frame looking house, Teresa, said Mother Jennifer lives here?

Dean, said Teresa you will not be mean, Dean asked Teresa you are so angry, talk too me Teresa tell me what you are so upset about, Teresa, said Mother I am sorry, Teresa, thought, no way.

Jennifer standing at the front door hey Mom, and Teresa, Teresa waved hello, and Dean, gave Jennifer a hug, Dean, said is Hank here? Jennifer said yes mom, you and Teresa come on in, Hank is out in the back working on the car.

Dean, said Jennifer I open a bank account down here, right here in canton, so it's not far away to drive too, Jennifer I put some money in there for you and Hank,

Teresa sat down and looked around, Teresa thought you have got to be kidding me, My stuck up sister as become the house wife, with needle point, wow.

Teresa thought.

Jennifer said Mother you did not have to do that, Teresa and Mom, I forgot to ask you can I get you something to drink, it's kind of warm in here, and Teresa said, my God, the heat in this house could cook a pork steak, how do you stand this heat Jennifer. ?

Jennifer, looked at Teresa, Teresa I had the same attitude you did when I first came down here, all I can tell you as your sister, these people down here are kind and they care, and they have love , real love in there hearts. Jennifer said, that's where you can start, is drop the attitude, Teresa, sighed Mother, can we go to Grandma's so I can unpack.

The back door shut and in walked Hank, Hank smiling reached out his hands and said Hello, you must be Teresa, I am glad I finally get too meet you, Jennifer has said wonderful things about you,

Teresa smiled back and said it's nice to meet you too,

But we are just now leaving me and mom, Teresa said sorry we have to leave so soon, but I need to take a shower, before I sweat to death,

Hank looked at Teresa, oh you must be used to that cool northern air, but I hear it gets hot up north too.

Teresa said yes, but people, most people that is have air conditioning. Jennifer, said Teresa I will be over later and help you get used too it down here,

I have a few tips for you. Teresa waved well by and Teresa said Mother please come on, this heat is making me sick.

Dean, hugged Hank and Jennifer good by, Dean said Jennifer; before I leave I want you to know that I know money is tight,

But there is enough money to get your self so air conditioning for your home, and other stuff.

Dean said I know what it is to be pregnant and I always felt hot, even in the winter time, so I know this has to be misery for you.

Jennifer, wiping off the sweat, Jennifer said, well I am very grateful for what you have done and I love you Mother,

Teresa is out side honking the horn in the car, Dean, said by Hank . Hank said I think you have your hands full with Teresa. Dean, waved good by and Dean got in the car, Dean, started the car and Teresa put her face right by the vents, the cool air blowing in her face, Teresa said Thank God, for air conditioning.

Dean, drove around one corner and then a next corner and there was Grandma's house, Teresa said oh, my gosh I was just getting cooled off,

Mother is it always this hot down here?

Dean turned off the car. Teresa said, I will get the suite cases Mother I can get both of them, I will be inside in a minute,

Teresa got her suite cases, Teresa looked around and no one was around, Teresa opened one of the suite cases, and yes, there is the money I got from the safe, Teresa

, shut the suite cases, and went inside the house. Dean was on the phone , when Teresa walked in, Teresa, said as her Mother was on the phone with Ed, Mother I am going to unpack and put my clothes up,

Teresa , open the first suite case, all the cash was , Teresa sighed, and thought you have not one this one Dad. Teresa put the suite case under the bed.

Dean, came walking in and said ,

Teresa this used to be my old bedroom , Teresa said I see , Mother we have to get a air conditioner for my bedroom if every body else wants to sweat until the eye balls fall out, that's there choice, I can not live like this, This is crazy, hot, there is not wind, Dean, said the attic fan is on, Teresa, said as she pulled clothes out of her suite case, Mother this much sweat is going to break my face, and make my hair oily looking

, Dean, sat down on the bed, with a stern voice, I just got the phone with your Dad, and Teresa you can not be down here messing up ,

Teresa, said oh I get it, only Dad , can screw up and get by with that. Dean, got up and said Teresa I am not going to argue with you, I will get you a air conditioner , but after talking to you Dad a few minutes ago, your Dad is still pretty angry with you, Teresa, looked at her Mother and said you tell Dad, I am angry with him.

Grandma, walked in and with her warm smile, and kind eyes, and gray hair, walked up and gave Teresa a long hug, Teresa, thought, what is going on here, Grandma said, now I had a chance to talk to Okle and she said something about she powder your bed sheets, Teresa, interrupted her Grandma, all of sudden, Teresa, said Grandma , I can put powder on my sheets, Grandma said,

Well child I was going to tell you, my back is not as good as it used to be, and I would have trouble making your bed and all,

Teresa, stopped and looked at her Grandma, and said I will clean my own room, Dean, had a smile on her face, Dean, thought what a relief. Teresa is not demanding something to be done.

Grandma, said now I have supper in there for you all, please come on and eat, Teresa said I will be right in Grandma, I am going to wash my hands, Grandma and Dean, walked out Teresa went in and ran cold water over her face and hands, at least for thirty seconds, it felt good.

Teresa, dried her hands off and went into the kitchen, and sat down to an older table, Teresa, said Granma what are we having?

Grandma said nothing until we say Grace until the Lord for this meal. Teresa, said ok, and listens to Grandma, tell the lord thanks for this meal and too bless us with kindness and wisdom to each other.

Teresa, grabbed the ice tea, which was so good, then Teresa looked at table full of food, Grandma Excuse me but what is this food? Grandma, smiled and put a big helping on Teresa's plate, them there are butter beans, the other are green beans with smoked bacon, and others lima beans, and fresh corn bread with butter, and cabbage.

Teresa, thought oh my gosh I wish I had McDonalds right now, I have never seen so much green food on a plate.

Teresa, ate a little bit of the food, and said, Grandma, this is really good, I am not that hungry, I want to take a cold shower too cool off, Grandma said oh, is your window open because the attic fan is on? Grandma, my window , but the attic fans brings in the 110 degree hot air right threw my window,

Teresa, stopped and said Grandma I know you are used to living like this, but tomorrow my mother is going to by me a air conditioner window unit.

And Teresa, walked out and took a cold shower, Teresa, could not believe her Dad still is angry at her, not with all what he has done.

Night time came quick, and Teresa walked back in there, where her Mother and Grandma were sitting,

Grandma, said smiling come sit down Teresa, I want to talk to you just for a second, Teresa, sat down on the hard chair, Grandma, Teresa thought she has the kindest voice I have ever heard, and then Grandma, said with now on Sunday's we must go to church. And I want you too try real hard in school, Grandma, said I know you are a smart girl, and I bet you good get straight a's if you wanted too. Teresa, could went numb for a second , Grandma, what do you mean church every Sunday,

Dean, sat back and let her Mother explain this too Teresa, Well, church is a great thing Teresa, I want too ask you something

Teresa, have you ever been saved? Teresa, said laughing Grandma, saved from what? Grandma, looked at Dean, and said Dean, has Teresa ever been too church, Dean, said when Teresa was about three years old Mama, Ed did not want to go to church, Ed wanted to go to the farm, and Grandma, said looking at Teresa and Dean,

Grandma, said with watery eyes, Dean, thanks a crying shame, this child has never been in church, how is Teresa, going to know JESUS if you don't head in the right direction, Grandma, said well Church on Sunday's Teresa. Teresa, said, ok. I can try, Teresa, thought I have tried a lot of things, Teresa, said Grandma, I am really tired. I am going to get ready for bed, Teresa, laughed yea I have been saved from a man , that trashes my mother,

Teresa, thought they have some really odd sayings down here.

Dean, said Teresa, I need to register you for school tomorrow, and don't say another word about the air conditioner you will get one, Teresa, said, well mother I noticed there is only one phone line in this house, Teresa, with her hand on her hip, said no can do, I have to have a phone, Dean, said Teresa go to bed we will talk about this in the morning.

Teresa, went in the bathroom and through cold water on her face, and thought, my gosh, who lives like this, and then likes on top it.

Teresa, folded back her sheets, and to Teresa's surprise there could feel the powder on her sheets, and it felt good, Teresa, thought that strange,

Grandma's back is to bad too do this, and I did not see my mother do. Teresa drifted off too sleep, and woke up to a sweat on her face,

Teresa, said oh my gosh, got up and washed her face, Teresa looked at the clock and it's three am. Teresa, walked out side very quietly and, my gosh, the mosquitoes are the size of humming birds, and why is it this hot at three am.

Teresa, looked around for a minute, and the stars were brighter down here, it like the stars were so large, and the moon was so bright,

Teresa, thought now that is pretty cool, never seen the stars and the moon so bright ever.

Teresa, walked back quietly and washed her face and hands with cold water, and went back to bed.

Next thing Teresa heard was her Mother's alarm clock going off,

Teresa, said wow that is loud. Nothing likes okle's voice. Teresa, just waking up, thought me really miss Okle, and Larry,

Dean, took a shower and got ready, and Teresa did the same, Dean, drove her daughter to Canton academy, Teresa, said wow they have iron gates just like Julius school he went too, Teresa, said Mother what is it with the iron gates, Teresa

said oh I know, they are afraid people will escape and get a life away from here. Dean, said Teresa that is not true

, Teresa, said really mom, that's what you did, isn't it?

Dean, looked and seen the angry in in Teresa's eyes, mixed with pain, Teresa, all you have to do is go to school down here, and you have your whole life in front of you,

Dean, pulling through the gates, and pulled into a parking spot, Dean, got and Teresa, slowly got out, as they walked in and Teresa, sat there, and listened to the rules for rules they had at this school, Teresa, said fine.

The principal said in front of Teresa, Mrs. Whitehurst, your daughter does not appear happy to be here, Teresa, wanted to say so many things, but for once did not say anything,

Dean, said this is going to be a little adjustment for my daughter, like it was for Jennifer, The principal said as he leaned his head back Ugh I see,

As Dean, made out the check , Teresa is really smart and out going, Teresa will get used to it. Teresa thought I like it already, this school has air conditioning.

The principal said as he gave Teresa, her paper work for her locker, and the rules of the school, the principal of the school, put his hand on Teresa's shoulder , kid you will like it ,after you make a few friends and get too know people. Welcome to Canton Academy. Teresa said nothing.

Dean, and Teresa thanked the principal for his time and Teresa would have her uniforms, Teresa, thought I can't wait. It's like the heat, the shit just gets worse. Now there going to dress me up like a Barbie doll.

Dean, and Teresa once back at Grandma's house , the phone rang , Teresa said to her Mother I have to take another cold shower, I am that hot, and then Mother can we please get the air conditioner for my bed room, Dean, tired of the conversation, said yes , Teresa.

Ed, was on the phone , someone had put sugar in the gas tank of his Brand new Cadillac, Ed, said I am telling you ,
Teresa is behind this, Teresa came out of the shower, and over heard, her Mother saying , No Ed, I am not going to make Teresa get out of the shower, and come to the phone, and something the dealer ship is told him this is going to cost a lot of money,
Dean, said Ed I will talk to Teresa and have her call you, But Teresa, loves you and would never hurt you Ed, Teresa over heard, Ed, how can Teresa be driving you nuts when she is over 500 hundred miles away from you. Ed, please calm down again I will speak with Teresa about this matter, Dean said not to change the subject is Larry, Julius and Okle doing ok? There all fine, but our son as went off and marred so girl named sandy, Ed, said what a joke.
Dean, said wow Julius got married and did not tell us, that is horrible, Ed, said I was just as pissed off as you Dean, and was going to fire him, over this, Ed said if you can't step up and be a man and tell his own parents he got married, How can Julius run this business. Ed, said but I know I can not fire him, because no one will hire Julius because of his fingers,

Any body that takes a look at his fingers are going to say no way, Ed, said if he wasn't my son, I would have the same thoughts,

Dean, I will let you go, I love you and miss and I hope you will be home soon, Dean, said she loved Ed back, and said Jennifer said she would like you to come down, are at least thing about coming down too see her Ed. Ed said Dean, I love you we can talk about Jennifer later, Ed hung the phone.

Teresa heard most of the conversation, Teresa, shut the door, and got out a letter and pencil and wrote Judy a letter,

Teresa, heard her mother coming and Teresa still had the pencil and paper in her hand, Dean, noticed it the envelope and said Teresa, who do you plan on writing a letter too, Oh, Mother I thought I would write Okle a letter, I think she would like to hear from me. Dean smiled yes, she would.

Dean said well why don't you write your letter later, and let's go get you air conditioner for you window, your uncle Dad will put it in for you. Teresa, said, let me walk next door and tell them Hello; I have not been over there since I got here. Dean said I will wait here for you.

Teresa, put the paper and pencil on her bed, and walked out side across the lawn, and my Gosh, sweat is on Teresa's face, Teresa knocked at the door, and three little poodles yapping at the door,

Aunt Polly answered the door, and had a big smile, and said come on in, Aunt Polly said oh don't mind those little dogs of mine, there bark is bigger than there bite,

Teresa, said I wanted to come over before me and my Mother leave to go shopping and say Hello, Aunt Polly said well I am sorry you can't stay long, Aunt Polly said let me have a look at you, my gosh you are still so tiny and skinny, and your hair is blond, like it was when you were just a little girl, Teresa smiled ,

Aunt Polly, my mother is waiting , Aunt Polly said in that case Oh, well Thank You for coming down, we are going to have neck bones for dinner,

Teresa, turned around fast, and said what bones are you having for dinner? Aunt Polly said oh that's right your not used to the southern food, Aunt Polly said you will like it, and if you don't , well then you do not have to eat it, But Aunt Polly said, you know if never hurts to try something different.

Teresa said ok. Aunt Polly said Teresa, just one more thing, Now I know that you used to driving your self places,

But your Mother as already said that your Daddy said you will not be driving ,

Teresa said what? Aunt Polly, said didn't your Mother say anything to you about you will not be allowed to drive, it's your Daddy's rules, Aunt Polly said , your Uncle Dade will drive you any where you need to go, now the piggy wiggly store is just around the corner, Teresa said thanks for letting me know

And Teresa said good by and shut the door, Teresa, thought bones, these people down here eat bones, so help Dad , you set me up, you knew these people are not normal.

Teresa, reached Grandma's house walked up the porch, and inside was just as hot as hot side, Teresa, thought do not turn on the oven, we will die from the heat. Grandma was up and cooking and hot and muggy in this kitchen, Teresa, said Grandma it's so hot, how do you always have a smile on your face?

The good Lord Teresa, makes all kinds of days, some are hot, some rainy, but complaining about the weather that the Lord gives you , it's not going to help any, Plus a person is not to complain for no reason, Teresa, said I am not complaining hot is hot and cold is cold ,

Teresa, for some reason could found her self , not trying to make a point with her Grandma, Teresa said to Grandma where is my Mother, Grandma said oh your Mother is I think taking a shower,

Teresa said well I am glad someone is not hot right now.

Grandma, said why don't you have seat and talk with me until your Mother is ready?

Teresa, sat down, and calmed down, and looked at all the pictures Grandma had hanging on the walls,

Teresa, noticed she was on the wall too, there were a couple pictures of Julius, Jennifer and Teresa, Teresa, said Grandma, where did you get these pictures, of me and my sister and brother?

Grandma, said I think I got them pictures some from your Mama, and some from Okle, they sent them too me,

Teresa said, why did you put pictures of us on your walls of you house though? Grandma, says that's what a person is suppose to do, Grandma asked Teresa, back home where you Dad is , there must be pictures of you kids hanging on the walls of your home Teresa, Grandma noticed the silence,

Teresa said no Grandma, there is not one picture of any of kids on the walls,

My Dad and Mom has art, and some type of boats, and merrils that hang the walls. Grandma, said well's that's just plum odd.

Teresa looked at her Grandma, and felt a connection, like some one else agrees with me Teresa thought, Dean, walked through still beautiful Grandma said.

Teresa said Mother can we go now, the sooner we get my air conditioner the sooner I will be in a better mood, Dean, sighed and grabbed her purse and car keys, Dean, told her Mama, we will be back,

Dean, turned around and seen Teresa standing by the car, Mama, Dean said Teresa can be a handful at times, Teresa can be hard headed,

Dean said I am leaving now, and Grandma, was going to finish cooking breakfast, and have something for Dean and Teresa to eat when they get back.

Dean, got in the car and started , Teresa got in, and put her face by the air conditioning vents of the car, my Gosh, as Teresa kept her head on the dash board, no wonder you left from down here, it is too hot. Mom, what are neck bones? Teresa, sitting back and the cool air blowing right on her face,

Dean, lit up a cigarette and said, it's pork, Teresa, said well if it's so popular , why have we never had it. Teresa, your Dad does not care for that kind of food, Teresa, said I have had it, Dad does not run every thing,

Dean, said calm down Teresa, you don't even know if you like neck bones or not, Teresa, looked at her Mother and said, do you like them, Dean, looked real quick at Teresa, and said Yes I do, but I have to pay attention to the road.

Teresa said all I am saying is you like this food and because Dad does not care for it, how does that stop you from eating what you like?

Dean said there just neck bones, it's not that important, Teresa, said Mother it's the point, which you just go with the flow of Dad's rules. Teresa said Bull shit.

Dean, said to Teresa, there will be no cursing down here, I can tell you that right now.

Dean, said all your Dad is doing is making you grow up and learn things the old fashion way, and that way you will have respect ,

Teresa, said Mother Dad and respect do not belong in the same sentence.

Dean, pulled in to world of wonder appliances, Dean said as she stopped the car and let him keep running for a minute,

Dean said Teresa I want to tell you something, and even thought it is your Dad's idea, I am going to stand behind your Dad on this, once a week you will be seeing a Psychiatric Doctor.

Teresa, said and why would you let Dad do that , and why would you agree with him Mother, Dean, said your Dad feels it would be best, I have done discussed this with your Uncle Dade, he will drive you up the Psychiatric Clinic

, Teresa said you did not answer my question? Why are doing this?

Dean, said as Teresa and her sat in the car, your Dad feels you have so much angry in you, and you are making bad choices, and maybe a professional Psychiatric can help you figure things out in a way you would understand.

Dean, said Teresa, we can not sit in this car all day, don't you want to get out and get your air conditioner,

Teresa, said hold on Mother, Dad is the one who needs professional help, Dad, screws around on you, Dad does all kinds of crazy shit,

Teresa said I am not done Mother, Teresa, said because he has money too buy you cars and Mother he buys off the police,

Dean, said there you go again you are being over dramatic. Dean, said to Teresa, you need to really look in the mirror at your self Teresa,

Dean turned off the car and opened her door,

Teresa got out and they both walked into the store, Teresa said loudly Dad does not need to see a Psychiatric Doctor, he needs to check in Psychiatric Clinic for about a year, and Dad needs to realize he is the one who is the one in a nut case. Teresa said at least I do not go around saying people are dead and really there alive.

Dean, said I have no idea what you are talking about Teresa, but you are embarrassing me, stop it right now.

Teresa, seen hurt in her Mother's eye's and said nothing.

Dean, walked in and the man at the counter looked familiar, His name tag said Bob,

Dean, said Hello, can you please help me with an air conditioner I am looking for a window unit.

Bob, said yes, he leaned over the counter, taking a good look at Dean, Teresa said what is wrong with you Bob, it's rude to get in some one's face,

Dean, nudged her daughter, Bob, said Waudean is that you, Dean, took a close look at Bob, and said oh my gosh it has been for ever since we have seen each other.

Bob, walked around the counter and gave Waudean a big hug, Bob said with his deep southern voice, it's been ages since I have seen you,

I left for years at went up to the northern part of Mississippi,

Then, my Mama passed away and I just started my own business right here in canton. Dean, smiling I am happy for you, you seem to be doing well for your self.

Dean, said this here is my daughter Teresa, I am looking for a window unit to go in Mama house, my daughter is going to school down here, and Teresa will be living with my Mama, Bob, said glad to meet you Teresa,

Teresa gave a half smile, it's a joy to meet you too Bob.

Teresa, noticed some country music was playing on Bob's radio, Teresa, having no patience, just get the air conditioner , mom give me the car keys I will wait out side,

Bob, noticed the rudeness in Teresa,

Dean, said here the keys, do not leave Teresa, Bob, said changing the subject, well what kind of unit are you looking for Dean, Dean and Bob walking down where all the window air conditioning units are. Dean, looked at Bob, said I want Teresa to have a good run, Bob, said I have a really nice window unit, but it sure is expensive, Bob said it cost so much money I only bought one of them,

Dean, said well Bob do you think air condioner will last a long time? Bob, said if it does not, I will fix my self, a for ever warranty.

Dean, smiled, let me see if Bob,

Dean and Bob dean did a lot of talking and Teresa could see from the window, Teresa went in and walked up too her Mother, and said Mom , my stomach is growling I am that hungry, can I just please drive and go get something to eat, I will get something to go, what ever place I go too.

Dean, thought Teresa will not be driving after I go back home to Missouri, Dean said yes, but be care full, Teresa,

Dean, said to Teresa before she walked out of the old store, do not be gone long.

Teresa walked out, and she drove around and nothing, Teresa, kept driving,

As she crossed the rail road tracks

Teresa pushed the button to let the window down, and Teresa smelled the best BBQ in the world, Teresa, pulled into a parking spot, and walked into an all black BBQ restaurant.

Teresa walked in said Hello, all the Black folks turned and looked at Teresa, not a bad stare but a strange stare, Teresa, said can I see your menu?

The black woman said with a smile as she handed Teresa the menu, the black woman said my name is Nellie, you are not from around here or you? Teresa stopped reading the menu and said no. I am not.

But, Nellie, can I have a some ribs, and, Teresa, said yes, ribs is all I want, Nellie, said those ribs are just now ready, I will get you a half portion, Teresa said fine, Oh, Nellie Teresa said and a cold soda, Nellie said soda, what is that, Teresa, with her eye brows down, you know coke or Pepsi, Nellie laughed, child we call that pop down here. Teresa, shook her head, ok one cook pop,

Nellie said it will be just a couple of minutes, Teresa laid down the menu, and looked around and it was a old wore out looking building, Huge fans every where, Teresa waited for her food as she noticed she was the only white person in this entire restaurant, and Teresa did not feel uncomfortable,

Nellie came back and said that will be four dollars even. Teresa handed her a five dollar bill and said keep the change Nellie,

Teresa, quickly grabbed her food and walked out, Nellie came out side, you for got your change, Teresa waved good by.

Teresa, started the car, and oh the cool air felt so good. Teresa open up the box and took a bit of the ribs, my gosh these are the best ribs in the world, and drank her soda, Teresa, was thinking of the word pop, Teresa smiled, that lady sure was nice.

Teresa, ate a lot of the ribs, and thought I will save some for her Mother; Teresa drove back across the rail road tracks, and pulled into the same parking spot her Mother had parked in.

Dean, came out and said Teresa , did you want to drive back to Grandma's, Teresa said sure, Bob said I will be over later to install that air conditioner today, Teresa said and we will be waiting on you. Dean, said Teresa why do you have to be rude all the time,

Teresa said I not being rude, I told him the truth, we will be there, or at least I will be there, if I am not with the nut doctor.

Teresa, said Mother here are some left over ribs, you have to try them they are so good, Teresa pushed the bag towards her Mother,

Dean, feeling her heart beat faster, Teresa, where did you go to get these ribs, Teresa, said well I had to drive over some rail road tracks and it's right there,

Mother, you should go there, they have great menu of food.

Dean, lit up a cigarette, Teresa, you can not ever go over there again, Teresa, stopped the car as she came to a stop sign, Teresa looked at her Mother, why?

Dean, said Teresa down here Blacks live on one side and whites on the other, and we do not cross the tracks, and the Black folks they do not come over on this side either, Teresa, said that is about the most retardest thing I have ever heard,

Dean, said Teresa it has always been like that, it was like that before I ever left here to go to college up to Missouri.

Teresa, said no wonder you got the hell out of here, that's not normal, Dean, said start driving Teresa, we can be at this stop sign for ever,

Teresa, drove back to Grandma's house, why would any one come up with those kinds of rules,

I am confused Mother, Teresa, said you did not have a problem when I was little me playing with Ronald and Donald, and they were black.

Dean, said Teresa, I can not explain, that's just how it is down here. Teresa pulled back in Grandma's drive way, and got out; Teresa said if you are not going to eat those ribs, I am.

Teresa grabbed the ribs and walked into the house, Grandma said oh, I see you got you some thing too eat,

Teresa said Grandma do you want some ribs, Grandma smiled, I would love to just taste them, Teresa said help your self,

Teresa noticed how the white part of town looked down on the black part of town, Teresa said Grandma, do you hate Black people too?

Grandma, smile came off her face, oh my Lord Child No, and don't you ever hate any one because of skin color, the good Lord makes us all.

Grandma, said you poor child this must be confusing for you. Dean, over heard the whole talk Grandma and Teresa were having and walked in where they were,

Dean, said mama, I had to tell Teresa about crossing the rail road tracks, and how it is down here, Grandma said

The Lord made one world and the good Lord made it , where we all can live. Dean said you do not know Teresa, Mama,

Teresa will walk over there just to get ribs, if Teresa wanted them. Grandma, said I never did agree that blacks on one side, and whites on the other,

Grandma, said as she looked at Teresa, it never did make sense to me. But who am I to say anything.

Teresa, said Grandma is it true you do not know how to drive, and my Mother is the only female in this family that drives? Grandma, said yes, the men do that Teresa,

Teresa, said Grandma, what do you think if I showed you how to drive then you would not have to wait on any one to take you any where, Grandma ,smiled you sure do have a high spirit in you Teresa, Grandma said, as it was getting hotter in the house, I am to old to learn something like that,

Teresa looked at her Mother and said when is your friend Bob, going to be here, you know mom the air conditioning man?

Dean, said Teresa he will get here as soon as he can.

Grandma gave Dean a plate of food, Teresa looked at it, and said I am going to my room, and let me know when Bob get's here.

Teresa walked out, and over heard her Mother telling her Grandma, Teresa is angry at her Dad, some of it I understand and then it's like Teresa is angry at the world.

Dean, said Mama, I really do not know if that angry will ever come out of Teresa.

Grandma, grabbed Deans' hands and said, there is a reason,

Teresa is here, do not worry, The Lord has a surprise for us all. Grandma said while you were gone Jennifer called, I meant to tell you sooner, Dean, said is Jennifer ok?

Mama, said well she seemed like it, Dean, said I will call her now, I will be leaving late tonight,

Teresa, thought how can you just leave me down here, I hardly know these people. Teresa shut her eyes and thought of all the rides her and prince had together. And drifted off to sleep.

Teresa, woke up and went into the front porch where Grandma was sitting reading her Bible, Teresa sat down next to her, Teresa leaned over, and said what are you reading that's so interesting,

Teresa, said I know it's the Bible, but what part do you like the best, Grandma, put the Bible in Teresa lap, and said, read right there, **Proverbs 20:22** Do not say, "I'll pay you back for this wrong!" Wait for the LORD, and he will deliver you.

Teresa, holding the bible open, Grandma what does that mean?

Grandma, said well I am no preacher, but I will explain it the best way I know how, Teresa, did not care about the sweat any more as Grandma said, Teresa it' like this, have you ever been angry at anyone and wanted to get even with them or hurt that person like they have hurt you?

Teresa, looked up, at Grandma soft kind eye's, Teresa said Yes Grandma, I have, at times wanted that, Grandma says and through you whole life you will be tempted to even up the score or call it getting even if you wish, Teresa, did not move, Teresa

eresa listened to every word that came out of Grandma's mouth,

Grandma, said, look here where it says, Wait for the Lord, Grandma, Teresa said how long does it take the Lord,

Grandma, that is a good question, it's called Faith, faith is putting into the Lord's hands, and the Lord does see all ,

You the Lord knows what you did and what you want to do, Grandma said as Grandma patted Teresa legs, Teresa, said Grandma, feeling so much love from her Grandma, Teresa said what if someone killed some one, Grandma said, well , the Lord is not going to approve of such actions, The Lord brings a person in this world, and takes them out.

Teresa said, I know about the haven and Hell part, Grandma, said Hell is hotter than this house Teresa, with evilness, and heaven is kind of, and loving and gentle , and Teresa, is it all about how you make your choices living on this earth, the Lord made for all of us.

Teresa, closed the bible, and seen Bob driving up , with the air conditioner in the back of his truck,

Teresa, said Grandma what happens to a person , who kills another person, Grandma, says, looking at Teresa, well that person should ask Jesus to forgive them, and that person must repent from there sins, Teresa, was into this conversation so much,

Dean, had to touch Teresa on the shoulder, Teresa, for the second time, Your air conditioner should be ready in just a little while,

Teresa, said ok Mom, But Grandma is talking right now ,

Dean, walked back to show Bob where the window unit should go, and Uncle Dade, walked over, and they were talking, Dean, noticed Teresa never left her Grandma's side, Teresa, crossed her legs,

Ok Grandma, Teresa said what happens to a person who is not nice to there family, Grandma, says well, what do you mean?

I mean Grandma; let's say there is a man who cheats on his wife and does stupid things, Grandma, when the lord stops that man from doing that,

Grandma, said

The Lord will give a person every day to make choice on rather to be a good person and live by the way of the Lord, or not.

Teresa, said so you are saying in a way, God made us, gave us some rules, and if we do what God says we go to heaven, Grandma, smiled at Teresa, I see a lot of questions in you?

Grandma said as she got up, we will talk Teresa,

But I am going to give you an example right now,

Teresa, confused, watched Grandma,

Grandma said , come on with child, Teresa followed Grandma in the house, and Grandma grabbed a big picture of Ice cold water in a picture and some glasses , Grandma, said can you help me Teresa carry some of this,

Teresa, grabbed the heavy picture of Ice water, and followed her Grandma out side, Grandma, said Hello , Uncle Dade, Bob, and Dean all turned around, with smiles , Hey there Bob, Uncle Dade said, Dean, smiled at Mama,

It's just too darn hot out here; I thought you all might like a cold glass of ice water, Grandma reached for the pitcher of water,

But Teresa caught on quick, and said Grandma I will do this, and Teresa poured all the glasses full of Ice water,

Bob, said well Dean, your daughter sure was raised up right, Teresa is so polite. Dean, said Thank You, Teresa, Bob, and Uncle Dade "Thank You for putting the air conditioner in, and walked away,

Teresa, thought my Grandma is some woman. Teresa went into the house, and sat by the fan.

Grandma, said Dean, do you have a minute I need to speak with you just for a second, Grandma, and Dean walked over by the clothes line, away from every one, and the sun beating down on them

Dean, said Mama what is wrong, you seem like you have something on your mind?

Mama, said to Dean, as she picked the clothes to be hung up,

Teresa, has never held a Bible in her life? That girl Teresa does not need a head doctor, or the shrink word as Teresa calls, it.

Mama grabbed dean's hands and said I am telling you as your Mama Dean, that girl needs to know the lord, and where kindness and love come from.

Mama, said I think you and Ed are making a mistake making Teresa making her go to a head doctor to see what's wrong with her.

Mama and Dean, heard Jennifer's voice as she was walking up the drive way, Jennifer said Hi Grandma, and Mom, Jennifer said it looks like Teresa is getting air conditioner, Dean, said yes, it's about the only thing that would make her happy.

Jennifer, said Mom, I know this is hard on you, but trust me when I got sent down here, at first I thought I was go nuts, it's another world down here, compared to you and Dad and the way you raised us.

Jennifer, said Mother, I love you and you're a great Parent, and nothing against Dad, but, Teresa for a little while may have trouble adjusting to the difference of everything from food to this thing called life.

Grandma, said now let's all get in the house, the clothes are hung up, and its cooler in the house, all three walked in the house, Teresa was in Aunt Polly's old bed room.

Jennifer said I can not wait to be a Mother; I can not wait to hold this child in my arms.

Teresa was inside and she had started a letter to her Dad, and how she wished he would die.

All the pain cheating on her Mother, and Dad, you do not care. Dad, how do you make fun of people likely Larry, and okle, that's right Dad, it takes so much money to do that bull shit, just like it,

You send kids off like they are bad products, and you are the mean one, you are the one who needs a shrink,

When you get old I am going to send you far away, and I am going to do with your money. , Teresa heard something and looked up and quickly saw her Grandma, Teresa put her hand over the letter she writing to her Dad,

Grandma, said Teresa are you busy, Teresa shook head no, Grandma, said well with your Mama leaving and all tonight, Jennifer has invited us all over to her and Hank's house for supper, Teresa, said Grandma, that house old and small,

Grandma, said you sure do got a point there, But I want to ask you something, Teresa, looked back up, as she folded the letter up that she writing to Dad, Yes Grandma, what is it? Grandma, said I am not going to tell you have to go over to your sister's house for supper, but it is so rude and unkind, on your part, to not spend time with your family when you have a chance to do so?

Grandma, said would you like to spend time with your family, instead of cooped of in this room? Grandma said, with a smile it's a choice, and Teresa you and I talked about choice of Life. Grandma, said just let me know I will be in the kitchen, if you do not come in the kitchen in about five minutes of less, I know your choice Teresa.

Teresa, put face flat down on the bed, and took a deep breath,

Teresa thought I am so confused, Teresa, felt something she never felt before, a need to be there for her family, really be there for them, to hear what they have to say. Teresa thought how bad can it be, Teresa, saw her reflection in the mirror as she got off the bed, and Teresa stopped, gosh, I have an angry look, and I am not even angry. This is my choice to go.

Teresa washed her face, combed her hair, and went into the kitchen, and said as walked next to her grandma, I am ready when you are.

Grandma, and Dean, said this is so nice. Jennifer said Teresa is you really coming over,

Teresa, said yes, Jennifer said Teresa I am asking you not to make fun of our house, I know what you think, and feel, because Teresa I know you and you have no problem expressing your feelings,

Jennifer said come over here just for a minute I want to say something you, Dean, said Jennifer we will be in the car waiting for you and Teresa,

Jennifer said ok, Mom, we will be there in just a few minutes, Teresa, getting aggravated,

Jennifer what do you want, Teresa, we do not have the house mom and Dad have, and we don't have the cars either, but we do not have the insanity they have either. Teresa, said, Jennifer if I did not want to come over I would not be coming,

But I want to, and by the way your Husband is kind of cute, and Teresa, said Jennifer has hank, you know check out other woman, Jennifer said no, he does not, and that would have to be so painful to see and feel that, Jennifer started walking to the car and Teresa followed.

Jennifer and Teresa and every one is the car,

Teresa, was the first one, put the air vents pointing towards the back seat, I hate to be hot, Grandma spoke up, well I am about to freeze, Grandma asked Dean to please pull over, Grandma said Dean, I just do not know how you take this cold, I need a sweater to be here in this car, me and Teresa will change seats, Teresa, thought, it is hot as hell down here. How do these people stand this heat.

Teresa said Great idea Grandma, Dean, said ok, Dean pulled over and Teresa and Grandma, switched seats. Jennifer said I only live around the corner she said to Teresa,

Teresa, said I know that Jennifer, but my complexion means something to me, Jennifer,

Teresa, said you have got a oily looking face all the time, and you have got the size of a cow,

Jennifer, started to cry, Jennifer said Teresa you are just like Dad, you say things that hurts people's feelings and you do not care,

Teresa, said you are so sensitive Jennifer, you always have been, you cry over everything, Dean, stop it both of you. Grandma Said well, I hear we might have storms tonight, Teresa, said all I know is I have air conditioning,

Jennifer said Teresa one day you will see the world will not revolve around you. And Jennifer said I know you never thought Dad would send you off, you were and are Daddy's little girl, who can not do any thing wrong,

Teresa said you're just mad because you are poor, Grandma, reached her arm and touched Teresa, and said if you can not say any thing nice, then you should not say nothing at all. Grandma said Teresa you wanted to know about God, early, God would not be impressed with what you said.

Teresa, found her self so confused when her Grandma, said things like that, God, and saved. Dean pulled in the drive way, and they all got out of the car, and walked inside, Jennifer walked in and washed her face, Hank greeted everyone with a big southern come on in welcome.

Teresa, noticed the grease on Hanks hands, Teresa said don't hug me unless you plan to wash your hands in bleach.

Teresa said to Hank I am not trying to be rude, but that is really disgusting. Hank, went and washed his hands and then was talking to Jennifer in the Bath room, Hank was saying your sister , is about the rudest person I think I have ever met in my entire life, Hank said are you sure you and your sister Teresa have the same parents, ?

Jennifer said, yes Hank looked closer to Jennifer's face; Hank said you have been crying, did you sister Teresa upset you? Jennifer knew Hank would not stand for anyone upsetting her, Jennifer looked at Hank and said , no, it's my mother leaving and me being pregnant and all,

Hank hugged Jennifer, and said you are the most beautiful woman in the world, you eyes have love in them for the whole world,

Hank said but I just do not know how much more I can take of your sister Teresa,

Teresa, yelled hey Hank, I am in the same house, small house at that, and I can hear you.

Teresa said if you have a problem with me, come and talk to me about it. Jennifer looked at Hank and said please not today.

Hank walked out, and said, Teresa, I do not have a problem with you; I just really love my wife. Hank said, I am sorry we do not have a big enough house for you, but I hope you will be comfortable here until you all leave, Teresa, sighed,

Teresa said when is dinner, Hank said, it's on the table now, Jennifer is getting the salad, and then you can eat.

Teresa, went in and washed her hands, came back out and sat down at the small kitchen table, everyone scooted there chairs closer together, and some how it all worked out,

After supper, Dean said Jennifer and Hank I must tell you Thank You both for having us over, the meal was very good.

Grandma hugged Jennifer and Hank as the sun was starting to go down, Jennifer said Teresa and Mom, did I show you the baby's crib?

Grandma, I know you seen, yes child your crib for your baby is beautiful. Dean, said no, Teresa said where is it?

Dean and Teresa and Jennifer walked in to Jennifer bed room , when I bring the baby home, the crib is going to be right by my bed, Jennifer stood there with a smile, and said well Mother and Teresa what do you think,

Mother looked at the crib, and said Jennifer I think you have done a wonderful job, I see you are sewing, and have made a lot of nice things for the baby, I am so happy for you,

Mother walked away and looked at the pictures of Hank and Jennifer's wedding,

Dean found her self think of Hank, Teresa, said it looks great. Jennifer said well I am glad you like it. Jennifer said you can even baby sit if you want,

Teresa, said I do not baby sit, and I do not hold little babies, Jennifer said why are you so mean, Teresa, said Jennifer, I am not being mean, to you are to you baby that will be here soon, Jennifer babies are so little, and I just can't handle it, Jennifer said, but he raised a mean dog to attack people , in fact you trained that dog, and now you are sensitive to babies?

Teresa, walked out, and said I tried to be honest with you Jennifer.

Grandma said I am getting tired, yaw all, Dean, said yes, and I still need to get ready to head home. Teresa, said let's go.

Dean and Grandma hugged Jennifer and Hank good By, Jennifer said mom, please call me when you get back home, or have Okle call so I know you made home safe

. Dean said I will. Teresa just walked out and went to sit inside the car.

Dean, and Grandma followed and Grandma, said I felt a rain drop or two, Dean, said mama, you always could tell if it was going to storm , With everyone in the car, it only took about five minutes to get back to Grandma's house,

Teresa, was the first one out of the car and Grandma never locked her house, and Teresa walked in and turned on her window air conditioner,

Grandma, went and got her night gown on and Teresa, said Grandma, are you going to take a bath, no I will let you take one first, I keep my self and my soul as clean as possible, Teresa, a little sweat never hurt anyone. Grandma, do you think I was mean to my sister , Grandma said Teresa, I think you have a big heart and your afraid to show any kind of feelings.

But the good lord can turn any one heart around, Grandma, said Teresa, But the good Lord, gives you the choice to ask him to change your heart,

Dean, walked in with her luggage, and said it's getting late, and I better get on the road, Grandma said you sure you just do not want to spend the night and leave early in the morning,

Dean said Mama I would love too, but Ed and the business and just things back home need to be taken care of.

Dean gave Mama some money and said this should help with the bills, and I will be sending you money every month, I open a bank account in canton, and you will have no problems getting money Mama,

Grandma said well Dean I sure thank you, but I have all I need, Dean, said mama with Teresa here your bills will go up, that I can promise you.

Dean, called Teresa, Teresa, came in and seen the luggage, well I guess you are leaving going back to Dad ugh? Teresa, said mom, you tell Dad, this is not over, this is just the beginning I do not give a crap how much money he has, You tell Dad mom, I know too much on him. Dean, raised her eye brows, Teresa, calm down and stop being so angry.

Dean said Teresa gives me a hug, I have to leave, and I love you, and be kind Teresa. Dean, waved good by, as the rain started to pour down.

Teresa noticed the tears in her Mother's that she was trying to hide.

Dean stopped and got coffee, and headed out on the highway.

Teresa, took a cold shower, came out and unfolded the letter she had started to her Dad, and Then Grandma, walked right in, and said Teresa, we are going to bed now, do you need anything before we go to bed,

Teresa, said we have to go to bed now,

Grandma said yes child , and I was hoping you would say a prayer with me, Teresa, holding the letter in her hand still,

Grandma got down on her knees , and ask Teresa to do the same, Grandma, put together Teresa's hands to show her how to pray,

Grandma said and it was storming out side, and the wind was blowing, Lord, you know you have given us a place to sleep tonight, and the weather is bad, strong storms, please let Dean make it home safe, and keep us safe Lord , we love you and thank you for this day. Please Lord guides us and protects us. Amen.

Teresa, said Grandma, my Dad say's there is no God, Grandma hugged Teresa, and said Oh child, please do not listen to such mess.

Grandma, said I promise ;you there is a God, Teresa said but how do you know for sure, Grandma got off her knees and told Teresa, to sit on the bed, and said for one thing, Grandma, said as she laid her hand on Teresa hand, Teresa, God got you out of a place, that says there is not God,

That's just for starters, Teresa, said then why would God let my mother go back to the same place God removed me from,

Grandma, said Teresa, life is about choices, no one made your Mother get in that car and go back any where, But you Mother is not a bad person,

Grandma, said you never what tomorrow holds, Teresa, said to Grandma, I guess I am tired

Grandma hugged Teresa, and Teresa said Good night, Teresa laid in bed, and the cool air, felt so well on these cotton sheets.

Teresa laid there in bed, thinking my Gosh; my Dad has got a really nice wife, and a great Mother, Teresa thinking of prince her horse, and how bad she missed him.

That horse was all I had. And my Dad sold him. Teresa rolled over and went to sleep.

The morning came quicker than Teresa wanted it to, Grandma, was touching her on the shoulder, Good Morning Teresa, wake up,

Grandma voice, Teresa heard, Teresa stretched her arms out and pulled back the covers and got up, Grandma said I will be in the kitchen waiting for you, Teresa, went in side the bath room, washed face and hands, combed her hair, and went into the kitchen, Grandma said with that kind smile,

Teresa sit down and eat your breakfast,

Teresa, seen ham, biscuits and gravy, and a bowl of white stuff, Teresa, said Grandma, what is in this white bowl, Grandma, said grits child. Teresa, said grits, what are grits?

Grandma, said take your spoon stir the butter on top of your grits in the bowl, Teresa, did it slowly, Grandma, said now Teresa if you do not like them, you do not have to eat them, Teresa, said I will try them, Teresa, took her spoon and got just a little bit of grits on her spoon, Teresa, said the only thing missing Grandma, is salt, I love salt on every thing.

Grandma, see there you tried something and you liked it. Grandma, said I know this is very new to you Teresa, but from now on, when you come to this table to eat, I want you to try and remember to tell the Lord, thank you for this food today.

Teresa, said well after breakfast, don't I have to see the shrink today? Grandma said with sad eyes, Yes, I believe you do.

Grandma said as Teresa ate her breakfast, you know I know in my heart there is nothing wrong with you, Grandma, says we all get angry, but keeping stuffed up in you heart and soul, will only make it worse, Grandma, says, Teresa, when you go to that doctor, you tell him just wants on your mind, Teresa, finished breakfast, and said , thanks Grandma it was good, as she pushed the plate away from her, Teresa, said I am going to take a shower and then I will be ready.

Teresa, thought how does my Grandma takes this heat, my gosh.

Teresa, came out of the bath room, and heard Grandma singing, something about God and Jesus, Teresa, looked in the mirror, and said ok Doctor; here I come ready or not.

Teresa said as she walked in the kitchen and Grandma was still singing,

Grandma, why does this heat not bother you at all, it's like an oven in here. Grandma, laughed child I never had air conditioning growing up, and I guess I just got used to it, Teresa, looked at the time,

Well Grandma, why do you hang out your clothes when my mother bought you and brand new washer and dryer, Grandma, said I do use the washer and dryer, the washer all time, but the dryer only on rainy days, Grandma, said it's not good to take advantage of a good thing. Grandma, said because you might get used too it, and it not be there one day, Teresa, heard the honking of her uncle Dade,

Teresa, got up , and said well I have to go now Grandma, while I am gone will you call my mother and make sure she got home safe? Or did she already call?

Grandma, said you mother called she is fine. Teresa walked out and got in Uncle Dade's old pick up truck,

Teresa, said hello, and it's hot in this truck, Teresa, rolled down the window, and uncle Dade, drove her to dr. smith's office. Uncle Dade, said too Teresa before you get out of my truck, you are suppose to be here for thirty minutes, now I need to run to the piggley wiggly for your Aunt Polly, and I will be back here waiting for you, Teresa, got out and shut the old truck door, and went in, and Told the lady at the desk who she was and,

The lady at the counter, said just have a seat you are next Teresa. Teresa said is this all paid for? The lady looked up and seen Teresa was speaking too her,

The lady motion Teresa, to come up to the counter where she was, By the Teresa, my name is Elda, and your Mother has paid for the visits up front. Teresa, said I do not have to sign any thing, Elda, said No, your Mother took care of all the paper work that needed a signature,

Teresa walked away and waited for her name to be called; Teresa looked around more art on the walls, Teresa, and thought at least it is peaceful looking pictures. Teresa heard her name being called and the Doctor was tall, with salt and pepper hair, and glasses, Hello, Teresa, I am Dr. Smith, as reached his hand out to shake Teresa's hand, Teresa, gave a little shake. And walked in.

Well, Dr. Smith with dark framed thick glasses said you have a seat and get comfortable, Dr.Smith said there is ice water in that picture if you get thirsty.

Thanks, Teresa said. Dr. Smith, can we just hurry up, and start this question and answer game.

Dr. Smith said I see you are anxious to get started, so the questions began . Doctor Smith, could tell Teresa was not telling all of the story. Thirty minutes came and went. and Dr. Smith was righting away, Dr. Smith, said I have written you a prescription, and held out his hand for Teresa to take it, Teresa looked at the prescribtion, Dr. Smith said it will help you with the anger you have. Teresa, grabbed the prescribtion,

Dr. Smith looked at the clock, and said I will see you next week, and we made some progress to day, Teresa, said screw you and put that in your notes to my parents, and no, Dr Smith you made some money today. And walked out.

Teresa, put the written prescription in he pants pocket, and walked out, passed Elda, Elda said Teresa, you are suppose to be back here , Teresa, stopped Elda, and said look lady, I know when I have to be back, and Teresa went out side to the hot heat of the day,

Teresa seen uncle Dade's truck and walked over and got into the truck, Teresa, could feel the hotness of the truck seats,

Uncle Dade, with a smile said well how did it go in there, Teresa, looked at her Uncle Dade, with a giant smile and arms in the air and swinging her arms back and forth and said Great, I feel better already. It's working. It's a miracle! I tell you Uncle Dad, the drugs he gave me, I feel so much better, man I could use a cheeseburger about now. Uncle Dad, looked at Teresa, and said that Doctor gave you drugs,? Teresa, put her arms down, no, but I feel like I wanted to give the Doctor drugs., his ass is crazier than me.

Teresa, said to her uncle Dade

if my sister has problems, we can maybe get a discount, Uncle Dade, said a discount, Teresa, said yea, you know two for the price of one at the nut ward.

Teresa said maybe the Doctor will run that special. The Doctor can treat both of us, and my parents will get a discount. Uncle Dade, said ugh child you might need a nap some time to day, I believe all this is over whelming to you.

Uncle Dade said you know your Mama, wants only the best for you, Teresa, said yes I know. Teresa said Uncle Dade and if my Dad wants things even better for me, then he will send me to Japan, on a one way ticket,

Uncle Dade, said we are stopping by your sister's house, to while were out and see if Jennifer needs any thing, Teresa, said ok.

Uncle Dade made a few turns and here we are , Uncle Dade got out of the truck and seen Teresa, still sitting in the truck ,and Uncle Dade , said Teresa get out of the truck and come see your sister,

Teresa, sighed open the truck door and got out, and went in to see Jennifer, Uncle Dade said it will be alright Jennifer, Teresa, seen Jennifer crying,

Uncle Dade said is Hank at work Jennifer, Jennifer wiping her eyes, yes, Uncle Dade said Teresa you stay here with your sister, and I will be back in a little while, Uncle Dade, pulled out of Jennifer and Hank's drive way and went to his place of work,

Teresa, said Jennifer what is wrong, did you break a nail? Jennifer said

Still crying more now, Teresa, realized her sister was really hurting, the kind of hurt Teresa tried to show, but get her self to cry.

Teresa walked up and said Jennifer what is so wrong? Teresa said I know I need to be nicer to you, but I am here now, for you.

Jennifer, sat down on the couch, and said it's the baby, Teresa, said what do you mean it's the baby, it something wrong with it?

Jennifer said Teresa, I am so afraid that this baby will have no fingers and toes just like Julius,

Teresa, said that was a freak thing, that hardly ever happens, it was just one of those things, Jennifer, said yea, I sure hope your right,

But Jennifer, putting her hand where the baby is, Jennifer said God please let this baby be born with all parts, Teresa, said is there anything else bothering you, Jennifer said yes, Jennifer said you know if my baby has no fingers or toes, Jennifer said, Dad will disown his Grand child.

Teresa said no he wills not, Dad has got problems Jennifer, but Teresa found her self telling white lies, and things her Dad never said.

Jennifer said yes he will , he got rid of Julius, the minute he could and Dad never really did any type of fishing or boating with Julius, are just hanging with his son, and if a man can do that, who is too say Hank, could not feel the same way.

Teresa said Jennifer, before I got sent down here, Dad, said he wished he would have never sent you down here, and you were smart, and other good stuff dad said.

Jennifer, stopped crying Dad said something good about me?

Teresa, said sometimes, he would have a few drinks Teresa said you know Dad,

Then, he would say how he felt. Jennifer said that is strange why Mother would not tell me that then, Teresa, said Mom, most of the time mother went to bed when Dad got started drinking or getting drunk, and do you blame her?

Jennifer said no, and I can see mom just going to bed, than dealing with Dad drinking.

Uncle Dade was back in the drive way, and Uncle Dade walked in the house, and seen Jennifer and Teresa being normal and talking, no screaming at each other.

Jennifer, said uncle Dade where did you go, Well uncle Dade said as upset as you were, I went and talked with your husband Hank, just too make sure you and Hank were not fussing with each other, and Hank is going to come home at lunch time, and take the rest of the day off, so Hank can be here for you. Uncle Dade said that Hanks just loves the heck out of you Jennifer, Hank is a good man.

Jennifer, said thank you Uncle Dade, but I think I was just having the baby blues, it sadness and it comes and goes.

Teresa, smiling and laughing, I know the perfect Doctor, and we can go together, Jennifer knew what Teresa was talking about, Jennifer said, that is a great offer, Teresa, but I am just going to pass on that one.

Teresa smiled back, Uncle Dade said we'll me and Teresa need to get back home, and well will see you later,

Uncle Dade said now you call if you need any thing Jennifer and I will be here along with your Aunt Polly, she will be off work soon.

Teresa, waved good by again this time with a smile on her face, Uncle Dade and Teresa were back in the old truck and back at Grandma in about five minutes,

Uncle Dade, said Teresa, I am here for you as well as your sister, Teresa, said "Thank You' and shut the door,

Uncle Dade, drove off, and Teresa walked in Grandma's house, Grandma, said Teresa, is that you, Teresa, walked in towards the kitchen where Grandma could see her, Teresa said I am back and crazier than ever, Teresa, said Grandma, that Dr Smith, is a great doctor

. Grandma, said, Teresa, I know this just has to be hard on you, Grandma said when you get as old as me, you can tell when a person just needs to rest, Grandma, said

Teresa I am asking you to go in your bedroom don't think about any thing, I have laid something on your bed for you, I want you to try and get some rest, I can feel your soul , playing tug of war from here.

Grandma, said now go own child get some rest,

Teresa walked into the her cool bedroom and flopped on the bed, and ouch, Teresa bumped her hand on something,

Teresa turned over and it was a book, Teresa, picked it up and the book said the Holy Bible,

Teresa, open the Holy Bible, and inside, was written, to my wonderful Grandchild Teresa:

The Lord will always be there for you and protect you and guide you, but go to Jesus and pray what is on your heart, and the Lord will make a way. I love you Teresa,

Love, Grandma.

Teresa, realized she had goose bumps, and thought I have never heard the word love so much in my life, how does mom, life with dad un real.

Teresa, walked in the kitchen and hugged her Grandma, like she had never hugged another person, Teresa hugged with love for the first time in her life.

Teresa, said Grandma, Thank You so much, you know for every thing. Grandma smiled, sure thing honey child.

Teresa, said Grandma, can I please call my Mother , I just will talk for a few minutes, Grandma, said why sure, why you couldn't talk to your Mother,

Grandma, pointed towards the old black phone and said call your mother, Teresa, picked up the phone and called straight through, Teresa thought I am not calling collect, Okle may not answer.

Dean, answered the phone, Hi Mom, it's me Teresa, Hello Teresa, how are you today, I am really good and you mom, Fine,

Teresa heard Larry yelling, and then it went away, Teresa, said what is Julius and Larry doing, Dean, said Teresa, your brother has got married, to a young love he met a school her name is Sandy, she is nice girl,

But your Dad is not real found of her.

Teresa, said who does Dad like? Teresa said

Mom, tell Julius I said congratulations, for me, Teresa said

But mom I need to talk to Larry, is he around,

Dean, said yes, but Larry and your Dad are getting ready to go to the farm, and I think Larry just went out side,

Teresa, said shit, Mom, is okle there Yes,

Teresa, Mom just hand the phone to Okle I need to ask her something,

Dean, handed Okle the phone, Okle said Hello there Teresa, Teresa said hello back, Okle I have an important question for you, what is your question Okle said, Has my Dad and Larry got into any arguments since I have been gone,

Okle said, well as matter of fact they have, Teresa said were they bad arguments are my Dad being mean and making fun of Larry?

Okle said some of them were bad, Teresa, said Okle , tell my Dad there is a important call for him , and then walk away, Do not give my Dad a chance to ask who is on the phone,

Okle, said I would only do this for you Teresa,

Okle went and got Ed, and said phone call I am busy,

Teresa, could hear the conversation Ed said Okle you know to ask who is calling, Ed picked up the phone,

Hello, this is Mr. Whitehurst , Teresa, said if you take Larry to the farm and hurt him I will tell Mother about Lolita, and introduce who to her and then Mother can have he pick between you and Hank, Teresa said Dad with all the other bull shit I have on you, and I will make sure Mother and Hank get back together, and Teresa, said Don't call me on my Bluff, I stole a lot of money from you, and you had so much you do not have a clue what I can do with that money.

Teresa said you fuck with Larry Dad, and I will fuck with you,

Teresa hug up the phone.

Teresa knew her Dad and his temper and one person were already found Dead on Ed's farm. Larry would be a piece cake for Ed,

Teresa went and sat on her bed, looking around thinking, and wondering if Larry will be alright, Teresa, thought I knew it,

Dad is picking Larry, and now he is going to either work him to death on that farm, or kill Larry.

Teresa, said Grandma, I want to pray, Grandma, came running in. Well child let's pray, and they held hands, Teresa said I want to ask God something Grandma, Grandma's hands sturdy strong hands made Teresa have comfort in her first prayer, Teresa, started praying God I am new at all this praying stuff, but God you know where there is trouble, and I am asking you to not let me Dad hurt any one, Amen

Grandma, and Teresa eyes met, and Granma said , any time you want to pray ,

Teresa, I am right here, and you can talk to God all day long , it's your choice always remember that. Grandma, said I want remind you no cursing in my home, God gave us a place live and sleep with out any problems, and Grandma, said you can go around cursing , it's not pleasing to the Lord Teresa,

Grandma, I am sorry, I lost my temper and said some bad words, but the rest I meant, Grandma, said is there something I can help you with. Teresa said no.

Days rolled into to Months, and Christmas was here, Jennifer was due with her baby any day now, and Teresa was used to the school and the culture difference and one more visit to Dr Smith,

Letters and gone and come from Judy, as Teresa was reading one of Judy's letters, Teresa, finished reading the letter and put it away with the others,

Teresa, got off the bed and walked to the front porch where Grandma, was sitting there reading her Bible,

Teresa sat down next to her Granma, and said Grandma I have a favor to ask, Grandma, booked marked her Bible and put it to the side , Grandma, sounds serious, Teresa said Grandma, I want to be saved, I feel and know there is a God now. Teresa, wanted to tell her Grandma, I killed some one, but I did it for the safeness of my friend. But the words would not come out. Grandma, said I reckon you can be saved when you feel like it, But Teresa this is a serious relationship with Jesus. Grandma, reached for her bible, and said this is a manual for life. Teresa, got up and

Teresa said as soon as possible, Teresa said I have gone to church with you almost every Sunday, and I know there is a God, and I don't hate my Dad any more, I feel sorry for him, Grandma, said yes, Grandma, says you know you can always pray for you Dad or any body else, Teresa said Grandma, when I get saved, how long does the preacher hold a person under the water? Grandma, smiled and said not long at all, Grandma said you will be Baptized in the Father, the son and the Holy Spirit.

Teresa, said well let's do that this Sunday if we can,

Grandma, I am going to ask uncle Dade if he will drive me over my sister's house, is that ok with you Grandma, Grandma, said yes, you spending time with your sister would be nice, and Jennifer likes when you come Teresa.

Teresa, made the call and Uncle Dade took Teresa, over , Uncle Dade Knocked as he went in the house, and called for Jennifer, Jennifer was in the Kitchen, holding her back and Teresa, came and said what's wrong Jennifer,

Jennifer said, I think I am in Labor, and I can not get a hold of the Doctor,

Uncle Dade said where is Hank, Jennifer said he went to the store to get me some ice cream, I was craving ice cream so bad, but the pains in back are bigger than my cravings, Uncle Dade, said Jennifer get in my truck and Teresa, you wait here for Hank, and tell Hank I drove Jennifer too the Hospital,

Uncle Dade, drove Jennifer to the Hospital, and Jennifer is in Labor, Uncle Dade, called Jennifer house, Teresa answer the telephone, and said Hello, Hey Teresa, your sister is in Labor, the doctor here said the baby will be born today, Uncle Dade, said I know it is getting ready to storm,

Uncle Dade, said, make sure Teresa you tell Hank to go by and get your Aunt Polly, then come on to Canton, Hospital.

Teresa, said Hank is pulling up now I will tell him, Teresa , ran out the door, and grabbed Hank as he was getting out of the truck,

Teresa, said Jennifer is having the baby now Hank, Uncle Dade called and he said go by and get Aunt Polly, and then come to the Hospital,

Hank said oh my God, let's hurry, Teresa, put her seat belt on because Hank is driving crazy fast, Teresa, said Hank please slow down, I would like to stay alive,

Hank, said I did not realize I was going that fast Teresa, Hank pulled up to Aunt Polly

S drive way, and Aunt Polly was standing there waiting,

Teresa, opened the door and Aunt Polly got in the truck, rushing to the Hospital, Hank said I can not believe my child is coming today,

Teresa said if you do not slow down, this child may not have a Dad.

Hank pulled into the parking lot of the Hospital, Hank ran to the emergency room section, and some lady guided him, to where Uncle Dade was waiting,

Teresa walked fast with her Aunt Polly and caught up with Hank and Uncle Dade in the waiting room.

Teresa could hear the screams of pain, from her sister, Teresa, said to her Aunt Polly, how long is my sister going to scream like that?

Aunt Polly said some times it can be a long time, it just depends,

Teresa, said I am going to call my mom, and let her know were here, and what's going on with Jennifer,

Teresa, said a prayer before she made picked up the phone, Teresa dialed the operator, and Teresa said I want to make a collect call from Teresa, to 555 313 3131

The operator said one minute and made the call, Teresa heard on the other end the operator talking to Okle, saying a collect call from Teresa,

Okle accepted the charges, and the call went through, Hi Okle, Thank You for accepting the collect call, Okle said you know I will every time ,

Teresa said is my Mom there, no she is out right now, but she is suppose to be back soon, Teresa said Okle, has my mother had to take any special vacations since I have been gone? Okle said no Teresa; your mother has not had to go to the hospital for a nervous break down, Okle, said vacation my butt.

Teresa asked Okle is any one there, Okle said your Dad is, Okle the reason I called is Jennifer is in the Hospital having her baby and so I wanted to call,

Okle said oh, I can wait to know if it's a girl or a boy, I just can't wait.

Okle said hold on, I am going too get your Dad, Teresa thought oh God, and this man I hope can be nice.

Ed, came to the phone, and Teresa said Hello Dad, how are you? Ed, said fine Teresa and you? Teresa, wanted to say I hate you Dad, but Teresa was fighting her words and angry, and just said

i am good Dad, but the reason I am calling is Jennifer is in the Hospital having her baby, and it would really mean a lot to Jennifer if all of you came down, to see her new born baby.

Ed, said well I will tell your mother when she gets back, Ed, said is school going good for you, Teresa sighed yes, Dad, But I have learned a lot , and your money is my money , your just getting old, and I know too much about your business not to take it away from you when you get old. Grandma, heard it all, and shook head, Teresa said Dad I had to get that off my chest, and I am going back to be with my sister. You know the second child you sent away. Teresa said Dad or you still there ? Ed, said yes Teresa , Teresa said good, I have one word for you vasectomy, Teresa, cleared her voice, and said you people should have never had children. And by the way Dad, there is a God, and he will bring you to your knee's on day. Teresa said now I have said what I wanted and I am going back to be with my sister. ,

Dad, I want to get back with Jennifer, Teresa said yelling, Dad did you get that?

Ed, said Teresa look on the phone you are calling from and give me that pay phone number? Teresa gave her Dad the number that was on the pay phone, Teresa said Dad, if you can't get through, and we are at Canton, Hospital.. Ed said you spoke your mind on me, now listen to me Ed said, Teresa, don't fuck with me I will send you ass out of the country. Do you got that? I have the money too do it.

Teresa said Good by Dad and hung up the phone, Teresa, could not believe she just went off on her Dad, Teresa went back to Aunt Polly, as Teresa started to sit down, here came the doctor, Aunt Polly and Hank stood up, and the doctor said Hank , Hank reached out his hand and said I am Hank,

The doctor smiled and said , Congratulations you have a healthy baby girl, Hank said can I see my wife and child, The Doctor looked at all of them and first you Hank, your wife is very tired, and then the rest of you please keep your visit to about five minutes. The baby is being cleaned up right now,

Hank said as he followed the Doctor, in to Jennifer room, and Hank said I would have got you flowers, baby but I did not have time, Hank hugged Jennifer so hard, Jennifer smiled and cried and the same time,

The doctor walked in with the baby girl, all bundle up,

Jennifer reached her hands out far, Oh, my baby , Hank is leaning over to see the baby's face,

The doctor said here is your new baby girl and the doctor placed the baby in Jennifer's arms, Hank sat on the edge of the bed to be close to his family, and Hank yelled Thank You Lord for this family.

The doctor smiled, and said just a few more minutes, because the rest of your family would like to see the baby too. Hank smiled ok.

Jennifer and Hank said she is so beautiful, Hank said hone I know you have so many names for him or her, But now that our baby is in your arms, what name come to mind when you look at her face, Jennifer, said I would love too name her maybe after my Mother, but the name Crystal is what I would like to name our baby girl, Jennifer looked at Hank and said what do you think?

Hank said Crystal, that's kind of a different name , Jennifer said when you look at Crystal, is beautiful , Hank said that is fine with me, and what about a middle name , Jennifer said let's be fair, you pick the middle name,

Hank said I had a Grandma that passed away and her middle name was Maria, Jennifer said Crystal Marie , is great
,

The doctor said I am sorry to rush you out of here Hank, but your wife is tired and the other family members can all come in at one time, but can only stay for five minutes.

Hank got up and walked out side, Uncle Dade, said here is a cigar, I bought them a while back, so it's stale, Uncle Dade, said them cigars have been in the glove box in my truck for six months,

Hank took the cigar and Hugged Uncle Dade, Aunt Polly, and Teresa, I am Daddy,

Teresa. Looked back, and wonder did my Dad act that happy with any of us.

Teresa, kept her thoughts to her self, and they all walked in Jennifer's room where the Jennifer is smiling and looking down at her baby,

OH, Aunt Polly said let me take a look at her, Teresa, said I will be right back and ran out the door and found Hank, Teresa, said with all this going on my Grandma, she would want to be here,

Hank said I just got off the phone with your Grandma, and she said she would come up tomorrow, and see the baby, and Jennifer and the baby can get some rest.

Hank said Teresa, you know when you Grandpa died in the Hospital you Grandma never left his side, and ever since then, your Grandma has not wanted to be around a Hospital since that day.

Teresa said, well I understand, I am going to get back in there before they tell us we have to get out of the room, Hank said you better hurry.

Teresa ran back in side, and Aunt Polly was holding the baby, and smiling and oh my she is just a blessing , I believe little Crystal Maria , looks just like you and Hank , Aunt Polly said I sure do see the both of you in her.

Teresa, looked at this little life, so tiny, Aunt Polly said here Teresa you want to hold her , Teresa froze up, as she was holding the baby, Aunt Polly, said Teresa Crystal Maria is not going to break,

Teresa, handed back the baby and said maybe when she is not so tiny,

Uncle Dade held she and he said, I remember when your Aunt Polly gave birth, but in our case we had children, and they grow up and move away, and send cards, and they try to visit.

The Doctor walked back in and said I am sorry to tell you, But it's that time you all, It's time for Jennifer and the baby to get some rest, Teresa, reached over and hugged Jennifer, and said she has all her fingers and toes, Jennifer said I noticed that while they cutting the cord,

Uncle Dade and Aunt Polly hugged Jennifer good by and they would be up in the morning to see her and the baby.

Jennifer laid her head back and drifted off to the best sleep.

Hank was so excited he said I got to go the flower shop, and make sure I have some flowerer for Jennifer and the baby tomorrow.

Hank said thanks for being here you all, Hank walked out to his truck and left.

Uncle Dade and Aunt Polly and Teresa, were in the pick up truck, Teresa, said Aunt Polly I called my mom, but she was not there , so my mom will be calling you , I talked with my Dad, and told him Jennifer is having the baby,

Aunt Polly said that is nice. Teresa said I also asked my Dad if all of them could come down and see the baby. Aunt Polly said what was your Daddy's answer, Teresa, said he really did not give one, So I will call my mom if she has not already called when I get back to Grandma's,

The rain was starting and the wind came out of no where, Uncle Dade, said that wind sure makes it hard to keep the truck on the road; we best get home, and quick

Uncle Dade, dropped off Teresa and Grandma's house, and then left to go home.

Teresa, ran through the rain, and stood just for a second on the curved porch,

The lightning was so bright, and the rain was blowing to one side, and then the other,

Teresa, thought this is some bad weather,

Teresa, walked in the house, and Grandma was reading her Bible,

Teresa, yelled Hey Grandma, Jennifer had a baby girl, and she named her Crystal Maria,

Grandma smiled, that is a nice name.

The lights began to flicker off and on, and then Off.

Teresa, said Grandma, I can not see you, were are you, Teresa ran right into her Grandma,

Grandma, said I am going to light this lantern, and that will give us light,

And the lantern put off a lot of light, Teresa, said Grandma where did you get that, Grandma, smiled, Your Grandpa got this lantern many years ago, when we could not even afford Electric.

Not too much later the electric came back on and the lights were on, Teresa, sighed with relief. That was some storm; Grandma turned off the lantern, and put it back, with the matches in its place.

Teresa, said Grandma, good thing you had your lantern, are we would have been sitting in the dark.

Oh, Grandma, with the electric back on I want to call my mom, Grandma said go ahead, Teresa called straight through and Okle answered the phone,

Hi Okle, it's Teresa again, is my Mother there, no Your Mother and Dad , left to go to Mississippi, and Okle said we are having bad weather up here in Saint Louis, so you may not get a hold of your Dad on his car phone.

Okle, said who does the baby look like and what did they name her, Teresa said, she is a little baby girl, and Hank and Jennifer named the baby Crystal Maria, Okle said that is a pretty name.

Okle said I would have loved to come, but my place is here.

Teresa said did Larry come.

No Larry stayed here, Because your Mother and Dad, said they did not know how long they would be gone, Teresa said does Julius and his wife know, Yes, Teresa , I believe your brother is going to leave in the morning to Mississippi to come see you all ,

Teresa smiled well. Teresa said I love you Okle. Okle said I love you to Teresa, give that baby a kiss for me. Teresa said I will and hung up the phone.

Teresa, went in the kitchen where her Grandma, was and Teresa, very excited said Guess what Grandma, Grandma, smiled you tell me,

I am no good at guessing anything.

My Mom and Dad are on there way down here right now, they have already left, home and on there way, Teresa said and Julius and his wife are leaving in the morning to come down,

Grandma said well that is great, Praise the Lord, Grandma said see Teresa, it only takes one soul that can bring family together, not money. Grandma, said I know your angry at your parent Teresa, but you have to give the angry to the Lord, he will release you from it, but you get saved and come all this way with Jesus, and then you talk all mean to your Daddy, Grandma, said when a person gets right with the lord, you will run in to problems and angry, but control your tongue. God can take care of your problems. Teresa, said Ok Grandma, fair enough, But how long is it going to take God too take care of my Dad, he is pissing me off. Grandma, said, child you can not be loving God, and playing on Satan's field . It's one or the other. It's very simple. There are going to be many times a person that will push your buttons and make you made, that's when Teresa, you pray all the time. I have told you that over and over. Please listen. Teresa, took a deep breath, and said a silent prayer. Teresa smiled at her Grandma, and said Thank you. I really deep down do not want to be angry. Teresa, thought about forgetting the anger and thought I love my parents, I will just try harder and to be better. God put here for a reason.

Teresa said I can not wait to see my parents, Teresa said Grandma, with Jennifer having the baby, and Mom and the rest of the family coming down, and can I still go and get saved this Sunday?

Grandma, said of course child, in fact I hope your parents are here to see it.

The phone rang and it was Aunt Polly and Grandma talking about the baby, and Grandma telling Aunt Polly, Dean and Ed are already on there way down, and Julius and his wife will be leaving early in the morning some time.

Teresa, went took a shower, tired and what a day, that little baby Teresa thought, so tiny , Teresa said God thank You for letting her have all her fingers and toes.

Teresa, put on her night gown and went to tell Grandma good night.

Grandma, said I am right behind you, I am going to bed, too, I took my bath while you were at the Hospital

Teresa, was excited she knew when she woke up her parents would be here.

Teresa and Grandma, had been sleeping for some time, and there was some one banging on the door like crazy, Teresa, woke up and so did Grandma, ,

Grandma said, I don't lock my doors; no one does around here,

Teresa, thought for a minute oh Gosh, I did Grandma, when the weather was bad last night I made sure the screen door was locked so the wind would not damaged the door.

Teresa and Grandma, both heard Aunt Polly's voice calling please wake up, and the banging kept up,

Teresa ran to the door, and un hooked the latch on the screen door, and Aunt Polly came in and Uncle Dade followed, in the kitchen the all were, Teresa , walked in and Aunt Polly had been crying ,

Teresa said what is wrong? Aunt Polly , blowing he nose,

Your parents have been in a car wreck and, all I know is they are in Jackson , Mississippi hospital, I got a call ,and all we know is Dean and Ed are there, we do not know any thing else,

Teresa, said oh Uncle Dade, please take me to that Hospital in Jackson, now. Aunt Polly said get your clothes on, and Grandma stared crying right away, Aunt Polly and Uncle Dade, said Mama, as soon as we find out anything we will call you from the Hospital.

Teresa came back out, and they all walked out and got in Uncle Dade's truck and drove to Jackson, Hospital.

The rain was pouring down still, and the old wiper on Uncle Dade truck was taking a beating. Uncle Dade, pulled over with his flasher's on, and Teresa said why are we stopping my parents,

Uncle Dade did not let Teresa finish her sentence and said this rain is so hard I can not see any thing, so I pulled over until the rain lights up a little bit , so I can see the road.

Teresa looked at her watch and finally Uncle Dade got back on the highway, Aunt Polly said this rain is just something else.

Finally they reached Jackson Memorial Hospital, and Teresa, was the first one out of the truck and ran towards the emergency room sign.

Teresa ran in and asked do you have a Mr. and Mrs. Whitehurst in this Hospital? The lady, said calm down who are you, I am there daughter Teresa Whitehurst,

Aunt Polly and Uncle Dade caught up with Teresa at the counter, Aunt Polly explained who she was and said she received a phone call, that her sister and husband were in this hospital, The lady got up, and went and got some a charge nurse, and

The charge nurse had a name tag that said Faith,

The nurse reached out and pointed and said let's go over here and sit down so I can tell you all what is going on,

Mr. Whitehurst is in surgery right now, and Mrs. Whitehurst is not as bad as her husband,

Aunt Polly , said what happen, all we know if they lost control of the car and it might have been do to the rain, it's bad all over the state of Mississippi,

We will have more information on Mr. Whitehurst after the surgery, the doctors will know more. Mrs. Whitehurst is banged up quite a bit,

Mrs. Whitehurst did have to have her arm in a cast, her right arm is broken, but the doctor said it could have been a lot worse, and the doctors haven given Mrs. Whitehurst something to help her rest, she has a black eye as well, Faith said what I understand when they lost control of the car, the car the were in rolled over the highway, and down a hill, a truck driver is the one who called in.

Teresa, thought gosh if it was not for that truck driver, being at the right place at the right time, God knows how long my parents would have been stuck in that car.

Teresa, found her self praying to God, Teresa sighed God, please let both of my parents be fine, and thank you for putting that truck driver where you did.

And letting him be able to call in for help.

Aunt Polly said well we might as well get as comfortable as we can get, because I am not leaving until I see my sister.

Uncle Dade called Grandma, and gave her the news, and told and that he would call as soon as they heard anything and they would be not be leaving the Hospital,

Uncle Dade, said for right now do not call Hank , this is only going to upset them , and it's the middle of the night or morning, and this will up set Jennifer,

We want to see what the doctor's have to say before we alarm any one Grandma.

Uncle Dade came back and told Aunt Polly and Teresa the conversation he had with Grandma, and Uncle Dade, said Teresa do not call your sister, this will only upset her, we will wait until the doctor tell us what is going on.

Time seemed like it had stopped and finally the doctor's came out and said are you the family of Mr. and Mrs. Whitehurst.

Aunt Polly, wiped her eyes, and uncle Dade put his coffee down, and said Yes, we are, Teresa said I am there daughter,

The doctors there were two of them Pauline reached her hand out and said I am Pauline , Dean Whitehurst sister, and Ed sister in n law, the doctors, said Mrs. Pauline, your sister has a broken right arm, we have put a cast on that , there is not trauma to the head , but Mrs. Whitehurst is very badly bruised on the inside and out side of her body, she has a left black eye, and her feet hurt her, but nothing else is broken and Mrs. Whitehurst is very lucky ,

Now Mr. Whitehurst, we had to back spinal surgery on him , and he has at ten stitches on his forehead, Mr. Whitehurst, will not be able to walk for a long time, and he will need some speech therapy, The spinal cord was damaged and the trauma to the head and neck ,will cause much long needed therapy.

Aunt Polly said down, and said my God, thank God there both alive. Yes, the doctor said my understanding they were on a trip down here, Mr. or Mrs. Whitehurst will not be able to drive for a while. Maybe a long time, for Mr. Whitehurst.

Mr. Whitehurst the nurses are just now getting him in his hospital room and Mrs. Whitehurst are resting finally.

The Doctor said I know you all are so tired, but I am sorry to tell both all of you, you can see Mrs. Whitehurst for sure tomorrow;

But Mr. Whitehurst well let you know. If he is up for company.

Aunt Polly and all went back to canton, and tried to get a good nights rest, but the phone was ringing early and it was Jennifer, Uncle Dade told Jennifer what had happen , Jennifer said oh my Gosh, I feel like this is my fault they were on there way down to see me.

Uncle Dade, said Jennifer, your Mother and dad, were in car wreck , the rain was so bad, I can see Ed, now not pulling over , thinking he would make better time, if he stayed on the Highway , but now driving as fast, Jennifer , said yes, that does sound like my Dad,

Jennifer said I still feel bad,

Jennifer said I can not even to and see them I am in the Hospital my self, Jennifer said my Doctor is going to release me maybe later on today or tomorrow.

Uncle Dade said I am glad to hear that.

Teresa, finally woke up to hearing Julius and some woman's voice, Grandma was telling them about Mom and Dad, Teresa pushed off the covers, and went in and washed her face, and out of no where Teresa got on her knee's and thank God, for letting her parents live, and how she would treat them different, and got up off her knees, brushed her hair, and went into the kitchen,

Teresa hugged her brother Julius and was introduced to sandy, Teresa, thought she is really pretty, long black hair, and blue eyes, and she was very nice.

Teresa, called Uncle Dade, and said do I have to go to school today, Uncle Dade said no your Aunt has called the school and told them what happen with your parents,

The phone rang, and it Julius answered the phone, Teresa the phone is for you, Teresa walked over and grabbed the phone and said Hello, Teresa, it's me Bobby from school, Teresa said Bobby who, oh, I am sorry now I remember you Bobby, Bobby, was cute and on the foot ball team, and Bobby asked if he could come by, for a few minutes, Teresa said fine, here is my address, Bobby said I know where you live.

Teresa said fine I will see you in a little while, Teresa went in and talked with her brother and told Julius were canton hospital is to see Jennifer and the baby, and told Julius Hanks treats Jennifer really good.

Sandy reached over too Teresa, and said I am so sorry to hear about you parents,

Julius said some boy is at the door,

Teresa, turned around and it was Bobby, Teresa said come on in Bobby, Grandma looked surprised,

Bobby was introduced to everyone and wanted to know if he could take Teresa up and get a pop with her, Grandma said that will be fine, But have her back soon,

Teresa started to open the grand am, But Bobby beat her too it, and said we southern boys open doors for girls. Teresa, said really now.

Teresa, and Bobby talked and Teresa told Bobby , what was going on with her parents, and then her sister, Bobby said wow, you have a lot going on , you know when it rains it pours , Teresa looked at Bobby and said Do you go to church, Bobby said yes I do,

Teresa said well maybe we can go to church together, Bobby said that' sound fine by me.

Teresa and Bobby sat in the truck after getting there pop, and Bobby and Teresa both had a passion for animals.

Bobby invited Teresa to come out some time and ride horses on his dad's ranch.

Teresa quickly took Bobby up on his offer. Bobby and Teresa realized they had been gone much longer than planed.

Bobby started his car and headed back to Teresa's Grandma House, Bobby and Teresa switched phone numbers, and Teresa said Thank You for stopping by and the pop,

Teresa walked in and it looked like everyone was waiting on Teresa,

Aunt Polly was there and said we are all going up to see your parents, let's go.

The doctor called and said we could see your Mother and we could see your Dad, but not long with your Dad.

Everyone once at the Hospital went into see Mother, Teresa, about lost her breath; her mother looked so banged up, cut lips, bruised face and broken arm.

Dean, said how is Ed, doing, Polly said , I am going to go see if I can see Ed, right now, and come back and tell you,

Pauline asked the doctor could she see Mr. Whitehurst, and the doctor said yes,

Pauline went in and about lost her breath, Ed Whitehurst looked like he escaped death

Pauline, said Ed, you are going to be alright, it might take some time to get back on your feet, but going by the car wreck report, you and Dean are lucky to even be alive.

Ed, said with a stutter, that he knew, and asked how is Dean,

Dean is not as bad as you, she did not need surgery, but she is pretty banged up and will need time to heal.

Ed, said again with a stutter, Tell her I love her.

The doctor came in and told Pauline time is up Ed needs his rest,

Pauline out side Ed's room asked the doctor when do you see them being able to leave this hospital, the doctor said Mrs. Whitehurst can leave in a couple of days, maybe sooner, Mr. Whitehurst is will depend he did quite well on the surgery part , and seems to understand every thing that has happened ,

But the looks of things, Mr. Whitehurst may go home sooner than I though; he has no real pain, but well see.

A week rolled by Julius and Sandy , seen and met the new baby and Hank , and enjoyed lunch with them before heading back to Saint Louis, ,Julius said I have to leave I have that business to run. I do not have a choice.

But I will try and get back, but I hear mom will be getting out of the hospital sooner than Dad, and staying with Grandma,

Julius came back to Grandma's house and told Teresa good by and that he had forgotten to tell Teresa, Larry and Okle send there love and to call and keep they updated. With mom and Dad.

Julius and sandy did not waste any time getting packed and saying good by to every one.

And the left, to go back to Saint Louis, Julius set up a bank account for his mother, and would be transferring the money down to them.

Time went by and Jennifer and Hank and Crystal were just about the most loving family Teresa thought it was amazing to feel the love for her sister and her family.

Dean, came home and needed medicine and realized she had no money on her, Teresa, went and got the suite case from under the bed, and gave Dean, a thousand dollars,

Dean, looked up and said where in the world did you Teresa get this type of money and in cash, Teresa told her Mother is does not matter right now, what is important is you have money for your medicine. The past is the past mother. Tomorrow was Sunday,

Teresa, went to church and Dean went to with the rest of the family and Teresa, got baptized in the name of the Father, the son, and the Holy Spirit. Teresa came up from the water feeling, like a brand new person, all stress gone, and Teresa, held up her arms and felt the Holy Spirit touch her, Teresa, heard the words, praise Jesus as Teresa turned around, and there was Bobby in the seats.

After church service, everyone pretty much went back to Grandma's house at least family and a few friends, Bobby came.

And told Teresa, that was so cool to see you get baptized, Bobby said too Teresa, your face expression had a glow, I am not kidding, I

was glad to be there to see you get Baptized Teresa. Bobby said I see why your mom, and family here I am going to go home, I will call you later and Bobby hugged Teresa and left.

Ed, would be coming home soon, and Dean said Ed's ego is hurting more than his body, I know that man all to well. As she held Grandma's hand.

Days rolled by and Ed, came home in a wheel chair, Ed could talk but he did stutter a lot, and when Ed walked he had a limp.

Dean, said Ed's stutter and limp the doctors said they have done all they can. Dean , could see in Ed's eye's is ego could not handle walking with a limp, and stuttering and physical his life was at a slow pace for Ed.

Ed, will have to learn to work with this. Dean, said Ed will not be able to do business talking like that, and his image , and they way his Dean was telling her Mama, Ed's has this suite and tie every day, and travels, here and there all the time Mama,

Mama said as the breeze came through the window in the kitchen, well Dean, I think in my opion this is the Lords way of telling you both to slow down, because no one could believe you both lived out of the car wreck after seeing the car, there is nothing left of it.

Ed, and Dean stayed moved in at Grandma's house for now, and stayed in Aunt Polly's old room and an air conditioner unit was put in right away,

Teresa, went to the same store, and took the money from her suite case and paid cash for it, and said.

Please just install in as soon as you can, the huge window air conditioner unit went in that day.

Dean, looked at Teresa, Teresa winked at her Mother. And said did I ever tell you how much I love you?

Dean, said you sure have changed Teresa, Teresa, said that's because God takes all the angry and madness out of a person's life and yes, Mother there are still problems, God just resolves them different than, not being with God. Dean asked Teresa, how did you pay for that air conditioner, were still getting the bank account set up down here, Teresa, said, Mother just look at this way , I owe you. Dean said I really see a difference in you. Dean, told Teresa, there for a while I saw your future, either taking Julius business away, or something, but I am glad Teresa, you have given up all that angry. Dean, told Teresa, I have spoken with Okle, and for now and

Okle and Larry will stay at the house in Saint Louis, and Julius will take care of the business and he also will take care of Okle and Larry, as time

Ed and Dean, and decided to look for a house in canton.

Until Ed would in his mind get back on his feet.

Teresa, said Mom, what about that business in New Orleans, Dean, said your Dad has money invested I am aware of that, But for now Teresa, your Dad, will has to learn to walk and talk ,

Don't get wrong Teresa, your Dad, walks and talks but he is far from what he used to be.

Teresa, looked in mother's eyes and said, do you believe some things happen for a reason? Dean lit up a cigarette, I am sure they do. Dean, walked back in the house,

Teresa, walked in behind her Mother, and said Mom, where is Dad, oh your Dad is in the bed room , Dean, said why, Teresa, said I just want to check on him , that's all, Dean, sat down and lit a cigarette, and watched Teresa, walk in to where Ed is.

Dean, turned on the TV,

Teresa sat down on the bed, and said Dad I have something to tell you, Teresa flipped her hair back, and said Dad; I want to know do you remember making fun of Larry's stutter, and Okle's Limp?

Ed, shook his head yes.

Teresa, said Dad, I am telling you this in not karma; this is You Reap what you sow.

Teresa said I am not trying to be mean to you.

But, I am trying to tell you , it's not so much what goes around comes around , Teresa said Dad it's down right a person will reap what you sow. Teresa said Dad I know about the business you have in New Orleans, and I could run it. Ed shook his head no way. Teresa said I don't have to get involved in kick backs; I can a business with out that. Ed said. I don't think so. Teresa, said and for some reason Dad, I can not let the business in New Orleans, La, go.

Teresa, said Dad there is a Bible in this house, Grandma made sure of it.

When you get time, I am asking you Dad to read the Bible, and not your bank account records. Teresa said there is perfect example I am telling you Dad about God, I can run a business with out all the insanity.

Ed, and Teresa and a long silent look at each other. Ed said Thank You for letting me know there is a Bible in the house, I will read it Teresa. Ed would not talk about the business in New Orleans, la; any more with Teresa, Teresa realized I might just have to take it. And still keep it family.

Teresa, got off the bed and went hugged her Dad. Teresa, said I am leaving now Dad,

Ed, said Teresa, before you walk out that door, I want you to know Teresa

You can move in here with your Mother and me.

Teresa said Dad, thanks for the offer, but I am comfortable with Grandma, and I do not want her to be alone. Grandma Misses Grandpa, Teresa said.

You know life can really be strange, Grandma, has a lot of wisdom, not the kind of wisdom a person gets from a school,

it's chilling how smart Grandma really is.

Teresa said I will see you later, and I am glad you and mom moved here.

At least most of us are in one place , Teresa said I hope Julius and Sandy move down here, but one more thing Dad, Grandma, said sometimes the more money a person has, sometimes the more problems that person has.

Teresa, said, like I said Dad, Grandma is wiser that you think. And her heart is bigger than your bank account. At least Grandma can go to bed in peace and wake up in peace.

Teresa shut the door behind her as she left her Dad's room.

And Teresa, said Mom, I am going home to Grandma's. Teresa walked up and hugged her Mother and said I love you Mom, before I leave I want to tell you something,

Teresa, said looking in her Mother's eyes, Mom, I used to think you were a weak woman for staying with Dad,

I have now realized you are a very strong woman, to have stayed with Dad.

And mom, I know you have had a lot of pain from Dad, but I want to tell you Thank You for keeping this family together. Teresa, knew her mother needed to hear that. The smile on Dean's face, showed a smile and kindness , Teresa had not seen in years.

Dean, with wide eyes looked at Teresa, and started to cry, and said Thank You Teresa for saying that. Teresa, took her finger and wiped the tear away from her Mother's eye, and said, it's a good day

Teresa said God does not make bad days. Dean, smiled at Teresa, as she walked away, and shut the door. Teresa was thinking about the business in New Orleans, and the money that could be made and then , Ed , called Teresa back and Teresa heard her Dad calling her as she was about to leave, Teresa , walked back in and Teresa looked at her mother and said Dad can not make up his mind, Dean, had hurt in her eyes, Teresa went back there and said yea, Dad.

Ed, said Teresa have a seat for a minute, Teresa flipped her blond back and sat down, What is Dad, Teresa said.

Ed, said I signed forms that you will being going into the canton psychiatric ward, Teresa, eyes got big, what , and Teresa started screaming and waving her hands around Dad, why Dad, or you series Teresa said,

Ed said calm down, Teresa, it is for the best, have you forgotten about what you did to Fred,

Teresa, with a angry face said , no have you forgotten about the person you killed and was found on your farm , and by the way Dad, I know who was, I can still provide the details of that person,   Dad you have got by with nothing,

Teresa, stood up and said , I refuse to go to a nut ward, Ed, said with a cigar in his mouth, that's fine Teresa , but I will have the police come get you, Ed, said legally I am still over you, Teresa, said really, you think so? Ed, smiled, Teresa, I will have your corvette waiting when you get out , and maybe that will make you feel better,, Teresa, turned around and said , But the corvette, because it will help you sleep better. And God know Dad, your image, your kid driving a brand new corvette.

Teresa, sat back and said Dad how long have you signed me into a nut ward?

Ed, said Teresa with your angry, Dr. smith told me , he could do a lot with you in two weeks, or it make take more time, it depends on how you Teresa work with them.

Ed, said only if you try and help your self. It will go by faster.

Teresa, said you make me sick. Teresa, said and your Doctor said you have head trauma, from the car wreck , tell me Dad, is this where I am suppose to be glad you fucking alive, and did not die in that car wreck? Teresa, said to her Dad, oh one more thing, I got the accounts in New Orleans, and I know about the kick backs, Dad if you were not screwing around on mom all the time, you might have been smart enough to see I learned it all, and I got it all from you, and you Dad, did not even have a clue, that I knew all this, until right this moment.

Ed, shook his head, see Teresa, you just do not get who is in control here

, Ed said I sure the Doctor will help you sort your angry and problems out. Teresa, said Dad, this is not about angry, this is about me making you a poor man, and me turning the tables on you. I will show you when I got out of the nut ward you signed me into.

Teresa, stood up, and got eye to eye level, and said this is not over. You can bet everything you own on it.

Teresa, pissed off got up and walked away. Teresa, talking to God, help me God, fight this battle, with out looking my faith. Show me . God.

Teresa, looked up at the sky as she was walking, The clouds were dark and swirling and it was starting to Lightning all at the same time, the wind was blowing harder than before.

Teresa stopped and looked and the dark moving clouds with lightning striking in them and Teresa could feel the a hot humid breeze,

Teresa looked back at her mother and Dad's house, still thinking about the business in New Orleans, and being sent away. Teresa, said out loud, this is no southern rain; this is a Southern Storm coming.